Praise for
The Transformation of Things

"*The Transformation of Things* is an elegant and involving page-turner about perception, truth, and what's really true about each of our lives. Part mystery, part love story, part coming-of-age, it is a wonderful book. I could not stop reading!"
—Barbara O'Neal, author of *The Secret of Everything*

"Jillian Cantor's *The Transformation of Things* is a moving and delicate look beneath the surface of a life, a window into the world of 'what if,' one woman's unique journey through a tremendous personal challenge. It speaks to the power of the mind to heal itself, to uncover truth within fiction, and indeed to change one's entire perspective on what makes life important."
—Morgana Gallaway, author of *The Nightingale*

"A provocative novel that raises fascinating questions about marriage and how to find our way back when love falters. Thoroughly original, highly engaging, and wonderfully tender. I couldn't wait to see how it ended!"
—Laura Fitzgerald, author of *Veil of Roses*

"Remarkable and magical, *The Transformation of Things* is a surprising and honest look at the assumptions we make about ourselves and those around us."
—Maureen Lipinski, author of
A Bump in the Road and *Not Ready for Mom Jeans*

By Jillian Cantor

From HarperTeen

THE LIFE OF GLASS
THE SEPTEMBER SISTERS

The
Transformation
of Things

JILLIAN CANTOR

AVON

An Imprint of HarperCollins*Publishers*

This book is a work of fiction. The characters, incidents, and dialogue are drawn from the author's imagination and are not to be construed as real. Any resemblance to actual events or persons, living or dead, is entirely coincidental.

HarperCollins books may be purchased for educational, business, or sales promotional use. For information please write: Special Markets Department, HarperCollins Publishers, 10 East 53rd Street, New York, NY 10022.

FIRST AVON PAPERBACK EDITION PUBLISHED 2010.

Designed by Diahann Sturge

Library of Congress Cataloging-in-Publication Data
    Cantor, Jillian.
      The transformation of things / Jillian Cantor.
        p.   cm.
      ISBN 978-0-06-196220-2 (pbk.)
      1. Self-realization—Fiction.   2. Family—Fiction.   3. Domestic fiction.
      I. Title.
    PS3603.A587T73 2010
    813'.6—dc22   2010015002

10 11 12 13 14   OV/RRD   10 9 8 7 6 5 4 3 2 1

For my children: May all your best dreams come true.

Acknowledgments

First, I want to thank my agent, Jessica Regel, whose constant encouragement and enthusiasm for my work always amazes me. She is fabulous at what she does, and also a remarkable person. I feel lucky every day to have her on my side, as well as everyone else at the Jean V. Naggar Literary Agency, who truly are the best.

An enormous thank-you to Lucia Macro, Executive Editor at Avon Books. Her passion, enthusiasm, and insight have made her an absolute joy to work with. Many thanks also to Assistant Editor Esi Sogah, and to everyone else at Avon, who have helped transform this from a manuscript I dreamed of seeing in print to a real, bona fide book.

I am overwhelmingly grateful to my writer friends, a constant source of support. You all make my life infinitely richer and more well-read. Thank you to Laura Fitzgerald and Morgana Gallaway for support on the home front and for fabulous dinners and talks. Thank you to The Novel Girls, who have been blogging and chatting with me since the very beginning of my publication journey: Tracy Madison, Lisa

Patton, Lesley Livingston, and especially Maureen Lipinski, who also keeps me sane and laughing on a daily basis.

My family has always been supportive in everything I've done, and without them, I know I never would've had the discipline or the conviction to write this book. Thank you to my dad, Alan Cantor, for sharing his experience with herbal medicine with me, and my mom, Ronna Cantor, the most experienced reader I know, for telling me honestly that the beginning was much too slow in the draft she read. Thank you to my sister, Rachel Cantor, who I am also proud to call a friend, and who continually inspires me to give my characters a sister.

Thank you to my children, and to my husband, Gregg Goldner, for always, always supporting me, for giving me the time to write, and for sometimes believing in me much more than I believe in myself. And an extra thank-you to Gregg for reading what probably seemed like infinite drafts of this book and offering advice, and beyond that, for being my best friend and the best husband anyone could ever ask for.

Once I, Chuang Tzu, dreamed I was a butterfly and was happy as a butterfly. I was conscious that I was quite pleased with myself, but I did not know that I was Tzu. Suddenly I awoke, and there was I, visibly Tzu. I do not know whether it was Tzu dreaming that he was a butterfly or the butterfly dreaming that he was Tzu. Between Tzu and the butterfly there must be some distinction. (But one may be the other.) This is called the transformation of things.

—CHUANG TZU, CHINESE PHILOSOPHER

The
Transformation
of Things

One

When I first heard the news about Will, I was at the Pierce Avenue Salon, getting my hair washed. I had my head back in the sink, the roar of water rushing through my ears, the annoying voice of Jo, my hairdresser for the four years I'd lived in Deerfield, ringing against the water. She was saying something about her kids. My head was pounding from the sound of her voice, and I had my eyes closed, which is why I didn't notice it at first, the big flat-screen TV that hung up in front of me.

I heard the water turn off, in mid-rinse, so I opened my eyes. "Isn't that your husband?" Jo asked.

"What?" The idea seemed ridiculous. There was no way Will would be at Pierce Avenue in the middle of the day, on a weekday. Will was a judge, the youngest judge to have ever been elected to the bench in Deerfield County. Which, he once told me, meant he had to work the hardest, meant he had something to prove.

Since he'd been elected three years ago, I'd barely seen him, except for five-minute sex at six A.M., once a month when I was ovulating. We were trying to have a baby, though we'd never admitted to each other that we weren't trying very hard.

I was only thirty-three. I still had time. Why rush things? It was Will who was dying for the pitter-patter of little feet— little feet he'd never be around to hear. So each month when my period arrived without delay, I couldn't help but feel a little relieved, even though I feigned mock disappointment for Will's benefit.

"No," Jo said. "Up there. On the news."

I sat up too quickly, and I felt a wave of dizziness wash over me as I saw the shiny newscaster, Gary Adams, talking with a smile so wide and so white that he looked more like a puppet than a human being. I'd interviewed him once, in my former life, before Will and I had moved to Deerfield, when I'd worked as a writer for *City Style* magazine. He was just as annoying in real life as he was on TV, and after he'd called me doll three too many times, I'd been ready to scream.

Jo grabbed the remote from behind the sink, rewound back sixty seconds, and turned it up.

And then I saw it, incredibly, the picture of Will up on the screen. It was his professional headshot, the one of him in his black robe, where he looked both exceedingly handsome and way too serious. "Judge William Levenworth," Gary was saying. "Indicted by a federal grand jury this morning for bribery."

Gary was still talking, but I didn't hear it. It was as if the water were still rushing through my ears, and the world was thick and heavy and cloudy all around me. "Mrs. Leven-worth." I heard Jo's voice, but it sounded very, very far away. "Mrs. Levenworth. Are you okay? Are you all right?"

There must be some mistake. There was no way that Will

had been indicted. What the hell did that even mean exactly anyway? I vaguely remembered reading something about a state senator who'd been indicted recently, but I hadn't paid too much attention to it. Still, I knew it wasn't good. "Mrs. Levenworth!" Jo's normally annoying voice was punctuated with an extra bit of shrillness. "Mrs. Levenworth!"

I took a deep breath. "I think I should go," I said. "I'll call and reschedule."

I stood up, un-Velcro-ed the shiny black robe that was supposed to keep me dry, and when I did, my wet hair plopped against my back with a thud. I felt dizzy again, and the room swirled around me, the din of the salon, the rainbow colors of shampoo all lined up in neat rows by the sink. "At least let me dry it for you," I heard Jo saying. "You'll freeze."

I grabbed on to the edge of the sink to steady myself for a second. "I'll be fine," I heard myself saying, though I wasn't sure where the words were coming from, if I was really speaking them. It was early October and pleasant enough, in the low sixties—the perfect time of year in Deerfield. The time of year when the leaves changed color and littered the winding hilly streets—the time of year that usually made me a little gleeful that we'd moved to the suburbs.

I opened my purse, fished out a twenty-dollar bill, and handed it to Jo. "Here you go," I said. My motions were clumsy, and the money slipped to the ground, but before she even bent to pick it up, I started running, through the rows of hair chairs and mirrors, past the waiting area and the anxious stares of the women sipping lattes, and into the parking lot, filled nearly to the brim with shiny, expensive cars.

I hopped into my black Mercedes SUV, as if it were pouring rain outside and I was seeking some sort of refuge. I slammed the door shut behind me.

Inside the safety of my car, I combed my hair with my fingers, and I tried to scrunch it as if I'd intentionally left it wet, so it would curl. It still felt a little soapy, but I did the best I could with it in the rearview mirror.

As I drove, I thought about my last conversation with Will, last night at dinner. There was no indication anything was askew, that he was about to be indicted. Though our conversations didn't necessarily indicate much anymore.

"Janice brought her baby by this afternoon," he said, taking a sip of his wine and chewing carefully on his salad of organic greens and vegetables that I'd prepared after a trip to the farmers' market.

"Oh." I nodded and chewed. Janice was Will's clerk, or she had been before she'd had the baby and gone on an extended, if not totally permanent, maternity leave.

"She was cute," Will said.

"All babies are cute," I said.

"Pudgy little cheeks," he said. He looked up and stared at me for a moment, and something he was about to say caught in his throat, until he stopped himself.

"What?" I said, wanting to egg him on, wanting him to say something, anything.

"Nothing." He shook his head and finished off his wine. "I've got work to do." He stood up and walked his empty salad bowl over to the sink.

"I rented some movies," I said. I wanted him to stay, wanted him to wrap me up in his arms on the couch, something he hadn't done in so long, years maybe. I'd gone into the video store on a whim on the way back from the farmers' market, hoping that Will might have some time to watch something with me. "Do you want me to wait for you to watch?"

"No." He shook his head. "I have an early day tomorrow."

"We could watch them tomorrow night."

He shook his head again. "I'll be home late tomorrow."

Of course you will, I thought, feeling close to tears as I put the disc in the DVD player and sat down on the couch myself.

And now in the car, I felt close to tears again, felt this whirlwind of colors, emotions in my head, like the fall leaves that littered the ground, swirling and dying in the wind. I was almost grateful for the sound of the ambulance, for the need to pull over for a minute to let it pass, so I could take a deep breath and compose myself before driving the rest of the way home.

Exactly ten minutes after leaving the salon, I pulled into my driveway, and I checked my hair in the mirror. Frizzy and half dry. Not my best look. And then I opened the garage door and saw Will's car, a dark gray BMW, sitting there in the second bay: bright and shiny and sparkling clean, looking as new as the day he'd bought it two years earlier. It always amazed me, the way Will found the time to take care of his car, keep it waxed and sparkling, when he barely ever had time to make it home for dinner on a weeknight.

Will was sitting in the kitchen when I walked in—the kitchen that I'd painstakingly redecorated over the past few years, replete with black granite counters, cherry handcrafted cabinetry, and bamboo floors.

Being a judge's wife, a pillar of the community, had come surprisingly naturally to me. Our house was immaculate, beautiful, and modern. I'd created a very successful charity auction that earned enough money for breast cancer research to make me feel like I was actually doing something useful. I played doubles tennis at the country club, and I was a member of the exclusive Deerfield Ladies Lunch Club.

And now here he was, Will, slumped against the mahogany chair I'd ordered from the Crate and Barrel catalog, his head leaning in his hands, looking nothing like he did in the photo from TV. His blue eyes were red-rimmed, his brown wavy hair was disheveled, his red tie was loosened, and the top of his white starched shirt was unbuttoned. His suit jacket hung on the chair behind him.

I felt this deep and incredible ache for him in my gut, an ache that made me forget, for a few seconds, about the loneliness I usually felt when we were both home, in this house.

He looked up, suddenly noticing me watching him. "You heard?" he whispered.

"On the news," I said.

"Oh shit." He laid his head down on the table in his hands. "It's on the news."

I sat down, and I wanted to hug him, wanted to hold myself close to him and bury my head in chest. I wanted to smell just the faintest hint of his pine aftershave, a smell that once made me feel intoxicated. But I didn't move. I just sat there. "Why didn't you tell me?" I asked, after a few moments of silence.

He lifted his head up. "There was nothing to tell," he said. "I thought it would go away." *And you don't tell me anything anymore*, I silently added, which was probably the real reason. "It's lies," he said. "All of it." I nodded. "I never accepted any bribes. You know that, right, Jen?"

"Of course," I said. "Of course I know that." I stared at him closely, this man, my husband of five years, whose life moved next to mine, around and around and around, barely, if ever, moving together. And I wasn't quite sure what I really knew and what I didn't.

I had a lot of questions: Why would he be indicted for bribery if he hadn't done anything wrong? What did it mean exactly to be indicted anyway? But I couldn't find any words to actually ask him. I knew it would all pour out of him so painstakingly, as if each word was killing him, just a little bit, to choke out; as if each word was breaking him. And I couldn't bear to watch it.

"I'm going to fight this," he said. "I'm not going to resign. I'm not going anywhere."

"Of course you're not," I said, as if it was the most obvious conclusion.

He stood up. "I'm going to go call Danny." Danny Halloway was a lawyer who'd worked with Will at Farnesworth, Fenley, and Grimes (FF&G) before Will had left to become a judge. Danny was short with bright red hair and freckles, with a sort of young Ron Howard look to him. But anyone who mistook his benign appearance to mean an easy target was sorely mistaken. Danny, like Will, had been made a partner at the law firm before the age of thirty. He and his wife, Kat, had also been our closest friends when we'd lived in the city.

I thought about Danny and Kat—it had been a while since I'd seen them together. Maybe they should've been a strange fit—his gentle quietness and her loud affection—but you could always see the way they loved each other, every second that they were together, in the way they looked at each other, in the way they clung to each other in small moments.

The last time we'd been to their house in the city was just after the birth of their younger daughter, Arabella, and even though Kat was swollen and tired-looking, Danny had been sitting next to her on the couch, his arm around her, their thighs touching. Danny looked at her like she was the most beautiful thing he'd ever seen, and she said it right back, in the way she reached up and innocently tousled his red hair.

Will walked toward his study, the study I'd meticulously

decorated with a black leather sofa and thick, dark cherry desk and bookshelves, sitting against a light cherrywood floor. The room was very dark, very judgelike, but I always thought the beige damask curtains lightened it up just enough to make it homey. I'd been so proud of the way it had turned out, the way it looked like something formal and gracious enough to have made its way into a design magazine. And Will had given me nothing more than "It's nice." He followed this with "You know I really don't care much about curtains," because I'd pressed him to give me an opinion on something specific, pointing toward the window treatments.

I stood in the doorway, staring at those curtains now. "Have you talked to Danny lately?" I asked, thinking that it had been a month or two, at least, since I'd last called Kat.

He shook his head, and I watched as he dialed Danny's number. In another lifetime, Will and Danny had been best friends, and Danny was a great lawyer. If anyone would know what to do, it would be Danny, even if they hadn't talked in a while.

"Danny," I heard Will say, his voice gasping out, almost as if he was choking. "It's Will."

And from the look on Will's face, I knew that Danny was saying that he'd already heard, that maybe he'd seen it on the news the way I had. Will put his head down on the desk, hanging on to the phone with his right hand and holding on to his head with his left. "Okay," I heard him say. "Yes, okay. Okay. I will." He hung up.

"What did Danny say?" I asked.

He lifted his head up slowly from the desk and looked around the room, as if seeing it for the first time, seeing me standing there for the first time. "He wants me to come down to the office."

"Now?" I asked. Will seemed to be in no shape to go any-where.

"Yes." He nodded. He looked at me for a moment, and I had a feeling he was considering asking me to go with him. But then he stood up, grabbed his jacket off the back of the chair, and breezed by me. "Don't wait up," he called out behind him. "I'll be home late."

He didn't wait for my response, and as I heard the door slam to the garage, I stood there for a moment, listening, waiting, for something else. But as always, the only thing res-onating through our giant, well-decorated house was silence.

Two

To be indicted is to be charged formally for committing a criminal act.

It was right there in the *Deerfield Daily* the next morning, right alongside Will's picture, with the headline that read: "Young Judge Indicted for Bribery." The definition of *indicted*, along with that of *federal grand jury* (a group of jurors who decide if someone should be tried for a crime), sat in a little blurb box off to the side, as if the editor at the *Deerfield Daily* was expecting his readers not to know these things. And why would they? People didn't get indicted in Deerfield.

Well, actually, some people did—Will was the second in as many months. That state senator I'd remembered had been from Deerfield, too. The article also mentioned this, although it failed to say what had happened to the senator, which is what I was dying to know as I perused the article. But the *Deerfield Daily*, like most small-town suburban papers, was not known for its stellar reporting.

The town of Deerfield sat in the heart of Deerfield County, just around thirty minutes from Philadelphia. Deerfield County was filled with mostly middle- and upper-middle-class suburbs, but the actual town of Deerfield itself was the wealthy upper-class center—made up of expensive shopping plazas, developments of large, newer homes—or McMansions, as my sister, Kelly, liked to call them—and a world-class country club with a Jack Nicklaus golf course. Needless to say, I was sure that my neighbors, like me, would not be up on their criminal terms, even if some state senator had already been indicted last month.

Right next to the oh-so-helpful definition box, there was another box, a fact box, that offered these little tidbits:

> Judge William Kenneth Levenworth:
> Elected to the bench three years ago.
> The youngest judge ever elected in Deerfield County at the age of thirty-four.
> The only judge in Deerfield County ever to be indicted.
> Formally charged with bribery, obstruction of justice, and conspiracy.
> If convicted, could serve up to twenty-five years in prison and/or be fined $750,000.

Twenty-five years in prison. My stomach felt like it was capsizing, and my head was throbbing to the point where I had to close my eyes in an attempt to make it stop, to contain the ache. Will couldn't really go to prison. Could he?

I took a deep breath, and I read the article. The gist of what it said was this: that Will had *allegedly* accepted $250,000 from a lawyer to decide in favor of his client. The writer used the word *allegedly* about twenty times in one paragraph—everything about Will was alleged, a word that seemed both like a redundancy and a relief to me all at once.

The article didn't say the name of the lawyer, because he hadn't been charged with anything yet, but it wouldn't have mattered to me anyway. I never kept track of Will's cases or verdicts. And it wasn't something he ever talked about at home. Work was at work (and he was almost always at work). But at home, he was in his study, washing his car, watching football, or, on Friday nights, sharing dinner with me at the club. We ate steak or lobster, made small talk about the neighbors or the new paint samples. We each had a glass of wine. And that was that.

Will had plenty of money. Our house, our cars, my decorating, none of it came cheap. But Will had made really good money at FF&G, and he also made a very nice salary as a judge. So the idea of Will taking a bribe made very little sense to me.

I heard footsteps coming toward the kitchen, so I hastily tucked the paper in the silverware drawer, and hoped he wouldn't find it. "You're still here," I said, stating the obvious. It was after eight, and he never left for work later than seven. I hadn't heard him come in last night, and his side of the bed had been empty when I woke up, something that was not unusual, so I hadn't thought twice about it until now.

He nodded. "Danny told me not to go back."

"For how long?" I asked.

He shrugged, a heavy shrug, as if the weight of the world literally held him down, kept him stooping far below his normal straight six-foot stature. "He's talking to the prosecutor for me." He ran his hand through his hair. "I don't know. Trying to cut a deal."

"A deal?" Though I knew very little about anything in

Will's profession, I thought that cutting a deal was what guilty people did.

"Danny knows what he's doing."

I nodded. Will and I stared at each other for a minute, neither one of us sure what to say. "Do you want coffee?" I finally asked. "Or breakfast? I could make you something."

He shook his head. "No thanks. I'm not very hungry." And then he retreated back into his study.

I tried to remember the last time we'd eaten breakfast together, and I couldn't. It was something we'd done every day when we lived in the city—coffee and oatmeal at the kitchen table. I used to love to watch the way Will's blue eyes lit up first thing in the morning, as if every new day had the possibility to be something special for him, for us.

But that was a long time ago. A different life. I sighed and then headed upstairs to get dressed, as if this was any other day in Deerfield, any other morning. I was playing tennis at nine-thirty, and I didn't want to be late.

The Deerfield Country Club sat at the end of a long, winding drive on top of a hill. It was surrounded on all sides by tall, leafy oaks and thick, lush evergreens. The building itself was large and white, with thick columns out front that looked oddly more like something out of ancient Greece than modern-day suburbia.

The inside was lush and luxurious, appearing more like a five-star resort than a simple tennis and golf club: hallways with thick red carpeting and expensive artwork on the walls. But today, as I stepped inside, I noticed only one thing: the instant and almost deafening quiet.

And then it hit me, that feeling I'd had in junior high school, just after my mother had died of breast cancer. Back then, everyone knew what had happened. Some of them had been to the funeral or even sent cards. But the first time I'd walked back into school that day, after she was dead, there was the unbearable quiet, this silent penetration of eyes, then whispers, about me, not to me. They all knew she was gone, knew I was suffering, but no one knew what to say or how to move, so for a few minutes, as I'd walked down the hall to my locker, the world had been eerily silent. I just kept looking down, watching my feet take one step after another. Counting them. One, two, three, four . . .

I did it now, staring at my too-white tennis shoes collapsing against the deep red carpet that led to the locker room.

And once inside I ran into the bathroom and shut the stall door. I felt dizzy, the blue tile floor swirling and dancing beneath my feet, and I tried to steady myself by sitting down on the toilet seat and taking a deep breath.

Danny was going to know what to do. Everything was going to be fine. Will was a judge. Will was a good judge, or I assumed he must be. This was a mistake. He'd done nothing wrong.

I took a deep breath, and I felt a little better, until I heard the unmistakable twitter of Bethany Maxwell's laugh. Bethany was one of the women I played doubles with and also my friend. Her husband, Kevin, owned a company that made fireproof materials, which had taken off of late. So they were literally rolling in it, as she liked to casually slip into conversation as often as possible.

She was talking to someone, but her voice was muffled, far away, fuzzy, and I couldn't make out her words at first. Then, all of a sudden, her voice became clear, and I heard her say, "Did you see the paper?"

"I did." I was pretty sure that was Amber Tannenbaum,

Bethany's doubles partner, whose husband was some big-shot CFO in New York City.

"I mean really," Bethany said.

"Jennifer's nice enough, but who's going to want to be her friend now?" Amber asked.

Tears stung hot in my eyes, and the door of the stall started swimming in front of me. *Who's going to want to be her friend now?*

I thought about another woman whose name I couldn't even remember now, who used to play doubles tennis with Bethany and Amber before they invited me. *She just didn't fit in with us anymore*, Amber had told me, crinkling up her nose, when I'd asked what had happened.

No. Bethany had shaken her head, while my partner, Lisa Rosenberg, had remained silent. And I'd thought it wise not to bring it up again.

I wiped the tears out of my eyes quickly and shook my head. Then I flushed the toilet, hoping that would be enough for them to move. It was.

When I walked back into the locker room, Bethany and Amber were standing there together with Lisa, who was not only my doubles partner, but also my next-door neighbor. Lisa was putting her hair in a ponytail, while Bethany and Amber were applying their makeup in the mirror. Yes, these two ladies never played tennis without their lipstick. *It doesn't hurt to look beautiful when you're sweating*, Amber would say, and make a face, as if the thought of sweating was really too much to bear.

"Oh, sweetie." Bethany ran and gave me a hug, and I had this strange detached feeling, as if I were watching this unfold like a scene in a movie, from somewhere far away, somewhere distant.

"We heard." Amber patted my shoulder.

"He's totally innocent," I said, enunciating the word *innocent* more than necessary, and looking directly at Amber, who didn't even flinch.

"Of course he is," Lisa said. "I didn't believe it for a second." I smiled at her, because I believed her. Lisa was always the most genuine of all my country club friends. She was the one who'd introduced me into the tennis club, and also the one who'd gotten me involved in the Deerfield Ladies Lunch Club.

The mother of twin five-year-old boys, she'd been a prosecutor in what she called her former life. But just after the boys were born, she and her husband, a plastic surgeon, retreated to the suburbs, and Lisa, now five years away from putting hard-core criminals in jail, was a little overweight and a little ragged around the edges from the demands of the boys, which she called never-ending. *Do not have kids*, she implored me. *Don't do it. You'll lose your ass and your waist and your sanity.*

Oh, it's not all that bad, Bethany would say. *Don't scare her.* Bethany had an almost two-year-old who was so perfectly behaved that her nickname was Angel. Bethany had not lost her ass or her waist—in fact she'd emerged through the pregnancy even thinner and perkier than before.

I've got two words for you, Lisa had whispered to me on more than one occasion. *Tummy Tuck!* And sometimes Lisa even called her this behind her back.

Tummy Tuck hugged me again. "If there's anything we can do," she said, "you just say the word."

"We can play tennis," I said. They were all still staring at me. "Hey, I'm sure it's all going to blow over in a few days anyway."

I grabbed my racket from the bench, and I headed in the direction of the court.

Lisa and I won, two to one. Maybe because every time the ball came my way, I heard Amber's voice saying, *Who's going to want to be friends with her now?* So I kept slamming the ball into Amber's court so hard that it was impossible for her to return it.

When the game was over, the other ladies went to take showers, but I snuck out, before I could overhear anything else that I didn't want to, anything else that would literally make me want to slam a tennis ball down someone's throat.

Three

Once I got into the car, I popped in my Bluetooth and checked my voice mail. My most recent message was from Will wondering when I would be home. I nearly ran a red light when I heard it. Will *never* wondered where I was or when I was coming home. And then there was a message from my sister, Kelly, which said simply, "I just saw the paper. Call me."

I quickly called Will at home, but he didn't answer. I wasn't in the mood to talk to Kelly, so I put that off until later, and instead I called my herbalist, Ethel Greenberg. Though we didn't have an appointment, I asked Ethel if I could stop by. She didn't ask why, and it was clear she'd either seen the paper or just didn't care. "I'm free all morning," she told me.

Ethel Greenberg's office was actually a small, converted detached garage, the inside of which was filled with rickety metal shelves of herbs. Floor-to-ceiling bottles of herbs.

The first time I'd gone to her office was just after we'd

moved out of the city, just after the lump I'd found in my breast had turned out to be benign. Back when I'd worked at *City Style*, I'd done an article on Eastern medicine, and I'd interviewed her.

On my first visit she'd spent five hours monitoring the electrical impulses from my body, checking, as she called them, my meridians. She was a small Jewish woman in her sixties, very grandmotherly, which immediately put me at ease, even after she looked me straight in the eye and said, "You're right. There is bad energy. Underneath here." She held her hand close to my chest, somewhere in between the territory of my heart, breasts, and lungs. "It is small now," she'd said, "but a small crack is rarely just a crack. It's the result of something bigger, something worse, lying just beneath the surface."

I'd nodded, and instead of feeling terrified, I'd felt relieved. Someone else could feel it, the sense of doom I'd felt hanging around in my body for years. And she also told me she could do something about it: a series of herbal remedies that she said would flush my body of toxins.

No one—not my friends, my sister, or even Will—knew that I went to her, because I knew they would think it was insane, think that Ethel was some sort of Eastern medicine quack, but Western medicine had failed to do anything to save my mother. I was a bit undecided myself whether anything Ethel gave me actually helped, but I also didn't think it could hurt.

Now I was on Ethel's maintenance plan, a visit every few months and herbs every night before bed.

I parked my car in Ethel's driveway and rang the bell by her office door. She opened it up right away. "Jennifer." She ushered me through the door. "Come in."

She cleared a box filled with pill bottles off a chair and

motioned for me to sit down. The office was always filled with clutter, something like the den of a mad scientist, and I sometimes wondered if I was Ethel's only patient, though back when I'd interviewed her, it had seemed like there had been others.

"How have you been feeling?" she asked.

"Good. I'm just running low on herbs, and I was in the area," which was not a total lie. I was actually completely out of herbs.

She cocked her head to the side. "Everything is good? Are you sure?"

"My husband," I said. "You saw the paper." Because it was clear from the tone of her voice that she had. Ethel was not a mind reader, only a smart old lady obsessed with the way natural herbs could improve the body's function. This was what she told me the first time we met. "I'm not a psychic," she'd said. "Not a miracle worker." She'd paused. "But that doesn't mean I'm not a healer."

"Yes." She nodded. "I did see the paper. That must be quite a lot of stress for you, Jennifer." Ethel had already told me to keep my stress level down, that stress in itself could prove toxic to the body, could suppress the immune system in ways that science had yet to fully imagine.

"A little," I said, feeling the dizziness I'd felt this morning at the club return, and I shook my head to try to clear it away. "But Will's innocent. It's all a big misunderstanding."

She stared at me for a few minutes and twirled a strand of gray hair around her finger. "Okay," she said. "But in addition to the usual I'm going to give you something else, something for calming."

"Okay," I agreed, willing to do whatever Ethel told me, not because I necessarily believed it would work, but because I

believed that *she* believed it would. And who wouldn't want
to trust in a little old Jewish grandma who was trying to keep
you whole?

She went to her shelves, and though any normal person
would be daunted by the sheer number of herbs, she always
knew exactly where it all was, immediately. She handed me
my four usual bottles, plus the new fifth one. "Let me know
if there's any problems," she said. "And I'll see you back in
three months." Then she bowed toward me as she always did
and said, "Namaste."

"Namaste." I nodded back. I always repeated it back to her,
even though I had no idea what it meant.

When I got back to my house, Will's car was gone, and there
was a note on the table that said he'd gone into the city to
meet Danny for lunch. It was funny to see the note there, in
his square block all-caps writing, as if he was neatly shouting
at me, which maybe he was.

Will and I didn't leave each other notes. We didn't talk
about whom we ate lunch with, what we ate, or what we did
in the space between breakfast and dinner at all. Or at least
we hadn't for the past few years. I'd never mentioned Ethel to
Will, not because I thought he would disapprove, as I knew
my sister, Kelly, would, but more because it just never came
up. Will didn't notice my pill bottles of herbs, or if he did, he
didn't ask.

I took a yogurt out of the fridge for lunch and got my list of
phone numbers for the other ladies on the board of the charity auction. The auction, which we always held the Saturday
before Thanksgiving, was only six weeks away, and we had
some planning and dividing up of tasks to do.

The charity auctions had been my idea, sort of my break

into the Deerfield social scene, if you will. Right after Will and I moved here, I met Lisa. Or I guess I should say she made a point of meeting me.

As the movers carried in our boxes, and Will and I stood in the driveway directing them, she walked over and handed me a plate of lopsided muffins.

"I made these for you," she said. "Welcome to the neighborhood." I guess she noticed my face as I looked at the uneven and oddly shaped muffins. "They're blueberry," she said. "My mother-in-law's recipe."

"Thank you," I said. "They look delicious."

"I'm not the greatest with presentation," she said. And that was Lisa in a nutshell; she really was very nice, and she tried hard, but there was always something a little too gruff, a little too edgy about her to really be a housewife or a refined lady of Deerfield. That was also why I liked her immediately. That—and there was a little something about her that reminded me of Kat.

I invited her to sit down in the driveway and share a muffin, and she invited me to join the Deerfield Ladies Lunch Club. They met once a week at different houses and, as the name implied, had lunch. "It's sort of like a book club," she said. "Only we eat, instead of read. And good stuff, too. Gourmet."

"I'm good with eating," I told her.

After a few meetings, when we were having lunch at Bethany's house, the women started talking about Helen Kemper, who I'd met once, only briefly, before she started undergoing chemotherapy for breast cancer, and who hadn't been back to the lunch club since.

"I wish there was something we could do," Bethany said, shaking her head.

"There's nothing anyone can do," Lisa said. "It's a private

thing." She said it like she knew, and I wondered if, like me, she did.

Then it occurred to me. We were a bunch of women, mostly smart, college-educated women, with time, probably too much time, on our hands. And the truth was, I was bored. After we'd moved out of the city, I'd fallen into a steady social life and an obsession with decorating, which all seemed to keep me busy on the surface, but sometimes underneath, it felt as if I was just passing time, just waiting for something real to happen. "We could have a charity auction," I said. Everyone stopped talking and looked at me, a little curious or a little annoyed, I wasn't sure which at first. "Raise money for breast cancer research. Or something," I added, just in case they all thought it was a terrible idea.

"That's actually very good," Lisa said.

Everyone else chimed in with nods and uh-hums. And that was how I made my place in the Deerfield social scene, as the organizer of the first annual and then the second annual and now coming up on the fourth annual auction. After Helen Kemper died last year, we renamed it in her honor, which, Lisa had said, making a lame attempt at a joke to lighten the mood, made us kind of like Susan G. Komen, except without the dreadful running.

And that was that. I was a member. Of the lunch club, of the country club, of the Deerfield high society. The women were all nice to me, and before I knew it I was part of the tennis team, and I was also being invited to parties and lunches. Though Kelly instantly made fun of it when I told her about it, I was surprised, almost awed, by the easy way I'd been accepted into life in Deerfield.

"Well, it doesn't hurt that your husband is a judge," Kelly said, just after Will got elected.

"That's not what it's about," I'd told her, annoyed at her inability to understand. Kelly had only a few close friends that she'd had and kept since high school. Her life was insular and revolved around her husband, Dave; her three kids; and her photography. "No one cares about Will," I'd scoffed.

But now, sitting there with my list of names and ten calls to make, I was worried that she'd been right all along. And I still couldn't get Amber's words out of my head—*Who's going to want to be friends with her now?*

As I went one by one down the list, each call started the same way. "Hi, it's Jen Levenworth."

Long awkward pause. Slow recovery. "Oh, Jen. I, uh . . ."

A sigh from me. "He's totally innocent. It's all a big mistake."

"Of course it is. I never thought anything else." Pause. "Oh, you poor, poor thing."

When I was done making the calls, I felt strange. Usually planning for the auction made me feel alive, but now my body was tight and heavy, and my eyes were having trouble focusing on the sheets of numbers. *Stress.* I pulled out the bag of herbs Ethel had given me and fished around for the new calming one. I swallowed the pill quickly with only a few sips of water, and then I sat and waited to feel something else, to feel calmer.

After a few minutes I felt tired, so tired, in fact, that I lay down on the couch and closed my eyes. I thought about Will, and the facts I'd read about in the paper. And then I was dreaming.

"Judge Levenworth, Jude Marris is here to see you."
I was sitting behind Will's desk, cloaked in his black

judge's robe. I reached up and rubbed my hand through my hair, short and curly. I was Will.

I looked up and met Janice's eyes. "Thank you." I nodded. "Send him in."

I was tired. No, exhausted. Case law to read. Verdicts to write out and decide. Lawyers to meet in my chambers. I pulled up my suit arm and glanced at my watch. Three-thirty. And I had at least four more hours of work. Better ask Janice to make some more coffee. And yet my stomach churned just thinking of it, the acid reflux I'd encountered since taking this job enough to put me through two bottles of Tums a week.

The door opened up, and Jude walked in. He was a thin, wiry man who was rumored to have a coke habit, and I'd gone against him once back when I'd been trying product liability cases as a lawyer. I'd won. No, I'd annihilated him. "Judge." He nodded.

I nodded back. "Mr. Marris."

"May I have a seat?"

"Go right ahead."

He folded his arms, then unfolded them again, shifting in his chair. I checked my watch, only three thirty-five. I sighed. "You know that matter we discussed last week," he said.

"I do." I nodded again. His client was a big-shot CEO who was being sued for sexual harassment. Mr. Marris had already been in last week, asking for a motion to dismiss, which I'd denied. "Well, I talked to the client, and he's willing to do anything." He leaned in closer. "I mean anything, to win."

"You'll be preparing a good defense then." I shuf-

*fled the papers on the desk, cuing him to get out, before
it got awkward and I had to throw him out.*

*"I don't think you understand," Marris said, lean-
ing in closer. "Listen to what I'm telling you."*

"Jen." Will shook my shoulder, and I opened my eyes and
saw him there, in our living room, looming above me. His
face looked dim, blurry, and I blinked to try to get my eyes
back in focus. "It's after six," he said.

I sat up. "I guess I was tired." But the words felt strange
coming out, my voice thick, and all I could think about was
what it felt like to be Will in my dream, how I'd felt so tired
and overwhelmed and not at all happy sitting in the judge's
chambers.

"Are you okay?" Will asked.

I closed my eyes for a second, trying to erase the dull ache
in my head, and then I nodded. "How was your meeting with
Danny?" I asked, remembering where he'd come from.

He shrugged. "It was fine." His voice sounded low and
stretched, so it was clear that it was anything but fine.

He stood up, and I knew he was going to walk back into
the study, and I didn't want him to. I couldn't shake the feeling of my dream, the feeling of emptiness. I reached out for
his hand. "Are you hungry? Do you want me to make some
dinner?"

He shook me off. "No thanks," he said. "I already ate."
And then he turned and walked into his study.

Four

The next morning I was still thinking about my dream, about how it had felt to be Will. I couldn't get it out of my head, really, the exhaustion, the annoyance, the sense of being displaced, and it was strange because usually I didn't dream. Sometimes, every once in a while, I'd remember a snippet of something when I woke up, but even then I couldn't quite remember if I'd dreamed it or just seen it somewhere else. But not like this, not something that felt so vivid, so tangible, that it still lingered in my mind as a weird sort of half-truth.

Will wandered into the bathroom as I was washing my face, and without saying anything, stepped toward me and put his hand on my shoulder, gingerly, as if he wasn't sure how to touch me, as if I were made of glass, and if he did it too hard I could break, shatter all over the beautiful beige marble floor. His hand felt strange on my shoulder, almost as if it was pushing me away, rather than pulling me closer.

But after a minute of hesitation, he moved his hand to the

back of my neck and did pull me toward him. He started kissing me, softly at first, and then harder, and I got this odd feeling from him that I'd never felt before, not from Will, tall, steady, confident Will. No, this was something else entirely: neediness. It had been a while since he'd kissed me like this, kissed me more than just a quick peck, and yet as soon as he did, it felt natural again, and I leaned into him and kissed him back.

He put his hand up to unbutton my nightgown, and his fingers felt warm as they grazed my bare skin. "I'm not ovulating," I whispered, as if this would be the only time, the only reason for sex. After I said it, I realized how stupid it sounded, and I wondered if my head and my heart wanted separate things.

"So," he whispered back. "So what?" And then there was something else in his voice, some of that urgency I recognized from years ago.

When we first got married, I would wait up for him to get home from the office, and even if it was ten o'clock and Will hadn't eaten dinner yet, he'd start kissing me, and wherever he found me in the apartment, the kitchen, the living room, the bathtub, we'd be having sex right there, as if there was no time to move to the bed.

But now Will scheduled everything. Every minute of every day, including, lately, sex—if you could count some of the quick, passionless exchanges as sex at all. I saw it there when I went in to vacuum the study, written on his calendar midmonth, just around the date when I told him I thought I'd be ovulating.

The lawyer's words from my dream swam in my head: *He's willing to do anything, anything to win.* And the words from yesterday's paper: *twenty-five years in prison.* I closed my eyes and had this horrible vision of Will in a tacky orange prison jumpsuit, his hand reaching for me across a partition.

I heard my cell phone ringing from the bedroom, and I pulled back. "I have to get that," I said, feeling both disappointed and relieved for the interruption. He nodded, but he turned away so he didn't have to meet my gaze, and as I ran to grab the phone, I heard his footsteps treading heavily down the stairs.

On the other end of the phone was my sister, Kelly. "Oh good," she said when I picked up. "You're alive."

"Yes." I sighed. "I'm alive."

"You sound out of breath."

"I'm not," I lied, closing my eyes and trying to breathe slowly, trying to forget the way Will's lips had felt, needy and yet warm.

I heard some screaming in the background and Muffet, the dog, barking. "Hang on a sec," she said. "I'm putting Hannah down for her nap." It made no sense, since she'd called me, but that was Kelly, always making me feel like I was the one interrupting her perfect life.

Kelly lived twenty minutes south of us, in Oak Glen Borough, right on the edge of Deerfield County. She lived only one neighborhood away from the one we'd grown up in, from the house where our father had lived until he'd retired, met Sharon Wasserstein on JDate, and moved down to Boca Raton with her.

But despite our physical proximity to each other, Kelly and I usually only saw each other on scheduled holidays and birthdays, and we didn't talk more than once a week or so. The truth was, I would rather talk to one of my friends than talk to her, and she was always busy anyway.

Kelly had three kids younger than the age of five, two boys

and a girl. Her oldest, Caleb, had finally started preschool this year, but she told me, the last time I'd talked to her, that the chaos hadn't let up. Once she'd described motherhood to me as drowning in a kaleidoscope. *There's colors everywhere,* she said. *So many colors that you can taste them, and nowhere to go and no way out.* She'd paused and then added with complete sincerity, *But I love it. Every minute of it.*

In addition to staying home full-time with the kids, she was also a freelance photographer, so dotting the walls, amid the clutter in her house, there were beautiful black-and-white landscape prints. They amazed me every time I saw them, the way my sister was able to capture something, a moment, in a picture, in a way that I never would've been able to see it at all. But that said everything, the way the world always looked so completely different to the two of us.

"Anyway," she said now, when she came back. I noticed it was stunningly quiet, and I wondered where she had to go to get it that quiet. The bathroom? "I was worried sick about you. Why didn't you call me?"

"I'm sorry," I said, mumbling something about being busy and planning on doing it right after breakfast. "And besides," I said, repeating my spiel from yesterday when I made the auction calls, "he's innocent. The whole thing is a mistake."

Unlike those other women, she wasn't so easily convinced. "Are you sure?"

"Of course." I jumped to answer her, but I felt my pulse starting to race, sweat starting to bead up on my brow. "It's Will," I said. "*Will.*" I looked up, and suddenly my bedroom felt too bright, the blues in the room too harsh, and I wondered if this was often how Kelly felt with the kids. Stress, I reasoned. And I blinked my eyes, until the room looked normal again.

"Will," Kelly repeated thoughtfully, as if she really was trying to picture it, him doing something wrong. *Yes*, I thought, *Will, the guy who refuses to drive even one mile above the speed limit.* If it was forty-five, he set his cruise control exactly at forty-five. "Still," she said, "you never really know how well you know someone, you know?"

"Kel, he's my husband." I left out the part about us not really speaking beyond simple pleasantries in months, the part about my dream, so oddly specific that it almost felt real. *How well did I know him now?* But I wouldn't give her the satisfaction of knowing this. Not when she and Dave had the perfect life, the perfect marriage. Kelly even had a doting mother-in-law whom she confided in—something I did not have since Will's mother was also dead.

"So what now?" she asked. "I mean, what's going to happen to him?"

"I don't know," I said. "Our friend Danny's working on it."

"It said in the paper he could go to jail." She said it quietly.

Tears burned hot in my eyes, and I blinked them back. "He's not going to go to jail," I said, just as quietly, trying to sound more sure than I felt.

I considered, for a second, telling her about our moment in the bathroom, and how a part of me wished I was still back there kissing him, feeling his hands on my body. But then she would probably tell me about her own glorious and spontaneous sex this morning with her perfect husband, Dave, and I wasn't in the mood, so all I said was "How are the kids?"

"Oh, they're fine. Everyone's good." She paused. "Jen, I really am worried about you."

"Don't be," I said, trying to sound absolutely sure. "Everything's going to be fine. I gotta go," I lied. "I'll call you later, okay?"

"Jen, I—" I waited for her to say something meaningful, something that would help, but all she said was "Don't forget to call me."

After I hung up, I cradled the phone in my hand for a minute and wished that I really had been able to talk to Kelly, that I'd been able to tell her about my moment at the club yesterday and the strange state of my sex life lately. But Kelly was the most judgmental person I knew—especially when it came to relationships.

Kelly and Dave had met in high school, and had been together ever since. They were one of those couples who, just to look at them, you absolutely knew they belonged together. They even resembled each other in this strange way—both on the shorter side, with brown wavy hair, green eyes, and a complexion just a shade lighter than olive.

They started dating right before our mother died. Kelly was sixteen, and she'd brought Dave home to meet our mother, just before she got really sick. It was the last time she cooked a big dinner, and I can still remember what it was, her sumptuous barbecue brisket and kugel—two recipes that seemed to have disappeared when my father sold the house, though secretly I imagined that my father's girlfriend, Sharon, stole them and was keeping them for herself.

My mother kept smiling at Dave and heaping more brisket on his plate. And he ate it all, complimenting her on how great it was. I was thirteen, and I didn't understand exactly how sick she was or how much Kelly liked him, and I left the table early, lying about having a lot of homework, but really I'd lain on my bed and listened to music.

After she died, Dave was at the funeral and the shivah afterward. He sat there on the blue-plaid couch that my mother had purchased and my father would eventually donate to Goodwill, and he had his arm around Kelly the whole time, as if he alone was sustaining her, was literally holding on to her so she would make it through the week. I stared at them with envy and annoyance. I wanted someone to hold me up, someone to still love me. With my mother gone, it seemed like it was never going to happen again.

When Kelly and Dave stayed together all through college and then got married right after, I told myself that it couldn't possibly last. That there was no way you could love the guy you started dating at sixteen.

When I was sixteen, I had sex for the first time with Joey Feldman, a guy that I dated for three months, who took me to the junior prom and then promptly broke up with me when school let out for summer. He had sandy blond hair and blue eyes, and he'd played soccer. There was nothing memorable about the sex except it sucked, the way every first time probably did, even with Kelly and Dave, though I doubted they'd ever admit that, even to each other.

For a long time I told myself that the only reason Kelly stayed with him, the only reason she married him, was because Dave had gotten my mother's approval, and that was something, maybe the last part of my mother, that she couldn't let go of.

Yet here they still were, thirteen years of marriage later, and you could tell by the way they looked at each other, the way they touched each other in seemingly insignificant moments, that they really did love each other.

And sometimes, that was reason enough for me to hate my sister.

I took my time, taking a shower, getting dressed, hoping that Will might have gone out. But he hadn't. He was there, sitting at the kitchen table again, head in his hands, just like he'd been two days earlier. He looked up when he heard me walk into the room. "It's over," he said. "It's all over." He had tears in his eyes, which I saw him trying to blink away, as if he hoped I wouldn't notice. I pretended not to.

"Oh, thank God. They're dropping the charges." I sat down next to him, the sudden absence of his burden making me feel light, ethereal, almost dizzy, again. I leaned in to hug him, but he shook me off.

"No," he said. "Danny struck a deal with the prosecutor."

"What kind of deal?"

"I'll resign," he said, refusing to look me in the eye. "And be permanently disbarred."

"I don't understand. You're innocent," I said. *Resign. Disbarred.* These didn't feel like words that were even in Will's vocabulary.

He shook his head. "I'm a judge," he said. "Was. I was a judge," he corrected himself. "I know better than anyone that innocent doesn't always mean something."

I was shocked to hear Will so cynical, Will, who usually talked about the law as if it was glamorous dinner party fodder. "It does to you," I pushed.

He shook his head. "It's complicated, Jen." He sighed. "Danny says this is the only option, and I trust him." He paused, then said quietly, "I can't risk it. Waiting it out. Going to prison." His voice cracked on the word *prison*.

"No," I said. "Of course you can't." But I wanted him to fight, wanted him to wait it out. Innocent people didn't just roll over and play dead. Innocent people fought.

"I know it's hard for you to understand," he said, as if for the first time in a long time, he actually did know what I was thinking. He looked at me, then looked down at the floor, the

Five

The *Deerfield Daily* did a stellar job of reporting it all, every last-minute detail, in a front-page article replete with enough definitions and fact boxes to make your head spin. *Resignation—notification of leaving a job. Disbarment— taking away officially the right of an attorney to practice law.*

Seeing it in print made it feel oddly real, as if the conversation with Will had only been a dream, something that couldn't have possibly happened until I read someone else's third-person account of the events.

After I read it, I waited for the phone to ring, for people to call and console me, but only Kelly did. "What are you going to do now?" she asked, and being completely unable to answer her, I lied and said I was in the middle of baking a pie and had to call her back, though I knew I wouldn't do it right away.

What I already knew for sure was this: It only takes a

bamboo shiny and unflawed. "If you want to leave me I . . . I . . ." He held his hands up in the air, not sure how to continue the sentiment.

"What's that supposed to mean?" I huffed. "Do you want me to leave you?" A part of me hoped he would take the bait, the bait he never took, that we could fight, get angry, yell, have makeup sex that felt real and passionate.

"No," he said quietly. "Of course not."

"Well, why did you say it?" I egged him on.

"I don't know," he said. "I just . . . I don't know." He paused. "If you need me I'll be in the study."

"The study?" I heard my voice rise.

"Danny faxed me the papers," he said, and then turned and walked toward the study, as if he hadn't even noticed, as if my annoyance hadn't hit him at all.

moment for your life to change forever. This was something I'd been keenly aware of since the age of thirteen.

All it took was one little thing, one rogue cancer cell that breaks into a lymph node, something microscopic, invisible at first. Until it multiplies, grows, a tumor on your liver and then one on your lungs, until it has gone from a stage one disaster to a stage four catastrophe—a stage from which there is no going back.

So in the quiet of my kitchen, staring at the article that shattered everything I'd thought to be true about Will, I sat there and waited calmly for the rest of my world to explode.

It was Lisa who knocked on my door, the next morning.

When I opened the door, I saw her standing there on the porch, with what looked like a smooshed pineapple upside-down cake in an aluminum pie tin. Four years later, and Lisa had not been able to up the presentation one bit.

"For you." She handed me the cake.

"You want to come in and have some coffee and a slice?" I asked her.

She shook her head. "I shouldn't. I'm supposed to be making the boys' Halloween costumes today. And that piece of crap sewing machine is not cooperating." I was sure it was not a piece of crap sewing machine at all, but a top of the line one that Lisa didn't really know how to use.

"I'm impressed," I said, and I really was. "You're making their costumes."

She rolled her eyes. "Yeah well. Chance and Chester wanted to be Peanut Butter and Jelly, and there's no store in the freakin' world that sells that. Believe me, I looked."

I nodded, and I waited for her to say it. Whatever it was

she'd come here to say. She didn't normally just drop cakes by my house.

"Look," she finally said. "Oh shit. I feel like such an ass-hole."

"Just say it," I said, dreading whatever it was all the same.

"Bethany's going to run the auction this year."

"Okay." I nodded. And though I probably should've been expecting it, I still wanted to yell or scream or throw the cake in her face, but my body, my head felt numb and incredibly listless, so I just stood still.

"And. The ladies don't think you should . . . Well, they don't want you to be in the lunch club anymore. And please, please, please don't hate me. I'm just the messenger."

I wondered if Lisa had argued, if she'd stood up for me, and though I wanted to believe she had, I thought she probably hadn't. Lisa and I were friends, but deep down I knew our friendship was secondary to her role in Deerfield. After all, she'd had that first, before she'd even known me.

"You could leave him, you know. No one would blame you if you did."

I shook my head. Despite the way the threads of our marriage had come apart lately, I could not imagine walking away, walking out the door for an auction, a lunch club. Her suggestion made me angrier than when Will had suggested it yesterday, because with Will, I'd known deep down that he hadn't really meant it, that he hadn't really wanted me to leave. But with her, it seemed like she genuinely thought I should or I might. I glared at her. "He's innocent, Lisa."

She cocked her head to the side, and she put on her serious prosecutor face. "It was just easier to believe before he resigned. And got disbarred," she said. "I mean, that's some serious shit, that permanent disbarment."

"Thanks for the cake." I held it up and pasted on a fake smile, an I-don't-want-to-discuss-this-with-you-you-crappy-little-friend smile. Then I closed the door, before she could say another word.

"Who was at the door?" Will asked. He emerged from his study, clad in sweatpants and a sweatshirt, his face stubbly from a week without shaving, his hair rumpled and uncombed.

"No one," I said, walking toward the trash can and dumping the cake in, tin and all. "Maybe we should move," I said. "Start over somewhere else, where no one's ever heard of us."

"I'm not going to hide," he said, as if it would be the act of hiding that would actually make him look guilty. "Besides," he said, "in this market, we'd never sell the house."

I turned to face him, looked him solidly in the eye, and said, "What now then?"

"I don't know," he said, and then he turned and went back in his study without saying another word.

That night, as I got ready for bed, my hands felt shaky, my heart felt like it was pounding too fast, out of control, and my head was throbbing worse than it ever had. I took my herbs with a full glass of water, and then I brushed my teeth and got into bed and waited. Waited to feel calm.

Will always knew what to do, always had a plan. The fact that now he didn't almost scared me more than anything else that had happened in the past week.

But after a few minutes, I did feel more relaxed. My body felt limp and warm and soft. My headache dulled to a mild twinge just above my eyebrows. *Ethel knows her stuff*, I thought, feeling a true sense of tranquillity from the calming herb for the first time.

Just on the brink of sleep, I thought about Lisa's messed-

up pineapple cake rotting in my trash can. I wondered if Will
would remember to take out the trash, or if I would go down,
find it there in the morning, and be forced to rehash my horrible moments on the porch.

*I was standing in Lisa's kitchen. I recognized it from
having had Ladies Lunch Club here—the pale green
color, the thick maple cabinets that nearly reached
the ceiling, the custom slate tile backsplash that
matched the slate tile floor. I was walking around,
from refrigerator to counter and back again, taking
out ingredients, squinting to read the recipe without
my glasses. Glasses? I didn't wear reading glasses.*

*But yes, I did. I picked them up. Lisa's reading
glasses—red-rimmed and oval, on a diamond chain
that Barry had bought for Mother's Day. I put them
on, and I could see.*

*I read the recipe for the cake. It was my mother-
in-law's recipe. I thought, That bitch is freakin' Betty
Crocker, and every time she looks at my cakes she grimaces. So my cakes look like shit? Big freakin' deal.
They still taste good.*

*I measured out the ingredients, just so, dumped
them in a bowl, melted butter at the bottom of the glass
pan, added brown sugar, pineapple, cake batter, and
then voilà, put it in the oven for thirty minutes. A cake
for Jen, I thought. And now I could be freakin' Marie
Antoinette. Let her eat cake.*

*I went to the bathroom, and then I stared at myself
in the mirror, tried hard to make myself smile. Even
smiling, I looked pale, listless, ghostlike.*

The phone rang. I walked slowly to get it. Something told me it could be Chance and Chester's school. Maybe they were hurt. Or sick. But the fog in my brain made it hard to worry, to think or feel. Everything was dulled and blurry. It felt hard to move, as if the air were thicker than water. And I was tired. So, so tired.

I picked up the phone, on the fifth ring.

The lady on the other end informed me that Chester had forgotten his lunch.

Of course I'll bring it down, I said, with the fake joy of someone who loved this fucked-up life, the life of someone who baked and sewed and cleaned and took care of everyone. My voice sounded ethereal, estranged, as if it was not coming from me at all but from somewhere just a little distance away, like the radio on the kitchen counter.

I lay down on the couch and thought about getting Chester's lunch, but I knew I had to wait for the cake anyway, and I was tired, so I threw a blanket over myself and closed my eyes.

Eventually I heard the buzzer for the cake, from far, far away, as if it was cutting through something like ice, to make its way toward me.

I woke up sweating, tangled up in the sheets, breathing shallow, rapid breaths. "Jen, what is it?" Will whispered. He sounded absolutely awake, and I wondered if he hadn't even fallen asleep yet, though it seemed to be almost dawn.

"Lisa's kitchen," I said.

"You were dreaming."

"But it felt so real." I thought about the feeling of fog, the deep and overwhelming sensation of trying to rise above a sea that was slowly pulling me under, and I could still feel it, still feel her.

"You should write it down," Will said. "Isn't that what writers do with dreams? Keep a dream journal or something?"

"I don't know," I said.

But after I watched him roll over and close his eyes, I got out of bed, went into the computer room, and rifled through the drawers until I found an old reporter's notebook.

Six

My mother had a soft voice, so that even when she was yelling it sounded like she was saying something sweet. After she died, I would dream about her, hear her voice talking to me in my sleep, and it always was incredibly soothing, until I woke up. I guess that's the way it is with dreams, they always seem much more surreal when you think about them after the fact than they do in the moment.

So maybe that's why I felt so unsettled, sitting there the next morning, reading over the dream of Lisa that I'd transcribed last night into my reporter's notebook. Or maybe it was because it was a Wednesday, and I was supposed to play tennis at the club, but I also knew that I wouldn't be welcome there anymore, that I was not expected to show up.

Will had taken to the couch, in his sweatpants and worn gray sweatshirt. He was flipping between ESPN and FOX Sports as I closed the reporter's notebook and checked the fridge. The only thing I had for dinner was a chicken, which had expired yesterday. It was unlike me to let things spoil in the refrigerator. I was usually on top of these things, but last night Will had been in his study and I'd made only a can of soup for myself.

I took the chicken out of the fridge and threw it in the trash can, right on top of Lisa's rotting cake. "Will, you didn't take the trash out last night."

He didn't answer so I slammed things around, making way more noise than necessary as I took the bag out and took it to the garage. "I'm going to the market," I announced, when I got back. No answer. "Will," I said louder.

He paused the TV. "What?"

"I'm going to the market. Do you want anything?"

He shook his head and put the TV back on.

I drove a little too fast to Whole Foods, accidentally ran a red light, and nearly swiped an old lady pulling into the parking lot. Still, she was in the middle of the lane, so I honked at her, only to see her give me the finger. I caught a glimpse of her, and even though I knew it wasn't, she looked oddly like my father's girlfriend, Sharon.

Maybe it was the gesture, something Sharon might do. But no, Sharon was much more backhanded than that, and I felt thankful that Deerfield news did not readily wing its way down to Boca. The last thing I needed was Sharon on my case about it.

As soon as I walked through the automatic double doors, I saw Amber and Bethany in their tennis whites, standing at the line by the coffee kiosk. I willed them not to look my way, not to see me here, unshowered, with my hair in a messy ponytail, wearing only gray yoga pants and a black hooded sweatshirt. I usually didn't leave the house this way, but I'd been so annoyed with Will that I'd wanted to make a statement, wanted to storm out in a huff so he would notice. Though I doubted he had.

And then, just as I'd almost gotten safely by them, Amber looked right at me, then looked away. She elbowed Bethany, who looked up, offered a half smile that looked more like a grimace (or maybe it was just too much Botox?), and then pretended to be incredibly interested in her soy latte.

I didn't want to make a scene, and I didn't want to run into anyone else either, so I turned and quickly walked out. Then I got in the car and drove to the Acme in Oak Glen, by Kelly's house, where I knew I wouldn't be able to find the organic foods I usually coveted, but where I also knew not a single person there would recognize me.

And so the days went.

Will on the couch during the day, in his study at night, not even coming out to eat, or at least not when I was home or awake, while I invented reasons to leave the house. Acme every morning, and then afterward, sometimes, a drive. Sometimes I drove by Kelly's house and thought about stopping in. She'd been calling me every day, just to see how things were going, but I'd been lying, telling her everything was fine, fine, fine. "A job does not define a person," I'd told her, trying my best to sound like I believed it.

"I know that, Jen," she'd said right back. "But still—"

Her *still* hung thick in the air between us, and I let it sit there, not bothering to explain more.

But here, a week and a half later, Will's stubble had grown

so thick that it was starting to look like something resembling a beard, and I couldn't be sure when he'd last taken a shower, much less shaved.

And then, as I left to go to Acme, I drove past the blue Daniels and Sons truck, waiting to turn into our driveway. I grimaced at the sight of it.

In the time between my mother's cancer "scare" and her stage four diagnosis four years later, my father quit his job as an accountant and bought a small landscaping company that he'd renamed Daniels and Sons. Though it was clear he was never going to have any sons, he thought it added an air of longevity to the title.

I'm not sure my father knew anything about landscaping before he bought the company, but he did know something about business, so during the worst of my mother's illness and then after her death, he threw himself into his work, growing the business from five employees to fifty. Daniels and Sons was a big name in Deerfield County now—I drove by those little blue trucks all the time, and they always made me feel unsettled. Made me remember the way my father had ignored us, the hours I was home alone after school and at night while my father worked and Kelly was out with Dave and then later off at college.

When my father retired six years ago, he gave the business to Dave. Just outright gave it to him, which Will told me was actually illegal for tax purposes. When I mentioned this to Kelly, she said, "So what the hell? Is he going to call the IRS or something?"

"No," I said. "I just thought you should know."

But my dad had wanted out, and Dave—the guy my dad said was the closest thing to a real son anyway, blatantly ignoring the fact that Will and I had just gotten engaged—wanted the business to stay in the family. Not that Will would've wanted the business, but it still seemed like my dad should've given it some consideration.

Nope. One day he was the CEO of Daniels and Sons, and the next he was packing up for Boca with Sharon Wasserstein. And Dave and Kelly were proud business owners.

Under Dave, the business was doing well. Or so Kelly reported at regular intervals, as if I would care, as if it would mean something to me. It didn't. After we moved to Deerfield, Will convinced me to hire them to mow our lawn, do our weeding, and plant our flowers, even though I had been strongly against it. "We can't just go hire someone else," Will had said. "Your sister would have a fit."

"We wouldn't have to tell her," I said, but then reluctantly agreed. Still, I made a point of not being home on Wednesday mornings when they showed up.

But today when I saw the blue truck pull down the driveway, with the trailer attached, when I watched the two men hop out and take out the tractor and the rake, when I thought about Will inside, lying like a lump on our couch, I had an idea.

I dialed Kelly's number on the drive to Acme, and as soon as she picked up, I said, "Will needs a job." If Will had known what I was asking, I knew he would've been mad, and not the kind of mad that I wanted him to get, but the kind of mad where he just glared at me, and then continued to sulk on the couch.

"Oh, Jen." Kelly sighed.

"It was Dad's business," I said. "Dad's business," I repeated for emphasis.

"I don't know," she said.

"Come on, Kelly." I didn't want her to make me beg, to make me tell her how much Will needed it. The silence on her end was so unusual for her that it made my head hurt.

"Fine," she finally said. "I'll ask Dave."

"Thanks," I said. "And have him pretend like it was his idea, okay?"

"He hasn't even said yes yet." But we both knew he would. Dave was a good guy, and he always did whatever Kelly asked. "What about you?" she asked. "Are you going to go back to work?"

Truthfully, I hadn't really thought about it, hadn't thought beyond the drive to Acme and what I might make for dinner. "I'm considering my options," I said, as if I had them.

After we hung up, I thought about it. What were my options? No baby. No friends. No charity auction to plan. Maybe going back to work *was* my only option now. I'd quit working just after we moved to Deerfield because it had seemed like too much to commute into the city every day, we hadn't really needed the money, we thought we might have kids at some point "soon," and I'd told Will I'd always wanted to write a novel. But all of that was only partly true, and though I knew Will knew it deep down, he never confronted me about it.

I thought about the feelings I'd had in my dream, as Lisa, and they felt oddly familiar. There was a certain numbness to my life in Deerfield, in my relationship with Will and my friends, even before everything that had happened in the last few weeks.

It occurred to me now how stupid I'd been to ever consider Amber and Bethany and the other ladies of the lunch club my friends—even my interactions with them had been superficial, anesthetized—conversations about recipes and cleaning and gossip about the ladies who weren't there. And then I thought about myself, sitting there the night before Will got indicted, watching that DVD alone, and I couldn't even remember what it was I'd been watching. The way I'd felt then, the way I was feeling now—it was the same way I'd felt as Lisa, as if I were trying to walk through water.

I tried to remember the last time I hadn't felt that, even the slightest hint of that fog, and I pictured myself sitting at my desk at *City Style*, Kat sitting across from me, laughing. Yes, I'd felt things then—joy and passion and hope and anger and sadness—and in a life in the suburbs, a life that was supposedly perfect, somehow those things had gotten lost.

Kat was an editor at *City Style* now, and I knew if anyone could get me my job back, she could. I pictured taking the train down to the city every day, entering back into the city life where most people wouldn't know or care who Will was. And it did seem like a good idea. So as I perused the pathetic fruit aisle at Acme and longed for the organic section at Whole Foods, I decided to give her a call.

"Oh, hon," Kat said as soon as she heard my voice. "Danny and I feel just awful about the whole thing." To her credit, she didn't mention that we hadn't talked in at least two months, or that the last time we had talked, things had been awkward. We'd lost some of our connection, our commonality: She was a working mom now, with two little girls to worry about, and I'd felt all my talk about the lunch club and tennis had seemed silly and mundane in comparison to what she'd had to say.

"Then come up for a visit on Sunday," I said, almost on a whim, wanting to see her, wanting to feel something again. "I'll make that lamb roast that you like." *As long as they sell lamb roast at Acme,* I silently added, guessing that they actually might not. Well, they were bound to have some kind of roast here.

She paused for a minute, as if she was really considering saying no, as if she, like the women of Deerfield, wasn't sure if she should be seen with me anymore, but then I heard someone else talking to her in the background, and I understood that I'd misjudged her. "What time do you want us?" she asked.

Seven

Once, years ago, I told Kat that I owed her for everything. It was the night before my wedding, when Kat had taken me to a bar in the city to celebrate my last night of being single. I'd had one too many Amaretto sours, and when I said it, I'd held on to her, hugged her, and whispered it loudly into her ear. But it wasn't just the alcohol talking—I'd really meant it. Because Kat was the one who'd set me up with Will.

I met Kat when I first started working at *City Style*, and we became fast friends. Then she got engaged and went on a mission to pair up everyone she knew. Her fiancé, Danny Halloway, worked at FF&G, and his best friend, Will Levenworth, seemed like the perfect person to set me up with, or so she said, again and again and again, until I agreed, if only to shut her up.

"No blind dates," I'd kept protesting, with an air of having had so many bad ones in the past that I was jaded. The truth was, I'd only ever been on one blind date before that one, but it had been a doozy. Kelly had set me up with Dave's friend's brother—the guy drank so much that by the end of dinner he was slurring his words and trying to grab my breasts across the table.

"What the hell?" I said to Kelly afterward.

"How was I supposed to know he had a drinking problem?" she'd huffed. "He's a perfectly nice guy sober." As if the whole thing was my fault.

So I went into my date with Will with trepidation, a turtleneck, and plenty of money for a cab home.

We went to the opening of an Italian restaurant, Il Romano, and I was supposed to be writing a review, so really it was a working dinner for me, something that made it feel less like a blind date, and not a total waste of time.

Will was early, already at the table, a little half-circle booth in the corner, when I arrived. I got a good look at him before he saw me. He was tall, with perfect, straight posture, thick brown curly hair, and, when I saw him up closer, these blue eyes that reminded me of the ocean on a perfect bright-sky day. He had broad shoulders, and a square jaw, and a really warm, infectious smile. A smile that made me feel at ease the moment that I met him.

"You're not what I expected," he said, when I sat down.

"Oh yeah?" I wasn't sure if it was a compliment or an insult at first. "What did you expect?" I was medium height at five-seven, with wavy brown hair and dark green eyes. I'd always considered myself cute, though not necessarily beautiful. I worked out, and I was thin enough. My breasts were on the small side, but since I'd discovered push-up bras in high school, I'd done a nice job of disguising this.

He turned red. "I'm not sure what I expected." He paused. "I'm not very good at this, I guess."

I laughed. "Me neither."

And then suddenly, I was. We both were.

After a glass of wine and an antipasto, Will started talking, about his parents, who'd both died in a car accident when he was in college; about how hard he'd worked to become partner at the firm to prove something to them, to himself.

And after two glasses of wine, I talked about my mother, for the first time in years. Though I thought about her all the time, I never talked about her. Kelly and I didn't discuss her, except every year on her birthday and her death day. Then one of us would call the other one and say something with the word *mom*, a word that had become so faraway and foreign over the years that it got stuck in my throat when I tried to say it.

We talked so much that I forgot to taste the food, to write down what I was eating, to think about whether I was enjoying it, because I was enjoying him, soaking him in slowly, like a very, very expensive wine.

And the night ended back at my apartment with a bottle of expensive wine. We were sitting on my couch, talking, and drinking. And then I was leaning on him, still drinking. And then the bottle was gone, and we were kissing, pulling off each other's clothes, so quickly and so clumsily that the top of my turtleneck split, which seemed incredibly funny to both of us.

Then we were both naked, and Will was running his hand across my stomach, down my thigh, saying it over and over again, "My God, you are so beautiful."

He reached down and pulled a condom from his wallet, so Will. So prepared. Always planning ahead. But I didn't stop to really think about anything then.

He barely had it on before I pulled him on top of me, not

thinking that we'd just met, that I barely knew him. Only that his skin felt perfect against mine, his body just right, just absolutely right.

In the morning, I woke up naked, leaning against him on the couch, and I couldn't remember much except that he'd called me beautiful, and that it had been the best sex of my life, drunk or not.

I'd walked into work smiling, despite the thick, dull ache in my head, the feeling that I was about to vomit. "So." Kat was waiting for me at my desk. "How was it?"

I shrugged. "It was nice." The understatement of the year, of course, but I wasn't sure if it was a fluke, a one-night thing, and I didn't want Kat going crazy over it.

She leaned in to get a closer look at me. "Shit," she said. "You're hungover."

"No, I'm not. Don't be ridiculous."

She wagged her finger at me. "You slept with him."

"Absolutely not."

"You are such a liar. Oooh," she squealed. "I have to go call Danny."

"Don't you dare," I called after her.

Two years later, Kat was my maid of honor and Danny was Will's best man as we stood in the backyard of a historic mansion and vowed to love, honor, and cherish each other through sickness and in health. *And indictment. Who would've thought to add that to the vows?*

Even now, eight years after I first met her, Kat Neely-Halloway was a force to be reckoned with. She and Danny were the ultimate perfect power couple, and she had managed to be promoted twice in the last three years, even after birthing two little girls whom she promptly dropped into day care after only six weeks' maternity leave each time. "Some people are cut out to take care of children," she'd told me over lunch, on one of the rare times I'd stolen back into the city after moving to Deerfield. "I'm not one of them." She'd puffed on her cigarette. "Hey, at least I can admit it, right?"

I'd laughed, though I couldn't imagine doing that myself. It seemed like if I ever actually had a baby, I'd feel this innate requirement to watch her every second, to make sure nothing bad happened to her.

And now, as she sat here on my back patio, amid the grassy, sweet-smelling suburban air, dainty blond-haired Kat still struck me as something akin to a fireball. We sat in lounge chairs together, watching her girls run around my giant green yard. I watched their images stretch and fade against the sunlight, and it occurred to me that this backyard was really meant for children to run in. It always felt a little empty when I sat out here all alone.

Kat lit another cigarette. "The suburbs are shit," she said, waving her hand in the air, letting the smoke trail out carelessly behind her.

"Oh, I don't know," I said. I would've disagreed with her absolutely two weeks ago, gone on and on about the virtues of the quiet and the nice friendly neighbors and the lunch club. "You get used to it, I guess."

Danny and Will were in the house, sharing beers and watching the Michigan game, Danny's alma mater. Will had even shaved and showered for the occasion, something that had made me feel just a little hopeful.

Kat and I could care less about football, and she said she was sick of watching grown men scream at the TV like children, so we'd retreated outside.

"The girls are getting big," I said. The last time I'd seen

them they were babies, not even walking. It was just after the younger one, Arabella, was born, and Will and I had gone down to the city with a designer pink layette and stayed only an hour. And here the older one was four and attempting a cartwheel.

"It's hard to believe," she said, taking another drag on her cigarette. "Someday they'll grow up and be actual people. Teenagers." She shuddered. "Women." Her voice trailed off. It was the first time I ever detected real pride in her voice when she spoke of her children, and I knew that underneath her tough-as-nails exterior she really did love them.

"What about you?" she asked. "I thought for sure you'd have at least one of your own by now. I mean, that's why people move to the fucking suburbs, isn't it?"

I shrugged. "Oh, I guess." I paused. "We've been trying. Sort of. It just hasn't happened yet."

"Sort of?" She sighed. "Danny takes one look at me and I get pregnant. It's like a fertility nightmare in our house."

I laughed. "That's not what most people would consider a fertility nightmare." I hadn't really thought much about my own fertility. I'd just assumed if I got pregnant, I did. And if I didn't, I didn't. I didn't see my life as eminently good or bad based on whether I could have a baby, though I knew Will didn't agree.

We were both quiet for a minute, watching the girls run around, doing twirls, dancing on the grass. "Look," Kat said quietly, "I can't get you your old job back." I was astounded by the way she could read me, even after the way we'd lost touch in the past few years. "Things are tight, and Hank thinks your replacement shits gold." Hank was the managing editor of the magazine, a wiry uptight guy who always looked nervous.

"Kat," I said, "I don't even know if I'd want my old job back." Though I felt a little disappointed even as I said it. Without it, I wasn't sure what I was going to do with myself, how I was going to feel something again.

She frowned. "I can get you something. Maybe a little freelance work." She paused. "But you'll have to go back to your old byline."

"You've already asked Hank?"

She shrugged but didn't answer. "Danny should've been able to do something more. I mean, what kind of a fucking lawyer is he anyway?"

"It's not Danny's fault," I said.

"So you'll do it?"

Jennifer Daniels. It had been a while since I'd thought of myself as anything other than Jennifer Levenworth, and just thinking of my maiden name, my old byline, made me more than a little nostalgic for my old life, for the days when Kat and I had sat around drinking coffee and exchanging answers in the *Times* puzzle over e-mail, while Hank thought we were hard at work on our latest assignments. "I'll do it," I said.

She smiled. "Great. Come down to the office next week, and I'll get you hooked up."

Later that night, after Danny, Kat, and the kids were gone, Will was in his study and I sat at the kitchen table wondering what kind of freelance work I was going to get. What would I—or Jennifer Daniels—be contributing to the magazine? I knew it would probably be shit. Hank gave all the good stuff to the full-time staffers. But I felt a little excited about it all the same.

Around ten o'clock Will walked out of his study. "I'm going to bed," he said.

"Okay." I stood up and pretended to be attending to the dishes, thinking that if only Will came over and helped me, his hand might brush against mine, and then I could lean into him and feel something again, any little bit at all of what I'd felt that first night we were ever together. But he walked toward the doorway, and I sighed. "I'll be up in a little while."

"Jen, I . . ." He paused for a minute. "Dave offered me a job."

"Oh?" I feigned surprise. "Doing what?"

"Sales," he said. "Weed control packages, lawn services, that sort of thing, I guess." I didn't look up because I didn't want to see the look on his face, the way this new job, this new profession would utterly fail to define him the way his old one had. "I start tomorrow," he said, his words sounding small and far away, as if he were shouting at me through a tube in the distance.

"Okay." I nodded, still unable to look at him. I didn't want to see it in his face, the way he knew, the way we both knew, that it was so much less than okay.

By the time I got into bed, Will was asleep, and I lay there in the darkness, thinking about Kat. About the way she'd looked at her girls, the way she actually loved them underneath, even though it didn't always seem that way on the surface. And then I thought, why had we ever left the city? What had we been thinking to come to Deerfield?

I was sitting at a table, holding on to a latte with one hand, a cigarette with the other. I took a puff of the cigarette.

"Hey," I said with a voice that was not my own, to the guy who sat down next to me. He was tall and blond, muscular, in his twenties. But his face was blurry, and I couldn't place him.

"Katrin, you smell great."

"Thank you," I said. It was the perfume. The perfume Danny gave me five years ago, that I hadn't worn since before the girls were born, since the days before spit-up and pee accidents. The perfume of lavender and rose hips.

I felt his foot underneath the table tap mine lightly, just enough to brush it, maybe accidentally. Or maybe not. Just enough to cause a tingle in my leg that traveled up straight through the center of my body, an electricity, an urgency, that I couldn't ever remember feeling, though I must have, once.

"I admire your work so much," he said. My work. I was still thinking about his foot, the tingling in my leg. I would totally fuck you, I thought. If you ask. All you have to do is ask. Please ask.

Eight

Will woke me up at seven with a kiss on the forehead.
My dream, Kat, still felt right there, right within my grasp. *I would totally fuck you.* I opened my eyes, and Will's looming face startled me.

"Jen," he whispered. "What should I wear?"

"What?" I rolled over and pulled the covers over my head. It took me a moment to remember that I was not Kat, but Jen, and that Will was not a sexy guy in a coffee shop whose image I couldn't even conjure now that I was awake, but my husband, who looked tired and worried and sad, and not at all in the mood to have sex.

"To, um, work," he said. "What should I wear to work?"

I groaned and pulled myself out of bed, rubbing sleep, the dream, away from my eyes.

Will's closet was filled with dark expensive suits, pressed

cotton shirts, and tie racks. Then off to the side were his golf clothes, khaki pants, and collared shirts. I picked out a pair of khakis and a navy golf shirt and handed them to him. "This?" he said. "Are you sure?"

It was such a contrast to the formal suits I was used to seeing him wear to work, but it was what my dad had always worn to work, and the kind of outfit I'd seen Dave in from time to time, so I nodded.

"Sorry I woke you up," he said.

"That's okay." I shook my head, unable to shake away the dream, the feeling of wanting something, someone, so badly. "I should get the day started anyway."

"What are you up to today?" It was a simple enough question, but one he hadn't asked of me for a long time, maybe the whole time we'd lived in Deerfield, so it caught me off guard for a minute.

"I don't know." I shrugged. "I may go into the city and see Kat. She said they might have some work for me. Freelance stuff."

He nodded and then kissed the top of my head. As he leaned in toward me, the smell of his pine aftershave invaded all my senses, and made the tingling in my legs from the dream return. I put my hand on his shoulder, and his skin felt smooth and warm from the shower. *I would totally fuck you*, I thought, and then felt almost alarmed by the sound of Kat's voice, Kat's words in my head. "I better get dressed," he said, pulling away. "I don't want to be late."

"Do you want some coffee?" I asked, unwilling to let him, to let the moment go. "I'm going to make some."

He met my eyes and smiled, and it looked like a real smile, the kind of smile you could see in his whole face, in the crinkly lines around his perfect blue eyes. "Sure," he said. "Coffee would be great."

As I made coffee, I thought about our life in the city, in Will's apartment that so quickly became our apartment after we got engaged and I officially moved in. We'd had coffee together every morning, no matter what. Will usually had to leave for work earlier than me, but still I got up and went into the kitchen to have my coffee with him before I even showered.

We had this thing that we did. Will started it. He'd said, "Tell me one thing you want."

The first time he'd said it was the first morning after I'd officially moved in. I'd looked at him, smiled coyly, ran my foot against his calf, and then Will was late to work because we ended up having sex on the couch.

But after a while, after we were used to being together, he said it, and I said something back, sometimes something silly, sometimes something real. *Tell me one thing you want.*

A good assignment from Hank.

Tell me one thing you want.

Another hour with my mother.

Yes. He'd nodded and reached for my hand, and I knew that he would want that, too, with his own mother. I knew it, just from looking at him, at the way he seemed both sad and surprised by my response—his eyes used to say it all, everything, so I knew exactly what he'd been thinking just by looking into them.

But this morning Will ran downstairs, looking something close to nervous in his khakis and golf shirt. I thought about asking him what it was he wanted. Just one thing. I thought about trying to see it in there, in his eyes, or about trying to run my foot against his leg under the table as I had that first morning. But as he took a quick sip of his coffee he didn't even look at me. Then he ran toward the garage. "I'm going to be late," he called out behind him, as if he owed it to me, some sort of explanation for not sticking around.

Nine

Walking back into *City Style* magazine, I almost felt as if I'd never left. Except my office was now occupied by the man who could shit gold, and Kat's office was right next to Hank's. Her new office was bigger and airier than her old one, with a window that looked out over the city.

"Very fancy," I said, when I walked in.

She sighed. "It's not bad, huh?

"Here," she said, pointing toward the doorway, "meet GS." I automatically assumed that GS stood for "gold shitter," but it turned out his name was Grant Stevens. I couldn't help but chuckle as I shook his hand and told him it was very nice to meet him.

Grant Stevens was extraordinarily attractive, not what I'd pictured at all after hearing Kat talk about him. He was young, maybe only a few years out of college, late twenties at most, muscular enough to be an underwear model, and he had sandy blond hair that fell into his eyes a little bit. There was something about him that struck me as familiar, very familiar. "Have we met before?" I asked him.

"No." He smiled. "Definitely not." He looked me up and down. "I definitely would've remembered."

"Oh." I blushed. But I still couldn't shake the feeling that there was something about him, something I knew.

"You didn't tell me he was so hot," I whispered when he retreated back to my—his—office.

"Is he? I haven't noticed," Kat lied.

I rolled my eyes at her, and I realized that I had missed this. Even Lisa—who I suspected was only a shadow of her former prosecutorial self—had been no replacement for Kat. "Maybe you're right," I said, looking around. "Maybe the suburbs are shit."

"Jen, I'm always right," she said. "But this place is shit, too."

"Even your swanky office?" I raised my eyebrows.

She sighed. "Especially my swanky office."

"I don't know," I said, staring longingly at the stacks of papers on her desk and all that I knew came with it: goals, responsibilities, deadlines. "I think you've got it pretty good here."

She leaned back against her desk and cleared her throat. "Okay, so I feel like a total asshole for dragging you down here, but Hank doesn't have anything real for you right now."

"Oh. Okay." I nodded, but I felt a little disappointed. No matter what Kat said about this place, it would have been nice to get back here, get out of my life, throw myself into the real world again.

"But"—she held up her hand—"he said you can compile the marriages, write 'em up real pretty and stuff the way those dumb brides like." She rolled her eyes.

I remembered that an intern had written up the weddings

when I'd worked here before. It was work that a monkey could do, with its eyes closed. But I smiled and told her I would love to.

"Here." She handed me the packet of handwritten notes from the brides. "I'm going to keep my eye on something better for you, okay?"

"I know you will," I said. I smiled at her, and then I felt it again, the feeling from the dream, the slow tingle in my leg, my body. "Kat," I said. "Is everything okay, with you and Danny?"

"What?" She laughed. "Why would you ask?"

"I don't know," I said. "Just a feeling."

"Oh, hon, don't worry about us. You've got enough stuff on your mind already."

"You would tell me," I said, "if there was something wrong, wouldn't you?"

Her phone rang. "I have to get this," she said, and she turned so I couldn't see her face. "But seriously, no worries, okay? We'll be fine."

We'll be fine, as if they weren't right now. But she already had the phone lodged between her shoulder and her ear, and she was yelling at someone about a deadline, so I gave a little wave and walked out, realizing I'd have to take it up again with her later, somewhere quieter.

Out in the hallway, I saw Grant standing by the copier. He turned, caught my eye, and winked, and his face turned light, almost glowing, the sunlight suddenly streaming in through the window, brightening his face into obscurity. I looked down to shield my eyes, and when I looked up again, I could see his face with complete and utter clarity. Then it hit me, where I'd seen him before. *I would totally fuck you.*

★ ★ ★

Out on the sidewalk I was shaking, and I had to stop and put the bridal folder in my purse to keep it from spilling everywhere. *It's not possible*, I told myself. *You must be mistaken. You cannot have a dream about a person you've never met.*

Ethel and her crazy calming herb. What the hell was in that stuff anyway? I took my cell phone out of my purse and scanned my contacts for Ethel's number, and then when I found it, I hit the send button with my shaking hand.

The phone rang three times, and then I got her machine. "It's Jennifer Levenworth," I said. "Call me immediately."

I'd barely hung up before the phone rang. "Ethel," I said, not even waiting to look at the caller ID.

There was a pause. "Jen, who's Ethel?"

It was Will. Will never called me. "Oh, no one you know," I brushed him off, hoping he'd let it go. "What's up?"

"Just wanted to say hi."

"Hi," I said softly.

"Hi," he repeated.

Silence.

"How's it going?" I finally said.

He didn't answer. I heard the beep from the other line and looked and saw that this time it was Ethel. "That's the other line. I should get it," I said.

"Ethel," he said. I neither confirmed nor denied. I didn't have time to go into who Ethel was now, not when she was beeping in and I desperately needed to talk to her. "Jen, I . . ." He paused. "I'll talk to you later."

"Jennifer," Ethel said, as soon as I switched over. "What is it?" It took me a minute to answer, because I felt a little bad about practically hanging up on Will. "What's wrong?"

I shook my thoughts of Will away and thought about seeing Grant, upstairs in the *City Style* office. I took a deep breath. "That new herb you gave me."

"Are there side effects?"

"I've been having dreams," I said. "Very vivid dreams."

"Ahh. Very good. If you're dreaming then you're entering into REM sleep. It's working."

I cleared my throat. "I don't think you quite understand," I said. "I had a dream last night about a person that I met today." *And I wanted to have sex with him. Or Kat did, and I was her,* I silently added.

"Jennifer, dreams are a representation of our subconscious. You must have seen this person before somewhere, even if your conscious mind didn't register it."

"No," I said. "I don't think I did." But she sounded so sure that I started to doubt myself. Had I seen Grant before?

Grant's picture must be in the back of the magazine, the same way my picture had been when I'd written for it, and I still got the magazine in the mail each month. I probably *had* seen it, seen him, without even knowing it, even realizing. "I guess you're right," I said. "It's just—it felt so real."

"This is all good news, Jennifer. Deep sleep is good. Very good. Deep sleep cleanses."

"Okay," I said. "Sorry to bother you."

"No bother. Keep on sleeping," she said. "Namaste."

"Namaste," I replied. As I hung up, I thought, *Shit, I really do have to Google that word when I get home.*

I did some window shopping in the city, and by the time I made my way home it was after six. Will's car was in the garage, and Will was already on the couch, his shoes and his belt hanging over the armchair, ESPN on the TV. "How was your day?" I asked, thinking for a moment about his telephone call, and that maybe now everything was going to be different between us.

"Fine," he said, not looking up.

I waited for a minute, and then said, "Do you want to talk about it?" He didn't answer. "Will?"

"Jen, I'm trying to watch something here," he snapped.

"Fine." I sighed and went into the kitchen to find myself something to eat: more canned soup, a quick dinner for one. I'd been stocking up every day at the grocery store.

As I sat there at the table by myself and ate it, I stared blankly at the newspaper, hearing the sound of the TV buzzing in the distance, a hum of white noise. I spooned soup into my mouth, not even registering the taste, feeling nothing at all like the way I had this morning, tingly and excited, but instead so much like Lisa in my dream, numb and empty.

Ten

With Will at work, I didn't feel the incessant need to get out of the house, so I started cleaning out closets. I came across some recent copies of *City Style*, and I flipped to the back to look for Grant's picture. Sure enough, there it was, his handsome, chiseled face smiling back at me. *So Ethel had been right*, I thought. My subconscious was smarter than I'd thought.

After a few days of cleaning and packing up trash bags of old clothes for Goodwill, I started to feel tremendously stir-crazy. I missed tennis, as much for the social interaction as the exercise, and I hadn't been back to Pilates either, because half the women in the class were also in the Ladies Lunch Club. I needed to do something, something to make me breathe hard, to make my blood flow. So one morning, exactly a week after Will had begun work, I decided to go jogging.

I drove to a beautiful wooded park, not too far from Kelly's house in Oak Glen, that had nice, winding trails. I started out running, slowly at first, my body feeling heavy and out of shape, sluggish, as if I were trying to move through something thick and unyielding. But when I was finished, after I lapped the multitudes of unfamiliar women pushing strollers along the meandering trail, I sat down on a bench and hung my head between my legs. I heard the pumping of my heart echoing in my ears, felt the blood rushing to my face, and then I did feel a little more alive.

When I got home I took a shower, and for the first time in a week I blew my hair dry with my big round brush and attempted to straighten it. Still it looked awful, so I distracted myself by trying to curl under the ends with my curling iron. Then I gave up and gave in to what I already knew: I desperately needed a haircut.

There was no way in hell I was going to go back to Pierce Avenue, back to Jo. There would be too many stares, too many questions. So instead I went downstairs and I called this little salon called Cuts 'n Stuff that I'd seen right across from the park. It didn't appear they did a brisk business because I booked myself an appointment, under the name Jennifer Daniels, for later that afternoon. I knew the place was a little tacky, but I was also positive I wouldn't run into anyone who might know me.

The lady whom I had an appointment with was named Cheryl, and I was a little skeptical when I first laid eyes on her. She was short and overweight, with shoulder-length, jaggedly cut hair that had chunky strips of bright red running through it. Whenever a hairdresser had seriously awful hair, I took that as a bad sign. But my split ends were, well, so split that I was starting to have seriously awful hair myself, so I stayed.

"What are we doing today?" she asked. She chomped on her gum, blew a bubble, and then popped it near my ear. She pulled up strands of my hair and held them up in her fingers. "You know," she said, "you should go shorter."

"How much shorter?" I'd only had the intention of getting a trim, but for some reason her gum-chewing assessment intrigued me.

"Like seriously shorter." She folded my hair up three times, so it went from shoulder-length to somewhere midway between my chin and my ears. "You totally have the face for it. You're lucky. Not everyone does, you know."

I turned my head to the side and tried to envision it. My hair had been basically the same length since high school. Sometimes I wore it curly, sometime I straightened it with a flatiron or a round brush, but the length had always been just around my shoulders.

She dropped my hair and looked at her watch. "But it's totally up to you." She shrugged. "It's your hair."

"Yes," I said, surprising myself even as I said it. "Cut it short. I could use a change." My words rang distantly in my ears, as if they weren't even coming from me, but from someone else, because my brain hadn't actually processed what I was telling her.

As she washed my hair, as I leaned my head back in the sink and heard the water rushing, rushing through my ears, I closed my eyes and remembered that morning at Pierce Avenue, that morning I'd heard about Will. When I sat up, I felt this odd sense of déjà vu, and for a minute, I was just as dizzy and disoriented as I had been that day.

I closed my eyes while she was cutting, to try to contain

the dizziness, the awkward feeling of nausea, and then when I heard the click of the scissors stop, I opened them again and looked in the mirror. My hair was short, really short, just below my ears, and angled slightly toward my face. Tears immediately welled up in my eyes because looking back at me was someone else, some entirely different woman whom I'd never met before. Cheryl frowned and held up her hands. "You said it's what you wanted," she said.

"I know," I said, trying to force a smile, though the feeling, the urge to start running, just to get out of there, rose in my throat like bile.

Once I got in the car, I thought about calling Kelly. Her house was only five minutes from here, and I hadn't talked to her since the morning I'd called her and begged for a job for Will. I knew she'd been working on a photography project, and I'd been resisting the urge to call her, as if bothering her when I normally wouldn't have was a confession of how un-fine I really was.

But it had been a while, longer than we usually went without talking, so I dialed her number. "How you doing?" she asked when she picked up, not sympathetic exactly, but matter-of-factly, as if it was a foregone conclusion that I should still not be doing well.

"I'm okay," I said. But I felt this haunting feeling that I wasn't, this deep sense of loneliness and numbness that I couldn't shake, maybe not even just my own sense of it, but Lisa's and Kat's, too, or my dream version of them anyway. "Anyway, what are you up to? I'm out your way . . ."

It took her a few seconds. Finally she said, "I'll be here all afternoon, if you want to stop over."

★ ★ ★

Kelly's house was cute, a split-level that had been built out of brick back in the fifties, when that sort of thing was still in style. She had a nice lawn in the front, and a small porch, with a garden filled with impatiens surrounding it.

The inside was a little small for the five of them, and often filled with clutter. And crayons. I swear to God, everywhere you went there was a rogue crayon. I'd found a red-violet floating in the toilet the last time I was here. Maybe that's why she thought motherhood was like being trapped in a world of crazy colors, as if Crayola had invented these tiny little waxy sticks to torture her.

I rang the bell, and I heard a thud, which I was guessing was three-year-old Jack. Caleb, nearly five, was at preschool, and I thought Hannah, who was barely even walking, was still too small to thud. In response to the thud there were screams, a barking Muffet, and the muffled sound of Kelly's voice. I had a feeling of déjà vu standing there, the same feeling I got every time I stood on Kelly's stoop. So much noise and so much clutter. Everything that my house wasn't, and yet I always secretly enjoyed it here, maybe even envied it, for a little while anyway, because it reminded me, in a way, of my childhood, of the life we'd inhabited when our mother was still alive.

Kelly answered the door with Hannah on her hip, Jack hanging on her leg, and the phone tucked between her ear and her shoulder. She waved me in, and I stepped gingerly, trying not to tread too hard or bump a toy that would explode into a fit of music—every toy in this house did.

She hung up the phone, gave me a half hug that was smooshed with kid. "Give Auntie JJ a kiss," she said. Jack obliged and Hannah tried to pull off my nose.

"Holy shit, she's strong." I rubbed my nose.

"Jen." She rolled her eyes toward Jack. "He's a sponge."

"Sorry."

"Go have a seat in the kitchen. I'm going to put Hannah down for a nap and put *The Wiggles* on for Jack." She paused. "I know. I know. I'm terrible. Letting the TV be his babysitter and all that."

"I wasn't going to say that," I said. And truthfully, it hadn't occurred to me that there was anything wrong with letting the TV distract him. Jack loved *The Wiggles*—it seemed like he was watching it every time I was over, and it always seemed to put him in a trance. Toddler drug of choice, Will had suggested once, watching as Jack and Caleb's eyes had both glazed over, as they'd cocked their heads to the side and held their mouths open.

She sighed. "Of course you weren't," she said, as if I was the bad guy.

Ten minutes later the house was stunningly quiet, except for music coming from the TV and, occasionally, Jack's almost girly-sounding voice echoing along. "Your hair is short," Kelly said, as she walked into the kitchen.

"I know." I nodded.

She reached up and felt the ends. "But I think it'll grow on me." I shrugged; I hadn't decided yet.

Kelly put up a pot of coffee and then unwrapped a few Tastykakes and put them on a plate. It amazed me to watch her, the way every motion seemed exactly right, exactly mom-like, as if she'd molded herself perfectly to fit into this world, this life. I supposed it must have been the way I'd looked on the tennis court, at the club, or announcing winners at the charity auction, but I wondered, if I had stood back and watched myself, the way I was watching her now, if I would've looked this at ease.

"Dave said Will has been doing well," she said.

"Yes," I murmured, though really, Will hadn't said a word to me about work, or about anything, for that matter.

"So tell me, how are you handling things?" Kelly asked, plunking the plate of Jelly Krimpets down in front of me. I told her about Lisa coming over with the pineapple upside-down cake and booting me out of my life. She chewed on her Jelly Krimpet and nodded. "Bitches," she said. She waved her hand. "You're better off without them." I tried to ignore the I-told-you-so look she flashed at me, something almost close to a smirk. "So what are you going to do now?"

"Kat got me a little freelance work." I left out what it was so she wouldn't roll her eyes or laugh at me, or point out what I already knew, that it was really just glorified typing.

"So you want to go back to work?" She paused. "That's not what I expected."

"You were the one who asked if I was going back to work," I pointed out, which was typical. I could never win with Kelly. "What did you expect?"

"I don't know." She shrugged. "I thought you might have a baby."

I didn't say anything for a minute or so, and then I said, "Well, anyway." I stared at the Tastykakes longingly, trying to mentally calculate how long it had been since I'd eaten something like that. Two years. Maybe three. "This would be the worst possible time for us to have a baby."

Kelly nodded. "There's never really a good time," she said. "Sometimes you just have to jump in and do it." She paused. "Like Dave always says, 'Shit happens, but flowers grow really well in shit.'"

"Is that like some kind of a landscaping joke?" I asked,

finally picking up the Jelly Krimpet and stuffing it in my mouth, letting the sweet, sweet jelly dull her questions. Why had I thought it would be a good idea to come over here?

"And what happened to your novel?" she drilled.

I finished chewing and shrugged. I didn't want to tell her the truth, that I'd never even gotten past the first chapter before I'd tucked it away in a drawer, and that I rarely ever thought about taking it out again. "How's your project coming?" I asked, wanting to change the subject, to take the heat off me.

"Good," she said. "I'm doing flowers, for a calendar."

I looked around at Kelly's photos—the one aspect of her house that made it seem grown up—the black-and-white landscapes on the walls. I examined the one that hung by the fridge, a close-up of a saguaro cactus from a trip they'd taken to Arizona the year before. It was so close that the individual needles looked like fingers, reaching out for something. Her photos really were beautiful, and it amazed me that somehow she managed it all: mom, wife, artist.

"Oh, by the way, I talked to Dad. He and Sharon are coming for Thanksgiving." I thought about the last time I saw my father and Sharon, last Passover. We'd hardly said two words to each other the whole night. Part of it was because he had never shown anything but disappointment for me, and the other part was Sharon, who was either unable or unwilling to shut up. She'd barely step foot inside Kelly's house before she'd be criticizing everything and everyone in her path. But even worse, she pretended to do it in a nice enough way, as if she was actually paying us some kind of backward compliment.

Last Passover, she'd started in with "The dinner looks

lovely, Kel." She'd wrinkled her long, pointy nose. "Now if only you could've dressed up a little more. Put on some makeup. You're too pale without it. And Jenny, oy God, you're too thin. Look at that waistline, Donny. You need to borrow a little from the middle of your sister, eh?" My dad—Don—to everyone but her—looked away, uncomfortable, not wanting to meet our gazes or stare at our waistlines either.

Dave had come up behind Kelly and put his arms around her. "Her middle is perfect. You can't have any." He looked at me and laughed, while Kelly blushed.

Kelly probably could afford to lose a little weight, but Hannah was only now just turning one, and Kelly said that with each child those last ten pounds became harder and harder to budge.

I liked my middle just the way it was—strong from Pilates and small from avoiding carbs for the last three years—despite the fact that Will hadn't said anything in my defense. He'd just stood there, holding on to a jar of gefilte fish that Kelly had put him in charge of, looking sort of dumbstruck, the way he always was by my family.

"Anyway," I heard Kelly saying now, and I knew I'd missed what she'd just been saying about our father, "it'll be nice to see him."

"Does he know?" I asked quietly. I hadn't talked to him since I'd called him for his birthday back in early August, and even if I had, Will's indictment wouldn't have been first on my list of topics.

She shrugged. "I didn't tell him." She paused. "But you should, Jen. He's bound to find out anyway."

I pictured Sharon's face contorting, her big nose seeming

even bigger as she scrunched her face up in a frown and whispered to my father, "I never liked that one. But you know Jen, she's not too bad-looking, but she's not a real good judge of character."

"You're right," I finally said. But I had no intention of talking to my father, much less telling him anything about Will.

Eleven

When I returned home, it was nearly dark, but our house was lit up and oddly alive-looking. I hadn't given one thought to dinner, and there was no way we were going for a quick meal at the club.

Judge Will never arrived home before eight, sometimes nine. I'd have dinner done at seven-thirty, and I was used to eating it by myself, then keeping it warm in the oven for him.

But when I walked inside, landscaping salesman Will was standing in the kitchen, amid a mess of pots and dishes, food boxes and cooking utensils. "Hi," he said. "I made us some spaghetti. And salad."

I stood there, my mouth wide open, not quite sure what to say. Will hadn't cooked for me since, well, ever. He always joked that he could make a mean anything-the-hell-I-wanted-off-a-take-out-menu. So I decided not to mention that I hadn't eaten pasta in something like three years. Plus

I'd already given in to the Tastykake, so the day was shot. "It smells great," I said, which was the truth.

He looked up from the stove and walked toward me. "You cut your hair," he said.

I nodded. "Do you like it?"

He reached up and touched the ends lightly with his fingers. "You look different," he said.

I stared back at him, at his khaki pants and his dark brown collared shirt, at the way his face seemed softer, and his hair was a little longer, more unruly, and I realized he looked different, too. But I liked it.

"Here." He pulled out a mahogany chair for me. "Have a seat."

I watched him move around the kitchen. He stumbled. The pasta water foamed over and started smoking up the stove, the garlic bread began to burn; he spilled some sauce on the floor. "Do you want some help?" I kept saying.

"No, no." He brushed me off. "I've got it all under control." So all I did was watch this person, this man, my husband, who was something more of a stranger right here in front of me than he had been a few weeks ago. Yet as I watched him, clumsy and trying so hard, I felt my heart beat a little faster, felt this warmth in my brain like I'd had a little too much wine even though I hadn't had anything to drink yet.

When the food was finished he put it all on the table, and then he placed a heaping pile of everything on my plate. "It looks delicious," I said, and I smiled at him. "You really didn't have to do this."

"I wanted to," he said. "I mean, isn't that what husbands are supposed to do when they get home early?"

I shrugged. "I don't know." And really, I didn't. None of my so-called friends' husbands got home early, and even

Dave worked long hours, so what did I have to compare it to? He sat down, leaned back in the chair, and smiled as I started eating. "You seem happy," I said, between bites.

"I made my first sale today."

"Congratulations." I smiled at him. "That was fast." I felt bad that it hadn't occurred to me before that Will might actually be good at this job. And why wouldn't he be? He was smart and handsome and well-spoken. I would've bought something from him if he'd shown up at my door before we met.

"I know." He nodded. "It was." He chewed carefully, as if trying to piece out what he wanted to say next exactly right. "Maybe I got confused over the past few years, hell, I don't know, forever. About what was really important to me." He put his hand on my arm. His fingers were warm, and I closed my eyes and imagined them on my waist, pulling me toward him, pulling me closer.

"You were a judge," I whispered, opening my eyes. "That was important to you."

"Shit, Jen, I don't know." He pulled his hand away and held up his wineglass. "Anyway," he said, "I made a sale. Life goes on." He clinked his glass to mine, and then swallowed it all down before pouring himself some more. I took a sip of mine. "You know," he said, when he finished the wine, "this is nice." He reached for my hand.

"This is nice," I repeated. I thought about all those times when all I wanted was Will to pay attention to me, Will to stop working and get out of his study and want to be with me. And now here he was, doing and saying all the right things. Yet I could see it in the way his face was stretched and tight and tired, in the way he'd drunk his wine too fast: Underneath, he wasn't happy here with me, with me and nothing else.

"I wouldn't blame you if you hated me," he said, interrupting my thoughts.

"Oh, Will, I don't hate you." I stared into his blue-sea eyes, a little glassy from too much wine, and I knew that I could never hate him. But I felt this oddly terrifying sorrow for him: His career had defined him, everything about him, and now, I knew, he was going to have to figure out who he was, who we were, without it. Sale or no.

"That's good," he said. "That's very good." He paused. "I don't want to lose you." The sound of his voice faded and dropped, as if he was whispering from the next room, and I suddenly had to strain to hear him. Still, the words rang softly in my ears: *I don't want to lose you.*

I wanted to say something back, but I was overwhelmed so all I could do was nod. I wanted all of it back, that life we'd had once, that life of laughter and passionate sex and good conversation. That life of being happy. Together. But I wondered if happiness was something you could find again, once you'd lost it, or if, after it was gone, there was no way to really erase all the things that had made it disappear in the first place.

"I know," he said. "I know." As if he really did know, as if he could tell what I was thinking. He touched the ends of my new, shorter hair. "I like it," he said. "It highlights your face."

"Do you really think so?"

"I do." He moved his hand down, so it covered mine, and then we sat there like that for a while, eating in silence. I wondered, if my neighbors were watching, if they'd be able to see it, the way, as the two of us shared our dinner at the kitchen table, the inside of our house had become just a little more illuminated.

★ ★ ★

After dinner Will retreated into his study. As I scrubbed saucy splotches off the counter I wondered what exactly he was doing in there, and why he still went in there every night. I didn't think he was working. But maybe it was a habit that was hard to break, the one thing from his old life that he couldn't let go of, that space of cherrywood and beige damask, that space that was completely and uniquely his. Or maybe it was just his way of getting away from me, of getting away from the awkwardness that might bloom in the space of an entire evening alone together. *I don't want to lose you.* And yet it felt so hard to find your way back to someone once you'd lost your way.

For a moment I wished I could go back in time, to when Will first told me he wanted to be a judge, just before we moved to Deerfield.

"I don't have to run," he'd said then, "not if you don't want me to." I saw it in his eyes, the way he wanted to, the way he silently pleaded with me to say yes. And I instantly knew if I said no that he might resent me for it, that I would be the one who'd stopped him from becoming someone great, something spectacular.

So I'd shrugged, turned away, and said, "You should do it. It's a great opportunity for you."

"Are you sure?" I could hear just the smallest lilt of excitement in his voice, the anticipation of a child. "It might be longer hours," he said. "More work."

I'd nodded, even though I'd been thinking that I really didn't want him to, that I hoped he wouldn't, that I wanted him here, with me. I stared at him and willed him to know what I was thinking, though even as I thought it, it seemed selfish. Life was short—this much I knew, and who was I to keep him from doing the one thing that was going to make him happy? So I pasted on a smile and gave him a hug. "You're going to be a judge," I'd said. "I'm so proud of you."

I finished the dishes and went upstairs, where I swallowed my herbs, brushed my teeth, and slipped under the covers. I thought about Will, about how I'd lied so he wouldn't end up resenting me someday. But lying there in bed, alone, Will still downstairs in his study, I thought, just before I drifted off to sleep, that maybe I was the one who'd ended up resenting him.

I was sitting at a desk, wearing Will's black judge's robe. I looked around. Will's chambers. Sitting in front of me was an appointment book, and I looked down and saw the name Jude Marris, circled in red.

I closed my eyes, and I felt the nausea rise and swell in my stomach, a ripple of anxiety that overtook me, until the bile rose so fast in my throat that there wasn't enough warning, no way to stop it from coming.

I quickly reached under the desk for the trash can, put my head down, and threw up.

I heard a knock at the door. Janice poked her head in. "Judge, Mr. Marris is here."

I nodded and wiped the sweat from my brow.

"Is everything all right?"

"Yes," I said. "Of course. Just give me a few minutes. Okay?"

I waited for Janice to close the door before I grabbed the trash can and felt the rest of my lunch coming back up.

When I woke up in the morning, Will was already gone, and I realized I must have slept late. I rolled over and grabbed his pillow and clung to it; it smelled faintly of pine trees and fabric softener. And then as I lay there, I wondered exactly what my dream had meant. What had my subconscious been trying to tell me?

I got up and got undressed to get in the shower, but I paused for a minute in front of the mirror, trying to size up my naked reflection objectively. I was still fairly thin, flat-chested, and getting a little cellulite on my upper thighs, but not bad for thirty-three. I ran my hand across my stomach, which was still smoother than satin despite the fact that I'd put on a few pounds in the last few weeks. I'd seen Kelly's stomach—wrinkly and pocked with stretch marks that made the skin gray and sag, and look like skin fitting for an eighty-year-old, not a thirty-six-year-old. "No more bikinis for me," she'd sighed.

I pinched a little bit of fat near my hips. That's what giving up Pilates and tennis, and giving in to carbs again, all at once, would do to a girl. Somehow, my morning jog wasn't making up for it.

All the women in the lunch club were thin—except Lisa, who was always struggling to try to get thin. But even she wasn't fat by any standard. I'd heard Bethany moan about having a twenty-five-inch waist, and Amber talk about doing four hundred sit-ups a day. And one time when Helen Kemper was going through chemo, and super-super skinny (I hadn't known her before so it was hard to say how much skinnier exactly), I'd heard Bethany compliment her, tell her she looked just like a model. "Yeah. Fantastic new diet," Helen said, and I detected the edge of sarcasm to her voice, even though I'd never really known her.

"Why?" Lisa threw her hands up in the air once in the locker room. "What's it all for anyway?" She was frustrated at not having lost weight after a week on the maple syrup cleanse diet.

"Oh, sweetie," Bethany said. "We have to stay thin and pretty or our husbands will find wives who will."

I'd seen a flicker of something, maybe fear or maybe annoyance, flash across Lisa's face before she'd turned to me and rolled her eyes.

I'd shrugged. I wasn't staying thin because I was worried Will would leave me for someone else. Because, in fact, he'd already left me, in a way, for something else. His career. And I always thought if I stayed thin and fit and pretty, well then at least I couldn't assign myself any blame. At least it couldn't be my fault.

I sighed as I looked at myself in the mirror now; I still couldn't shake the sick feeling in Will's stomach from the dream. And my limbs felt like Jell-O, too heavy for my body. *It was just a dream*, I repeated in my head a few times, but the awkward feelings refused to disappear. Is this the way Will had walked through life? Had he felt this way all the time?

For the first time it occurred to me that I'd known nothing about Will's life as a judge. Nothing at all. And it wasn't just because Will hadn't told me, but also because I'd never asked.

Twelve

By the week before Thanksgiving, Will had sold three yearly landscaping packages to three unsuspecting families in Deerfield. And by unsuspecting I mean that they had no idea that they were purchasing said packages from a judge—no, former (indicted) judge—only that they were buying them from a guy named William Kenneth who had driven up to their house in a little blue Daniels and Sons truck. The name William Kenneth left out something very important, of course, Will's last name, but it was Dave who'd printed up the business cards. And Will told me he thought the omission was actually for the best. Though I wondered if deep down it was soul-crushing, to have your identity taken away, just like that.

But Will said there were people who still recognized him anyway. These people knew him from the pictures that had been plastered in the *Deerfield Daily* for the better part of a week in the beginning of October. He told me he could always tell when that happened, when the surge of recognition flashed across an old woman's face, as he tried to explain the essence of their organic compounds, when a housewife suddenly asked him to leave after offering him an iced tea only moments before.

"People will forget," I told him, as he complained about it in the middle of getting ready for bed. "Everything gets forgotten eventually." I knew that some people wouldn't forget—Lisa and Bethany and the rest of the Ladies Lunch Club. But the other people, the ones who hadn't ever known us before in our life as "The Levenworths," those people who hadn't known him as anything more than a black-and-white photo, those people would let the image of the indicted judge slip away; they would forget eventually.

He rubbed his hand over the stubble on his face, the stubble that formed in the space between his new shaving routine, which only happened every fourth or fifth day now. "Yeah." He let out a dry laugh. "Before you know it, I'll cease to exist. Will Levenworth will be no more."

"Don't be ridiculous," I said. "Of course you'll exist."

I watched him pull off his pale blue cotton golf shirt, the one that I'd always thought had looked good on him because it really brought out his eyes. "You're ovulating this week?" he asked, popping his head out of the shirt. It sounded almost more like a statement of fact than a question, so I knew he must've noticed it on his calendar, and it popped out so easily, so carelessly, that he might as well have said, *Did you remember to buy milk this week?*

I shrugged. I actually wasn't exactly sure that those calendar days were all that accurate anymore.

Kelly had given me a book called *Fertile and Free*, back when Will and I had first gotten married. I'd flipped through it when we first moved to Deerfield, then put it high on a bookshelf, and had never bothered to take it out again. But this week I'd taken to reorganizing the bookshelves, and I'd come across it. I'm not sure what made me start reading it, but I'd sat there one afternoon and read through the whole thing.

I learned there was a lot more that went into figuring out when you were ovulating than just simple timing, that the fourteenth-day-of-the-cycle bit that Dr. Horowitz had hastily recited off to me at my last appointment was something of a myth, and that there were all kinds of ways to figure out when you really were ovulating. Special thermometers and charts and graphs and analysis of cervical mucus. I found it more than a little horrifying, the way the whole baby-making process seemed a hell of a lot more scientific and complicated than I'd ever imagined.

"Jen." He walked toward me, and he pulled me close. He kissed my forehead; the scratchiness of his face was rough enough to sting a little bit against my skin. His body felt warm against mine, and a part of me wanted to lean up and kiss him. "I really want a baby," he whispered.

"We've been trying," I whispered back.

"Let's really try. For real."

"I don't know, Will." I paused. "I don't know if it's the right time now."

He pulled back. "You never think it's the right time." It was true, even when I'd consented to try a few months back, I'd still mentioned that I wasn't sure I was ready. Then Will had reminded me that we weren't getting any younger, and I'd reluctantly agreed. The truth was, I wasn't sure I would ever feel ready, though this much I'd never admitted out loud.

But right now seemed like it might be the worst possible time, no matter what Kelly said about flowers growing in shit. I tried to imagine what it would be like for him or her, the baby, to be born into this world, with two parents who didn't exactly know how to talk to each other, and who didn't fit in with their surroundings anymore. There would be no Swedish pram walks with Bethany and Angel, no playdates with the neighbors, no swimming lessons or birthday parties at the club.

"Maybe we should give it a few more months. Wait and see . . ." I finally said.

He frowned and turned away. When he turned back to face me I couldn't tell if he wanted to yell or cry. "Why don't you just say it, Jen?"

"Say what?" I whispered.

"That it's not that you don't want to have a baby." He paused. "It's just that you don't want to have a baby with me."

"That's not it," I said, and I was so surprised that I felt as if I'd been punched in the stomach, the wind knocked out of me. It had never once occurred to me to want a baby with anyone else.

He shook his head, and I knew he didn't believe me. But I had no words to say it, the way I was really feeling, thick and heavy like the way I'd walked through the dream as Lisa, the world so foggy that my thoughts felt impossibly stuck in my brain.

Will went into the bathroom and shut the door, and I got into bed and closed my eyes, if only to stop the tears from coming. I thought about Kat, about what she'd said about how some women were meant to be mothers and others weren't. And maybe I was the latter. Yes, that's what I wanted to tell him. That it had everything to do with me, and nothing to do with him. But my head was too weighted with sleep for me to get out of bed to say anything.

> *I was sitting in the coffee shop, the whir of the espresso machine making it hard to hear. But there was a man talking to me, a voice, deep and sexy and smooth. "Katrin," he was saying. "Katrin, are you listening to me?" He put his hand on top of mine, looked me in the eye, and smiled.*
>
> *No, I am not listening, I thought. How could I be listening, when you're touching me? When all I can think about is your hand, your hand on my skin. "I'm sorry." I shook my head. "What were you saying?"*
>
> *He leaned in, just about to kiss me, his face close enough for me to notice that his breath smelled like coffee and grapefruit.*

I sat up, startled, the smell of coffee so strong in my nose that I was positive it must be real, that Will must be downstairs, brewing coffee. Only it was dark, so dark that I could barely see, barely make out the shapes of the furniture in the room. Will was snoring softly beside me, and when I took another deep breath, the smell of coffee slowly dissipated. But when I lay back down, I couldn't fall back to sleep right away; I couldn't get the image of Grant's face coming closer, coming toward mine, out of my head.

The next morning, Kat called to congratulate me. *City Style* was running my first set of wedding announcements.

I'd just gotten out of the shower when she called and I ran to get the phone in my towel, thinking it might be Will, and hoping I could find the words to tell him what I'd been feeling before I feel asleep last night. "How does it feel to have your name back in print?" Kat asked. As soon as I heard her voice, the image of Grant's face, coming closer, the smell of coffee and grapefruit, overtook my senses.

"Great," I said, after a moment. The truth was—well, aside from the obvious truth that it wasn't exactly my name—I didn't really care all that much about the wedding announcements.

"I know it's not much," she said. "But I thought they were very well written."

"Thanks," I said, because I knew she was trying to make me feel better. But I couldn't shake the feeling of Grant. *Grant's smell. Grant's hand.*

"How's everything going?" Kat lowered her voice to a whisper, and I wondered who she thought was within earshot. I wondered if it was Grant, if he was there with her, leaning over her desk, leaning in close.

"It's going," I said.

"And Will?"

I thought about the way he'd looked at me last night, with a mixture of anger and disappointment, and it was so different from the way he'd looked at me that night when he'd cooked me dinner. "Will's good," I lied. I paused. "Kat, you're not really the motherly type. What made you decide to have children?"

She laughed. "There wasn't any deciding about it, the first time around." She paused to contain her laughter. "I'm telling you, we could've made a fortune if Danny would've had the balls to sue Trojan."

I chuckled, picturing straitlaced, red-haired, freckled Danny actually filing a complaint against a condom manufacturer. And it was impossible to imagine. But who would've ever imagined Will wearing khakis to work and selling weed control either? "What about the second time?" I said.

"Ahh, the second time." She lowered her voice to a whisper. "Danny got me drunk, and he swears I said I wanted to get pregnant. But I honestly don't think I ever woulda said that, even three sheets to the wind. I think he liquored me up and took advantage, because he thinks being an only child would've scarred Sarah Lynne for life. Blah, blah, blah."

"Well, it all worked out," I said. "You have two beautiful children."

"Yes," she said. "I do, don't I?" She paused. "Look, you ever want to try on the whole motherhood thing for size, I could drop the girls off at your place for the weekend." When I didn't answer either way, she kept talking. "I'm thinking about renting them out to prospective parents. Talk about population control," she said. "Kidding. I'm kidding." She paused. "I'm telling you, though. Motherhood is the toughest fucking job you'll ever have in your life."

After I hung up with Kat, I got dressed, and checked the mail to see if my issue of *City Style* had arrived yet. It hadn't. I didn't feel like driving all the way back to Oak Glen again, so I decided to risk it and run quickly into Whole Foods to pick up a copy.

I was standing in the magazine section, thumbing through the issue, when I heard someone say my name, and I looked up and saw Lisa standing in front of me, hanging on to her overflowing shopping cart as if it was another appendage. *Oh shit.* I was never coming back to this store again.

"You cut your hair," she said. "You look different." She paused. "It looks nice."

"Thanks." I nodded. Then I looked back down at the magazine, hoping she would disappear. I knew she was right, that she'd only been the messenger for the other women, but also it was something else. Seeing her there, I saw it in her eyes, low and red-rimmed and moist—I saw the feeling I'd felt in my dream, the intensity of her sadness, the way it consumed her. Maybe Ethel had been right, that I'd only been dreaming what I already knew. And maybe, deep down, I'd known it the whole time with Lisa, that part of her was broken, a deep part of her, the part that dies inside you when you lose something unfathomable, a parent to cancer, the part that starts off small, but then grows and grows, enough to choke the rest of the life right out of you.

She cleared her throat. "How are you?" she asked.

"I'm fine," I said, not looking up again.

She grabbed on to the magazine with her hand and lowered it, so we were staring at each other, eye to eye. Lisa had a steely gaze when she wanted to—I'd seen it on her before when she was yelling at Chance and Chester for playing in the street—and I'd always imagined that once upon a time she'd been a formidable opponent in the courtroom. "I've been worried about you," she said. In the whirl of the supermarket noise, her words almost seemed to disappear, making hardly any sense against the beeping of the checkout counters and some announcements coming across the PA system. She frowned. "Bethany's making a mess of the auction." And then I felt the world go quiet, the rush of the market dulled by her words flooding my ears.

I closed the magazine, and for the first time since being booted out of the Deerfield social scene, I really thought I might just burst into tears. It was one thing to lose friendships with the petty and the spineless women of the lunch club, but another to hear that my baby, my auction, was falling apart. I blinked the tears back, and I shrugged. "So," I said, "what do you want me to do?"

Lisa appeared to be considering saying something, and even though I hated myself for it, a small part of me wanted her to ask me back, to ask me to come swooping in to save the auction, to save her. Even something smaller, even her saying that she would talk to the other women for me, plead my case—she'd been a prosecutor, for Christ's sake—would've been enough. But all she said was "You're right. I'm sorry. I shouldn't have said anything."

I nodded, and I watched her awkwardly turn the stuffed shopping cart toward the checkout. Her hair looked dry and brittle from being dyed and blown out one too many times, the skin under her eyes was starting to sag, and her butt looked downright huge from this angle and in those horribly tight jeans she was wearing. I knew it was harder for her to fit in than, say, someone like Bethany, but that still didn't feel like an excuse for abandoning me.

Thirteen

The night of the charity auction, I was sitting at the kitchen table, organizing my coupons in my Filofax, when Will walked in, dressed in a tuxedo. "You're not dressed," he said, seeming stunned. "Jen, you haven't even showered yet." He lifted up his arm to look at his watch, thinking perhaps that he was the one who'd erred—gotten the wrong day or time. I felt a steady sinking in my chest.

By this point, my ousting from the Deerfield social scene had become something I'd gotten used to, something that only bothered me a little bit, but it was also something that I hadn't mentioned to Will. At first I hadn't wanted to upset him, thinking he had enough of his own to deal with. And then it was hard to stop lying.

Now that we actually had started eating dinner together every night and having coffee together some mornings, there were questions: "How was your tennis match?"

"Oh, good," I lied. "We won." I invented a score in my

head, and a play-by-play of the action each Monday, Wednesday, and Friday afternoon, just in case he ever asked. I also
didn't mention that when I was supposedly playing tennis, I'd
been jogging in Oak Glen.

And Will hadn't noticed that the house was extra clean, his
closet extra organized. He hadn't noticed that I now cleaned
the spotless oven weekly or shined the bamboo floors bi-
weekly, or cleaned out the attic, or alphabetized some of his
old jazz records in the basement. Or, if he had noticed, he filed
it under "Things Jen Does That I've Never Been Around to
Notice Before."

I stared at Will for a minute now, handsome and sweet-
looking in his formal wear, and I had to close my eyes and
take a deep breath before I broke the news. "I guess I forgot to
mention it." I tried my best to sound breezy, casual. "Bethany
is running the auction now."

"What? Why would Bethany . . ." His voice trailed off as
he understood why, and then his face turned a shade of white
that made him look like a ghost, an apparition of his former
self, so he began looking oddly out of sorts in his tuxedo.
"Jen, why didn't you tell me?"

"It's no big deal." I shrugged and pretended to go back to
my coupon organizing, while blinking back tears. "It was a
lot of work anyway."

"But you loved it." He sat down next to me and covered
my hand with his to stop it, to stop me, from moving. "Jen."
I looked up. His eyes were a cool shade of blue in the slow
evening glimmer of the kitchen. They were sad eyes, anxious
eyes, and I had to look away. "You're not even going to go?"
he asked.

I swallowed hard. "We weren't exactly invited," I said.

He stood up and ran his fingers loosely through his hair. "That's ridiculous. This is your auction." He started pacing across the bamboo floor, the heels of his dress shoes clicking on each turn. "I'll call someone. Who should I call?"

"Will, don't." I stood up.

"You'll go without me." He held his hands up in the air. "None of this has to do with you."

"It's okay, Will."

I put my hand on his shoulder. He stopped pacing and looked at me, and I knew my own eyes were revealing more truth than anything that had come out of my mouth in the last month. "It's not okay. Dammit, Jen. Why didn't you tell me?"

"What's the point?" I whispered. I cleared my throat. "Besides, I've been busy. I have my freelance work, and . . ." I let my voice trail off because there was nothing else to add.

He sighed, reached out for me again, and pulled me to him, so my head was against his chest, so his heart was beating in my ear. Still loud and strong and steady, like the grandfather clock that had been in the hallway of my parents' house and now sat in the front hallway of Kelly's. He kissed the top of my head. "You're still here," he said, almost to himself, as if he couldn't believe it, and he said it so softly that I had this strange feeling that he was somewhere very far away, despite still being able to feel his heartbeat.

"I am," I said, feeling unbelievably sad about not being able to go to the auction, this deep, intense sadness. It worked its way from my stomach to my chest to my brain, until tears formed in my eyes again and threatened to spill over onto Will's white tuxedo shirt.

"I'm going to go change," he said. "And then I'm taking you out to dinner."

"You don't have to do that."

"I want to," he said.

I shook my head. "I'm really not up for dinner. How about a rain check?"

He sighed. "Jen, I wish you'd just—"

"Just what?"

"I don't know." He paused. "Throw something at me. Scream at me. Get angry, for God's sake."

I turned away from him. "I'm not angry," I said, but even as I said it, I thought that maybe I was. I just wasn't sure I was angry at him.

Will went upstairs to change, and I got myself a glass of Merlot and went out to sit on the back patio. It was a mild night, for November, and I was comfortable in only my sweater and jeans. As I sipped the wine by myself, I closed my eyes and thought about last year's auction—about the red dress I'd worn, about the veal piccata I'd gotten the club to serve for only the price of chicken. The night had flowed, people milling about, bids being placed, everyone kissing my cheeks and telling me what a great job I'd done. And this was it right here, the one thing I'd really and truly liked—no, loved—about living in Deerfield. Being in charge of something great, something worthwhile.

When I looked up now, I caught a glimpse of Lisa, in her own red ball gown, standing in her kitchen, the little heads of Chance and Chester bobbing up and down. Even from far away, I could tell by the way she held herself that she was tired, that she didn't even really want to go to the auction, and it didn't seem fair, that she got to go and I didn't.

I finished the glass of wine, and then I was too exhausted for dinner. I went upstairs, took my herbs, and got into bed.

I was walking down the plush red carpet in the entranceway of the club, holding on to Barry's arm. I looked down to adjust my dress. Red wasn't my favorite color, but Barry liked it.

Bethany was standing up ahead, by the door to the ballroom. She wore a black strapless gown that overemphasized her bust and her thin waist. I sucked my stomach in.

"Would you look at the tits on her," Barry whispered.

"Oh Jesus, Barry."

"What? I'm just saying. I wonder who did them for her. I bet it was Stevens. No, Markowitz."

I frowned. I had a headache. I wasn't in the mood for an auction, for a night of sucking in my stomach just to look half as thin as everyone else here, a night of listening to boring people talk about boring things. But I continued walking, one foot in front of the other, holding on to Barry's arm.

We each picked up a bid book, found our table, and sat down. Bethany had put us at a table with other doctors, guys Barry knew with wives I did not. Barry started talking to them, while I folded and refolded my napkin in my lap. "I'm going to bid on the golf lesson with Chuck Jagger," I heard Barry say to another guy, a high-risk ob-gyn named Killigan whom Barry had wanted me to consult with when I was pregnant with the twins.

I flipped through. There was nothing in the auction book that interested me: Dates and lessons. Yacht trips and dinners. I'd take friendship, real conversation, a challenge. How much for those?

I nudged Barry. "When are you going to have time for a golf lesson?" I said, thinking that I already never saw him.

He laughed and said, "Come on, Lisa," as if my question wasn't even a real one. As if he didn't already work twelve-hour days, and worry more about other women's breasts than mine.

Bethany walked to the front of the room; she was glowing. She was enjoying this, stepping in, stepping over everything Jen had done. She talked and talked. She got some bids, but she wasn't aggressive, not persistent, not even kindly nagging us to remember what the money went to and how much breast cancer needed us, the way Jen always did.

Then the golf lesson. Barry stood up right away. "Five hundred," he called out.

"Five-fifty," Bethany's husband, Kevin, said.

They went back and forth like this until Barry won the half-hour golf lesson for $1,025. When he sat down, I gave him a look. "What?" He shrugged. "It's for a good cause."

Fourteen

The next morning, Sunday, the details of the auction were splashed all over the front page of the *Deerfield Daily*. "Deerfield's Finest Donate Time and Money to Cancer Research," the headline read. They had raised $12,000 for the Helen Kemper Memorial Cancer Fund, which, really, wasn't bad, but last year we'd raised $17,500. I couldn't help but feel a little smug, and then a little sad. I shook my head. *Cancer research, for Christ's sake.* And I'd been booted out of that, of wanting to, of knowing how to, do some good.

On page seven, the article continued with a collage of pictures: Bethany in a black ball gown, smiling at the mike. Lisa's Barry standing up in a tux, bidding for an afternoon with golf pro Chuck Jagger. The article said he won it for $1,025, the highest bid of the night.

$1,025. It sounded familiar. Exact.

I went and got my reporter's pad, and there it was, written in my own writing. *Barry bought the lesson with Chuck Jagger for $1,025. Lisa is annoyed. She's already alone too much.*

I sat down, the paper shaking in my hands. There must be some mistake. I couldn't have really dreamed that, the exact amount of money, that golf pro. Was that the golf pro we'd booked last year? Had he sold for that much? I thought about Ethel, saying that my dreams were only my conscious discovering what my subconscious already knew, but how the hell did it already know this?

I grabbed my cell, found her number again, and called her, and even though it was Sunday morning, I left her a message to call me right away.

While I waited for her to call back, I paced the kitchen floor and tried to take deep breaths. There must be some logical explanation. There had to be.

I jumped when I heard my cell ring, and I ran to grab it.

"Ethel," I said, my voice trembling.

"Jennifer, is everything okay?"

"No," I said. "No. I don't think it is."

"What's wrong? Are you still dreaming?"

"They aren't dreams." I paused. "They're real things. Things that happened. To other people."

She was quiet for a minute. "The transformation of things," she said.

"What?"

"Have you ever heard of the Chinese philosopher Chuang Tzu?"

"No," I said.

"That's what he called it. He once said he dreamed he was a butterfly, and then he woke up and he was a man. But then he wasn't sure if he really was a man who dreamed he was a butterfly or a butterfly only dreaming he was a man."

I wasn't exactly sure what she was getting at, and I wasn't at all in the mood for some mumbo-jumbo Eastern medicine theory. There had to be an explanation, a rational one. Maybe the dream was just something I'd heard, something I'd guessed. Or it could be a coincidence. $1,025 felt like a nice round number, something I might dream up on my own.

But that's not what Ethel had been saying at all—she'd said something about transforming, about not being sure if you were one thing or another. And what the hell was that supposed to mean? Was she saying I really was Lisa, and I was only dreaming now, dreaming as Jen? I knew that couldn't be right—I could remember an entire long history of my life— Jen's life—a funeral in the snow at the age of thirteen, a blind date in an Italian restaurant at age twenty-six.

"I don't understand," I finally said, feeling even more confused now than before she'd called.

"It is funny, the way our mind can play tricks on us," she said. "Sometimes everything is not as it seems, Jennifer." She paused. "A dream is only a dream. Even Freud never thought they were real."

"A dream is only a dream," I repeated back, trying to believe it the way she seemed to.

"Jennifer, try to relax. If the dreams keep bothering you, we can adjust at your next appointment. But it's good that you're sleeping so well."

After we hung up I flipped back through my notepad, reviewing the dreams. Maybe Ethel was right, and a dream was a dream was a dream. But maybe she wasn't. After all, she'd told me once that she was not a miracle worker at all, only a healer. Maybe the dreams were real. And even Ethel didn't have the knowledge or the understanding of how that could be possible, how a simple herb could transform your mind into something so oddly metamorphic.

And if they were real, then there was so much I knew now, oddly so much more than I'd known when I'd been close to Kat or Lisa. And Will—what had the broken dreams about Will even meant? That being a judge had made him literally sick? I ached for Will, for the way his job had made him feel, and for the way I'd pulled away from him because I'd thought it was the job that he really loved, not me.

This is ridiculous, I told myself. *Listen to Ethel. Forget about the dreams.* Yet, no matter how many times I repeated this in my head, I still couldn't bring myself to really believe it.

After a shower and some coffee, last night's dream, the auction felt further away, felt like something that couldn't have possibly happened at all. I went and cleaned up the paper, and then lying underneath, I saw a note on the table from Will. MEETING DANNY TO WATCH THE GAME. HOME FOR DINNER. LOVE, WILL. *Love, Will.* He was shouting it at me, in all caps again, and maybe that was the only way he knew how to express it, like this, a silent but authentic battle cry. Then I felt a little sad, thinking of the way he'd looked at me last night, stunned and broken, like a sick bird.

Since Will was with Danny I decided to give Kat a call and see what she was up to. Back before we moved to Deerfield, before Kat had the girls, Will and Danny had watched football together nearly every Sunday while Kat and I had gone shopping or to lunch. When the weather was still nice enough, we'd sit outside, sip nonfat mochas, and do the *Times* crossword puzzle together. It was the only way either one of us could ever finish it, sharing answers. Kat said that didn't make us dumb, just resourceful.

It had been years since I'd done the *Times* puzzle on a Sunday. Not because I didn't have the time in Deerfield, but because I didn't have Kat.

"You busy?" I asked, when she picked up.

She sighed. "The girls are supposed to be at a birthday party in thirty minutes, and I haven't even gotten them dressed yet." She paused. "You all right? You sound funny."

"Yeah, I'm fine," I said, thinking of her and Grant in the coffee shop, and wondering if it had been real. If she was actually cheating on Danny. "I've just been—"

"Sarah Lynne, do not hit your sister with the hairbrush." The days of mochas and the *Times* puzzle were long over for Kat, too, though maybe in her case, not by choice. *Case in point, Will. Why we shouldn't have kids. Don't we already have enough problems as it is?* Kat sighed again. "If I disappear check the mental hospital. I may just have to check myself in." *Or Grant's apartment*, I silently added, though I had no idea if Grant even lived in an apartment or not. "Sorry," she said. "You were saying."

"Oh, nothing. I've just been having these vivid dreams. They're freaking me out a little bit," I said, leaving out the most important part.

"God, I wish I got enough sleep to actually dream." She sighed. "Or any time to think, for that matter." She paused. "Fucking birthday parties are the worst. And on a Sunday." She paused. "Hey, you wanna come?"

"After that hard sell?" I laughed.

"No, really, you should come. It's my cousin Emily's daughter. Remember her?" Emily. I did remember. The opposite of Kat in every way. She was such a devoutly religious member of some sect of Christianity that I couldn't remember, that she and her husband hadn't even kissed until their wedding night. She was a photographer who did some freelance work for *City Style* from time to time, a fact I always hid from Kelly because I knew it would make her bug me about trying to get her in, too. "Come on. I was going to sneak some vodka in my purse. We'll watch the kids bat a piñata around and get hammered."

"In the morning?"

"Okay. Buzzed. Slightly buzzed," she said. "You'd be doing me a favor, really. I hate going to these things alone. Having to talk to all the bitchy stay-at-home moms. Please? Pretty please?"

And though a birthday party did not sound exactly like refuge, I was eager to get out of the house, out of my own head, so I agreed to go.

Kat was right. The Sunday morning birthday party was hell. Screaming children running through a crowded downstairs, a piñata on the chilly back patio, at which the children also screamed.

"There's a lot of screaming," I whispered to Kat.

She passed over her Sprite can, which I'd seen her slip the vodka into after she'd first arrived. "Have some," she said. "It helps."

I shook my head. "No thanks."

She shot me a look. "You're pregnant?"

"What?" I laughed nervously. Had Kat noticed the extra five pounds and assumed? "No way."

"Are you sure?" She raised her eyebrows. "You said you

were having vivid dreams and now you don't want to drink, so I sort of assumed . . ."

"You have vivid dreams when you're pregnant?"

"Oh God, completely," she said. "When I was pregnant with Sarah Lynne, I had this dream that I was in Munchkinland, you know, in *The Wizard of Oz*." I nodded. "I was like the fucking queen Munchkin or something, and all the little people kept coming by to wash my shoes. And I swear to God, when I woke up, I really thought it was real." She paused to take a drink out of the Sprite can. "Oh, and then there's the sex dreams. Ironic, huh? Just when you turn into a beached whale, you can't get enough of sex. Though in the dreams I was never pregnant. Just really skinny. Like size zero. With boobs." She held her hands up to emphasize. "Big ones." Kat is more like a size six and probably a B cup like me, so it was clear that her dreams were more fantasy than reality. Nothing like mine.

I laughed nervously, looking around to see if Christian Emily could hear us, but she looked engrossed in making sure some kid didn't smash her daughter, rather than the piñata, with the giant red plastic bat. The kid's aim was despicable, and he kept hitting the picnic table instead. "No," I said. "Kat, it's nothing like that. I'm not pregnant. I swear. No sex dreams." I felt a little bit thankful that I hadn't had any. That would be weird. I'd never be able to look at Barry, or Danny, or Grant, or maybe even Will again, if I had a dream like that. "I did have a dream about you, though." She raised her eyebrows, and she chugged the rest of the can of Sprite. "You were with that guy Grant, who took over my old job."

"Oh, I was?" She looked away, toward the piñata, as if she found a half-smashed Dora the Explorer the most fascinating thing in the world.

"Are you sleeping with him?" *No, fucking him*, I thought, to use her terminology, her thoughts.

"Was I, in your dream?" I shook my head. "Too bad," she said. She took a cigarette out of her purse, but I pulled it out of her hand before she could light it. "What?"

"You can't smoke at a kids' birthday party." It bewildered me that I understood this and she did not.

"I wasn't going to smoke it for real," she said. "Just hold it in my hand and think about smoking it." I handed it back to her. She held it in her palm, clasped and unclasped her hand. "That's weird," she said. "That you dreamed about me and him." She cleared her throat. "There have been a few times when I've thought about it. Him. I mean, haven't you ever thought about another guy?"

I shook my head. It was true, I hadn't. Things hadn't been and weren't the best between Will and me, but I'd never thought about cheating, finding someone else. I just assumed things would get better eventually or they wouldn't. Another man never felt like the solution to anything.

"Well, it's different for you," she said. "You don't have kids. Kids change everything." She held the cigarette out as if thinking about smoking it, then clasped it back in her hand.

"How?" I asked.

"They just do." She waved her hand in the air. "You know, Danny works late. I work late. Then when we get home it's all about the kids, getting them dinner, and playing with them and bathing them and getting them to bed. Before you know it, it's ten o'clock, you have food crusted on your shirt, and you're more fucking exhausted than you could ever imagine. And then it all repeats. Day after day." She held the cigarette between two fingers, and I noticed her hand was shaking. "It happens," she said. "People fall out of love, after they have kids."

I reached out for her shaking hand. "It doesn't happen to you. You and Danny. You guys are fucking Kat and Danny," I said. I pictured them the way they were six years ago, wrapped around each other on the couch in Will's apartment, their legs inextricably linked as if they were one person, their laughter coming in tandem as Will told a story about work, and I could still remember wishing that Will and I could be like them, could be them. *They really are the perfect couple*, I'd said to Will after they went home.

He'd nodded in agreement and added, *Their happiness is so . . . tangible.* So if Kat and Danny couldn't survive, then what chance would Will and I ever have?

Kat laughed wryly. "That was a long time ago," she said, as if she, too, was remembering that same night—just about a month before Will and I got engaged, when she and Danny were still an entity of perfection. "Now we're just tired. And," she added, "we haven't had sex in six months."

I thought about the way Kat had felt when she was with Grant, that warm spark, the tingling in her legs. It must've been the way she'd felt once with Danny, and I knew it was the way I'd felt with Will. She had to be able to get that back with Danny. She had to. Because if she could, that meant that maybe Will and I had a chance, too. "Hey, you know what?" I said, without really thinking it through. "You and Danny should go away for the weekend and let me and Will watch the girls."

"Are you serious?"

"Yeah. Of course," I said, because once it was out there, I was totally serious.

"Okay, I'll talk to Danny about it. Maybe."

"Any weekend you want, okay? Will would be excited about it." He probably would, probably would think it was a great way to convince me that I wanted a baby, though, as I watched Sarah Lynne wildly swing the red bat, I knew it would probably do just the opposite.

"Thank you," she said.

"Just tell me one thing. Where were you, those times with Grant, when you were tempted?"

"In the coffee shop," she said. "The one below the office that we used to go to all the time." I nodded and I tried to look calm, though my heart was pounding rapidly in my chest. I thought about the smell of the coffee, sitting in the plastic chair while I felt his leg brush against hers. "Is that where I was, in your dream?" she asked.

"Oh no," I lied. "Of course not. You were at my sister's house," I lied again, surprised by how easily it came out. "Weird, huh?"

She reached over and squeezed my hand. "Thanks for coming with me." She paused. "And don't tell Will about the vodka. He'll tell Danny, and then Danny will be pissed, drinking when I'm with the kids, and blah, blah, blah."

"Don't worry." I squeezed her hand back. "Your secret's safe with me."

Lying in bed, that night, alone, Will still down in the study, I thought about him. And just before I fell asleep, I wondered what he would say if Danny had asked him about me, about us, the way I'd asked Kat.

I was standing in my office, staring out the window. Just below the courthouse, there was an entire world, people moving, doing things: a mother pushing her baby in a stroller, a family walking into the used book store across the street. I closed my eyes and imagined myself walking on the street, going somewhere, doing something.

I heard a knock at the door. "Come in," I called out, but I didn't step away from the window. I couldn't.

"Judge." I heard Janice's voice, and I turned away from the window. "Is this a good time?"

I sighed and gestured to the chair across the desk. "Have a seat." With the weight of the baby in her stomach, everything about Janice seemed swollen, even her eyes, which were dark brown, the color of chestnuts.

"It's okay," she said. "I'll only be a minute." She paused. "I just want to tell you that I don't think I'll be coming back. After the baby." I nodded. "I'm really sorry. I love it here, but Rick and I talked about it, and it's just too much time. I don't want to miss everything with her."

"Is that all?" I asked. I saw her eyes swell up, begging me to tell her it was okay. So I did. "Look, Janice. It's fine."

"Are you sure you're not mad?"

"No." I sighed. "I'm not mad."

"Okay. Good." She nodded. "I'll start looking for my replacement then?"

I nodded and turned back toward the window. The mother on the street was still there, sitting on a bench, lifting her baby in the air.

It's not fair, I thought, as I heard Janice walk away. Not fair that she can leave. Just like that.

I rolled over and reached out my hand for Will. He murmured and rolled toward me. "Where did you want to go?" I attempted to whisper into the darkness, but my mind hung somewhere in blurry half sleep, and I couldn't force the words from my lips.

Fifteen

Will spent most of Thanksgiving morning on the couch, watching football, while I spent it throwing my nervous energy into pies—pumpkin, apple, and pecan. I always did the pies because Kelly couldn't bake to save her life. She was an excellent turkey roaster and potato masher, but she managed to ruin every baked good she ever touched. Hence her penchant for Tastykakes.

I still hadn't told my father about anything that had happened to Will, or to me, for that matter, and I was hoping we'd be able to get through the dinner without it coming up.

As I sliced apples, I remembered a night from my childhood: It was snowing, and my mother was standing at the stove making soup, the bones of her face protruding in this unnatural skeletal manner, her chestnut wig on a little crooked. She kept stirring the soup, looking out the window, watching for him.

It was dark by the time he got there, long after the three of us had eaten the soup. "It's late," my mother had said when she saw him. "I was worried."

"Sorry," my father had grunted, sounding unapologetic.

In the end, she'd been in hospice care at Twelve Oaks Nursing Home. Her last night, my father had been working late, and Dave, who'd just gotten his driver's license, had taken Kelly and me over there after school.

After she died, my father always managed to find a way to be disappointed in me whenever he was around, which was rarely. When I was in high school, our brief exchanges were frowns and grimaces. I didn't get a scholarship to college like Kelly had. I was not a standardized test person, and my SAT scores had been too low. I didn't find a nice Jewish boy like Dave to date, lose my virginity to, marry, and take over the family business.

My senior year I'd dated a guy named Frank De'Anzo, a tall, lanky Roman Catholic, with a tattoo of a snake on his biceps that he liked to curl and uncurl just for fun. I "accidentally" left my birth control pills out on the kitchen counter just to see if my father would yell or really get angry. He didn't. He just handed them back to me, said, "I think these are yours," and then he frowned, a frown so heavy that it might have exploded under the weight of his disappointment if he hadn't then gone into the other room to watch the baseball game and forget all about me.

When my dad met Will for the first time he didn't react. He shook Will's hand. "Will's Jewish," I told him, putting heavy emphasis on the word *Jewish*.

"Half Jewish," Will corrected me.

"Half, whole, it's all the same." I waved my hand in the air.

My father frowned.

At my wedding, my father walked me down the aisle. He hadn't offered to pay the way he had for Kelly and Dave's wedding. Will said he could afford it, that there was no need to ask my father for anything. Still, he should've offered. And that's what I thought the whole time I held on to his arm, down the long white aisle that had been dusted with purple rose petals. *None of this is yours. None of this belongs to you.* When we reached the end, he hugged me squarely, still keeping me at a distance. As he sat down in his seat, he stared straight ahead, looking at Will and then back at me, and I thought I saw him frown.

So I could imagine just the look on his face if I were to tell him about Will, a frown that yet again would tell me how I was nothing to him but an utter disappointment.

Around noon, the phone rang. "Happy Turkey Day," Kat said, when I picked up.

I listened for background noise but heard nothing. "It sounds quiet. Where is everyone?"

"Danny took the girls to the park, and I'm supposed to be getting the turkey in before his mother gets here. God help me."

"You're cooking?"

"Danny thinks his mother is getting too old to do it, so he offered me up. I feel like a fucking sacrificial lamb or something. I can't do it."

"You'll be fine," I said.

"Seriously, though. I can't. I mean, I don't know how." She paused. "Okay, I have this fucking turkey sitting here, and I don't even know what the hell to do with it." I chuckled at the thought of Kat holding a raw turkey and feeling so bewildered. "You suburban bitches know this shit. So spill." Her words tumbled out together, a little slurred, and I wondered if she'd been drinking again. If the vodka in the morning Sprite wasn't an oddity at all.

I told her how to wash the turkey, take out the giblets, and get it in the oven. "Don't worry," I said. "Take a deep breath. You're going to be fine." I heard her clanking around in the background, the turkey slapping up against the counter, the water rushing over it, as she held on to the phone. While I waited, I checked on my pies to make sure they were browning evenly. And then finally I heard the slam of the oven door on her side.

"I did it," she said. "I fucking did it."

I laughed again, and I had this sudden flash of Kat sitting on a horse on a carousel, bobbing up and down, her long blond hair flowing out behind her. We were in Atlantic City for the weekend, the four of us, sometime just before Will proposed. The guys were trying to win us stuffed animals on the boardwalk, and Kat and I had chosen the carousel, chosen to spin around and around and around, the cool salty breeze whipping through us, making us feel like children, like two little girls on the playground.

"Oh," she said, interrupting the memory. "I almost forgot. Danny wants to go away next Saturday night. If that's okay. If you still want to watch the girls."

"Absolutely," I said, with much more confidence than I felt, thinking of the way it felt to be on the carousel, young and free and beautiful, and now wanting that all back, for both of us. "It'll be great. Where are you going?"

"I don't know. I told Danny he could choose."

"Atlantic City," I said.

"Atlantic City!" She laughed. "Oh God, that feels like a lifetime ago."

It did, and it made me sad, just thinking about it, the way a few years could change everything, the way love could disappear just like that. "Well, anyway, just let me know what time you want us to come over, and we'll be there," I said.

"Be where?" I heard Will's voice from behind me as I hung up the phone. He leaned down to kiss my shoulder, a gesture that I wasn't expecting, a gesture that gave me chills. I closed my eyes for a minute, remembering him on that trip, in the gorgeous suite we'd had in the Taj Mahal, with the deepest spa bathtub I'd ever seen. I could still picture the way he'd looked at me in that bathtub, the way his blue eyes were lit up and the color of sea foam, the way I'd slid on top of him into the water, and the warmth that had rushed over me, that had invaded my body so intensely that I'd never wanted it to end, never wanted to get out of the tub. "So where are we supposed to be?" he asked now, as he moved toward the oven to check out the pies.

I cleared my throat. "I told Kat we'd watch the girls next weekend, so she and Danny can go away."

"You did?" Will sounded as puzzled as I felt. And then it occurred to me, what the hell were we going to do with two little girls, for an entire weekend?

"You don't mind, do you? Because if you do, I can do it by myself." I hoped he wouldn't call my bluff, because the truth was I would be terrified doing it with him, much less alone.

He shook his head. "Nah, it'll be fine." He paused. "And besides, maybe one day they'll return the favor." His voice was softer when he said it, almost pleading.

"Yeah," I said lightly. "Maybe." And then to change the subject I quickly said, "Kelly wants us around four."

"I'll go shower then," he said. I stared at him for a second. His face was stubbly, and he was now in dire need of a haircut. It seemed plainly evident in his new face, his new demeanor, that he was no longer a judge. I pictured Sharon wrinkling her big nose, sniffing the air when we walked in, as if she could smell it on him, that something was entirely different.

"You're going to shave." I posed it as a statement more than a question.

He rubbed his chin. "I don't know. I was thinking about growing a beard."

"A beard?"

"You don't like the idea?"

I hated it. My father had a beard. Old men had beards and mustaches. Things that made your lips, made anything attractive about a man's face, disappear into this utter mess of scratchy hair. I shrugged.

"Yes, I think I might like a beard."

"Just shave for today, okay? For me? Please."

He nodded. "Okay. If it's that important to you."

I put my hand on his arm as he turned to leave. "Will, one more thing." I paused. "My father doesn't know about . . ."

He shrugged my hand off. "About your failure of a husband, you mean."

"No, that's not what I mean. It's just, you know I never talk to him. And, well, it's Thanksgiving. Let's not bring it up today."

"Fine," he said. "It's your family." His voice curled with something that might have been anger, or maybe jealousy, on the word *family*.

★ ★ ★

Sometimes I tried to imagine what Will's family might have been like. I'd seen pictures of them, his parents, albums and albums of a small, slight woman with a big toothy smile and a lanky bearded man, who Will grew to look like more and more as he got older. There were pictures of the three of them together, in museums, in cities, in Europe. Will's mother had been a law professor and his father a trial lawyer—until the summer after Will's freshman year in college, when his parents' rental car collided with a truck on their way to see the Anne Frank museum in Amsterdam.

Will told me once that he would've gone with them if it hadn't been for his summer job, where he'd been an intern with a big ad agency in Manhattan. It was only after his parents died that he changed paths, that he decided to switch to prelaw, to go to law school. At the ad agency, Will had asked for two weeks off to tag along on the trip, and his boss, who Will said was a big surly man who always smelled of cigars, told Will that if he wanted to go, he knew where the door was. There were a hundred other college students lined up on the other side, just waiting to take his place, just waiting, he said, for the goddamn opportunity of a lifetime. Will had chosen to stay.

Once, as he'd shown me an album of them together, the summer before that, on a cruise they'd taken around Scandinavia, he'd said it, barely a whisper at first, and then he repeated it louder. "I should be dead right now," he said. "I was supposed to die."

"No." I'd grabbed his hand. "No you weren't."

He shook his head. "You don't know. Maybe I was. Maybe I cheated fate."

"Maybe not," I said. "Maybe you actually weren't supposed to die at all. That's why you got the job, why you got picked out of all those other college students."

"Maybe," he said.

But I knew the feeling, cheating fate, or tempting it—it was the feeling that caught in my throat every time I got a breast exam, every time I reached for my breast in the shower to feel it in a circular motion, the way Dr. Horowitz had shown me, every time I did that and felt nothing, nothing at all.

Sixteen

We arrived at Kelly's at five minutes to four.

Will was freshly shaven and showered, and he smelled of Dove soap and pine aftershave, the scent I loved because I always associated it uniquely with him. And now every time I smelled it, it felt familiar, like coming home.

"You smell nice," I whispered to him, as we walked up Kelly's front steps.

He grunted out a response that might have been thanks, or might have been shut the hell up. It was hard to tell. It had just started snowing. The snow fell hard and fast in plump, wet, late autumn flakes, and Will had wrapped his scarf close to his mouth.

I took a deep breath as I rang the bell. I heard noises, laughter from the other side of the door, then Muffet barking.

Dave's mother, Beverly, opened it. "Oh, hello there, Jennifer." Her lip curled when she said my name. Beverly had never really been nice to me, and why, I wasn't sure. After all, she doted on Kelly, and deep down I'd always been jealous that Kelly had someone else, another mother after ours was gone. But tonight her frown seemed to crease a little more than usual. I smiled back in return.

"Hi, Beverly, nice to see you again." I nodded at her.

"How's the new house?" Will asked. He extended his hand. She didn't take it. Instead she grabbed the pies from me and stomped off into the kitchen.

Beverly used to live in a house just a few streets over from Kelly's, but after her own mother-in-law had recently died, leaving behind a vastly unknown and rather large fortune, she and her husband had bought a McMansion up in our neck of the woods. Tonight she was wearing her wealth, in the form of fur wrap and a large diamond necklace.

I felt this burning twisty fear in my stomach. *She knew. And she was going to say something about it at dinner.* But before I could really digest that thought, I heard Sharon's annoying shrill whine. "Oh, Jenny, sweetheart. Well, come on in and take your coat off. The cold doesn't do your complexion any favors."

Kelly walked in behind her, an "I'm the Mom, That's Why" apron tied around her waist, her hands encapsulated in two rooster-laden potholders that I knew must've been a gift from either Beverly or Sharon. I'd never seen them before, and I was sure Kelly would've thought they were just as ugly and tacky as I did. "Hi." She shot me a sympathetic look. "Will, Dave's in the den, watching football with Dad."

He nodded. I reached out to squeeze his hand, not a nice squeeze, but more of an I-know-you-hate-me-right-now-but-please-don't-fuck-it-up-for-me-anyway squeeze. He didn't squeeze back.

"Gotta baste the turkey." Kelly shot Sharon what I was sure she meant to be a smile but came off as more like a grimace.

"I'll help," I said.

Sharon swirled her drink in her hand, the ice clinking noisily against the glass, and the sound felt unnecessarily loud, piercing my eardrums. I assumed it was rum and Coke, what she always drank, no matter the time of day or the occasion. "Well, don't you girls worry about me."

We wouldn't.

I grabbed Kelly's arm and walked quickly toward the kitchen before she could follow us.

"You didn't tell me that your in-laws were coming," I whispered.

"They weren't," she said. "They were supposed to go Pittsburgh but Kathleen got the flu." Kathleen was Dave's sister. "And you know what germ-a-phobes they are." She paused. "You don't mind do you?"

I sighed. "Sharon's here. It doesn't get much worse than that."

"Oh stop, Jen. She's not all that bad." She laughed. "You did tell Dad about Will, didn't you?" Her tone had changed so fast, from one of conspiratorial friend to one of a chiding, derisive schoolmarm, that it shocked me a little bit how one person could be two different things so quickly.

"Not exactly," I said. I shook my head. "So don't say anything tonight, okay?"

She threw her roostered hands up in the air. "When are you going to just grow up and start talking to him already?"

"Why do I have to talk to him?" I said, pulling a carrot from a vegetable tray and popping it into my mouth.

"He's our father." She shook the roosters at the sky, in a gesture that might have been comical if she hadn't also looked so exasperated.

Beverly stepped into the kitchen. "Am I interrupting?"

Yes, I thought.

"No, of course not, Mother."

I pinched her arm, slight enough for Beverly not to notice, but hard enough for her to squirm. She knew exactly what it was, what I was saying, so I didn't even need to verbalize it. *I can't even believe you call her Mother now.*

She shot me a warning look back, which said, *Shut up. Don't lecture* me *about parental relationships.*

"Well, I thought you should know that Hannah is in the basement chewing on a Matchbox car."

"Did you take it from her?" Kelly asked.

Beverly shrugged. "I asked her to give it to me, and she didn't listen."

Even I knew that one-year-olds didn't know enough to listen to something like that. I rolled my eyes at Kelly, but if she noticed, she pretended not to. "Here." She handed me the roosters. "Can you baste?" And then she ran off toward the basement, Beverly in tow.

The eight adults sat around Kelly's dining room table, and the two older kids sat at the little wooden one Kelly usually had in her basement. Hannah was in the high chair, alternating between stuffing bite-sized pieces of turkey in her mouth and throwing globs of mashed potatoes on the floor. Every time she threw food, I watched Beverly grimace, watched the corners of her mouth turn down sharply, her eyes stare accusingly at Kelly, who was too busy running in and out of the kitchen, taking Jack to the bathroom, getting Caleb more

444

apple juice, to actually notice. Beverly struck me as what Kat would call a woman who was not meant to be a mother, and I wondered how she'd managed to raise Dave and his sister to be somewhat normal and functioning adults.

My dad and Sharon sat across the table from us, next to Beverly and her husband, Stan. Dave sat on the other side of Will, and Kelly, when she managed to, sat down next to him.

I tried to eat my turkey quietly, tried not to meet anyone's gaze, afraid they might talk to me directly. I chewed my food slowly, and sipped my wine too fast.

Will, who ignored the adults, made a silly face at Hannah, and she giggled, then spit out some turkey and giggled some more. "Don't." I nudged him. "She's eating."

He glared at me.

But this gave Sharon all the opening she needed. "Isn't that sweet? Look, he's good with her." I looked up and forced a smile, but then I went right back to my glass of Merlot, finishing it off. She nudged my father. "What do you think, Donny, could be some more grandchildren in the works, eh?"

The table got silent. Until Will finally said, "Maybe. We'll see."

"What's to see?" Sharon was talking with her mouth full now. Chewing the sweet potatoes messily and quickly, the way she'd just butted her big ugly nose into our business. "Jenny, you got quite a catch there. You're married to a judge. Take advantage of those smart little swimmers."

At the word *judge*, the room stopped. Even little Hannah seemed momentarily distracted from throwing her food. Dave had his fork suspended in midair, and Beverly looked mildly bewildered, as if a blood vessel had just silently erupted in her brain and had given her this odd moment of suspension, where everything in the room felt as if it were under water. But no, maybe that's just how I was feeling.

"What did I say?" Sharon asked. She shook the ice cubes in her empty glass, and then sucked one up and started crunching it with her teeth. "Oh, Jennifer, are you infertile? That's all you hear these days, bad eggs and in vitro fertilization. And oy, sexual diseases."

My father looked as if he hadn't heard a word, as if I was not his concern, as if any grandchildren from me weren't important enough for him to get involved. He quietly sliced his turkey, and then reached across the table for the gravy boat, all without looking up.

"Jen," Kelly said. I glared at her. *Not now*, I said with my eyes. *Let it go.* She shook her head. And then I knew she was going to say it, that she was going to tell them. That's the way it was with my sister. Everything was about controlling the situation with our father, doing what she thought was best without any regard for me or my feelings. Maybe she thought she was trying to help, but somehow she always made things worse.

She'd done the same thing after Will asked me to marry him. I'd asked her not to tell our father the details, not to tell him at all until I was ready, but a few days later, Sharon called me up and told me that they'd heard the news from Kelly.

I'm sorry, Kelly had said, when I'd called her to yell at her. *But he's our father.* As if that meant more to her than us, than our relationship.

You don't know, I'd told her. *You don't know everything about him.*

Oh Jen, she'd sighed. *Just grow up already.*

But I didn't want to watch her do it now, watch her act all high and mighty as she sold me out, so I stood up and walked into the kitchen. I heard Caleb's voice behind me, "Where's

Auntie JJ going?" *Sweet, sweet child. You cannot possibly understand what a bitch your mother is,* I thought.

Then I heard Kelly's voice, barely audible, a whisper. ". . . not a judge anymore . . . Daniels and Sons." Sharon gasped, and as I stood there trying to fully grasp what had just happened, the noise from the other room became suddenly muted, the air still. Then I heard the sound of Sharon's glass hitting the table, the ice cubes clinking so hard that they made a noise like shattering glass, or maybe the glass had hit the wood floor and actually shattered.

I smelled Will's pine aftershave, then felt his hand on my shoulder. "You want to go?" he said, his voice sounding soft and calm and small, but not at all angry the way I'd thought it would be.

Seventeen

We drove in silence. The roads were slippery and dusted with snow that, as the sun began to set, had started to change to ice. Will gripped the steering wheel tensely, with both hands, staring straight ahead. I thought about him staring out of his office window, wanting to leave, wanting to escape. And that's almost what it felt like we were doing now. "Do you want to stop and get some food?" he asked.

"No." I shook my head. "I'm not very hungry. But if you want to . . ."

"No," he said. "I'm fine."

When he pulled into the garage and turned off the car, he turned toward me. I knew he was watching me carefully, even though I was still staring straight ahead.

"I'm sorry," he said. "I'm sorry that you have to be ashamed of me. That— Oh, I don't know. Fuck it." He leaned his head against the steering wheel.

I turned toward him and put my hand on his shoulder. "I'm not ashamed," I whispered. And I wasn't. I was displaced, now floating around in the world with no purpose, no sense of who I was supposed to be. Not a real writer anymore. Not a fund-raiser. Not a friend. Not a lady of the club. Not a doubles tennis player. And not really even one half of the Levenworths—for all intents and purposes, the Levenworths ceased to exist and the two of us were just Will and Jen, not sure where to go or who to be, or how to be something together.

He leaned up. "Then why didn't you just tell him?"

"I don't tell him anything," I said. It was impossible to explain, the way I felt that every time I talked to my father there was an ocean roaring in my ears and obscuring every sound, making it impossible to really tell him anything or hear anything in return. It was impossible to explain that I didn't feel love for my father, that I didn't even really like my father, when I knew Will would've given anything to have his father back. It was impossible to explain the way I felt about Will right now, the way I felt this want, this need for him to make me feel the way he once had.

I leaned toward him, barely noticing the gearshift in my side, and I ran my finger along his smooth shaven cheek. He turned his head to look at me, and I kissed him. Not a quick kiss, not a little peck that we'd gotten used to giving each other as a formality, back and forth, the motion of emotion, without any real emotion at all. This was a long kiss, a slow kiss, a kiss that I felt pass with a tingly sensation down my legs. A sensation like the one I'd felt dreaming as Kat. This was the kind of kiss that made you feel warm, even when you were angry and scared and freezing cold.

He pulled back first, but he did not pull away, so I felt his breath against my cheek. Warm. "Jen," he whispered. "Jen. I—"

I thought about Kat and Grant, about how easy it was for passion to slip away, to transform into something else, and I didn't want this moment, our moment, to end. "Sssh," I whispered, and I kissed him again. I felt his tongue, pushing into my mouth, sweetly at first, then more insistently, and I closed my eyes. Will. This was Will. Me and Will. What I knew. What I loved.

And then the annoying jingle of my cell phone broke into the moment, and Will pulled back. He stared so intensely that I couldn't look away. "Are you going to get that?" he whispered.

"It's probably just Kelly," I said. But it kept on jingling. I sighed and rummaged through my purse until I found it. "It's Kat," I said. "I probably should get it."

He hesitated, then said, "Go ahead. I'll meet you inside."

I watched him get out of the car and start to walk away before I picked up the phone. "I burned the fucking turkey," Kat cried into my ear. I heard her, but I couldn't erase the feeling of Will, the taste of him. "Jen, are you there? Are you eating? Oh shit, I'm interrupting your dinner."

I cleared my throat. "No," I said, thinking that if she weren't so upset she would've noticed it, that something was different than it had been earlier, just from the sound of my voice. "I'm not eating. Tell me what happened."

Twenty minutes of consoling her, and two calls to Boston Market later, Kat had calmed down and had located a pre-cooked turkey. I went into the kitchen, where Will sat at the table, browsing through the gigantic pile of Black Friday ads. When I saw him sitting there, I felt nervous, the kind of nervous I'd felt the first time I saw him, sitting there in Il Romano, the glow of the candlelight washing across his face, telling me immediately that he was not just any blind date, he was someone special. "Everything all right?" he asked, not looking up from the paper.

"Kat burned the turkey."

He nodded. "Still, not quite as bad as our dinner, though, huh?"

"I'm sorry," I said. He nodded, and he distracted himself with the paper. I willed him to look up, to catch my eye, to remember kissing me. "You know it has nothing to do with you."

"It is what it is, okay?" He looked up, but he wouldn't quite meet my gaze.

"Will, I . . ." I wanted to say something about the kiss. No, that wasn't exactly true. I wanted to actually kiss him again, wanted to feel that passion from him again, but when I saw the way he looked right now, saw the sadness and the disappointment in his face, I knew for sure that all we'd had in the car was a moment. And in the course of a marriage, one moment did not mean all that much.

He stood up and gave me a quick kiss on the forehead. "I'll be in my study. Don't wait up. Okay?" And then I watched him walk away, and thought about the way I used to watch him, the way I used to look at him in disbelief, with a sense of wonder: *This man was mine. This man loved me.* And now he was always walking away.

I made my way upstairs, slowly, this new sense of disappointment settling heavy in my chest. One passionate kiss did not fix a marriage, did not repair the damage that had

134   Jillian Cantor

broken in slow and winding slivers through the years. I told myself this, but still, I couldn't stop thinking about it, thinking about him.

I took my herbs and lay down in bed, and I wondered if I thought about kissing him, thought about being with him, if it would happen in my dream. If thinking about being in that passionate place would be enough to dream me back there. And if I dreamed it, maybe in the morning I would wake up, and it would feel real. But then, just as I drifted off to sleep, Kelly's face popped into my head. The way she'd looked, looking at me, egging me on with her eyes. *Tell him. Tell him.*

Shit, I thought, *I'm going to dream about her.* And in the seconds before sleep, this annoyed me.

I was standing in Kelly's kitchen. I opened the oven door with my hands, which were covered in roosters. Hideous potholders that Beverly gave me as a gift for my birthday last year. I saw them and I thought of you, she'd said. As if she knew anything about me. Anything at all.

"Can I help, dear?" Beverly asked from behind me. I closed my eyes and spun around. Her face was tight and smooth—too much Botox—I could tell from her voice she was frowning, but there was an absence of emotion on her face, except just right around her eyes.

I wished I had my camera, so I could capture her, in this moment, with this exact nonexpression on her face, that still somehow to me conveyed disdain, disappointment. Dave never believed that I saw it there, never could see it the way I did. Maybe a picture would prove it to him.

"My mother loves you," he always said. "Just like you were her own daughter." No, not true. Her own daughter, Kathleen, could do no wrong, even when she did, even when she drank herself into a stupor and collapsed on the couch for an entire weekend. Even then, I'd never seen the look on Beverly's face that I saw when she looked at me.

"No," I told her. "I have everything under control. And Jen is bringing the pies."

"Jen is coming?"

"Of course," I said, "Jen always comes." Beverly rarely did. Beverly liked to spend the holidays with her daughter and her real grandchildren, my two little twin terror nieces. Who could blame them? If I had a mother like Kathleen, I'd probably try to set the kitchen curtains on fire, too. Or throw the contents of the sandbox down the toilet. Or any of their other various indiscretions since they'd been born five years ago.

"She's not bringing that man with her? Is she?"

"Her husband, Will?" I said, though I was positive she knew his name.

"You won't let him around the children?"

"Beverly, Jen says he's innocent. And there's nothing wrong with letting him around the children. He's not a child molester or something."

"Kelly, how many times do I have to tell you to call me Mother?" She sounded vaguely annoyed.

I nodded. "Sorry. I—I will." Mother, you are not my fucking mother. Mother. When I closed my eyes, I could see her, standing right there in front of me, her hair up in a bun, wearing the string of pearls my

*father-in-law bought her for some anniversary, telling
me that whatever is meant to be will be.*

*"And I still wouldn't want him around the children
if I were you. You have to teach them good values,
Kelly. Morals." She waved her hand in the air.*

*"Yes, Mother. You're right," I said. I swallowed
back the lump in my throat. As if she would know anything about morals, wearing a dead animal around
her shoulders.*

When I woke up the next morning, Will was already gone,
and there were four voice mail messages on my cell. Three
from Kelly, which all basically said, *We need to talk. Call me
back.* I thought about my dream, about the way Beverly got
under Kelly's skin—and instead of feeling sorry for her, I felt
even madder. She'd sold me out last night, for what, for her
mother-in-law? For Dave? I didn't call her back.

The fourth message was from my father, with Sharon's
whiny voice echoing in the background. He said they were
flying back to Florida this afternoon, and Sharon thought it
might be nice if we got lunch and . . . talked.

I was sure if I went to lunch with them he would be frowning while she would be swilling her rum and Coke, and telling me, with absolute certainty, that I should indeed not have
Will's baby, that his swimmers were probably little schemers,
just like him, and that I should leave him.

So I deleted all four messages, and went off to take a shower.

Once I stopped talking to Kelly, I couldn't stop dreaming
about her. I had two dreams about her the week after Thanksgiving. I remembered only pieces of them when I woke up

in the morning, but what I did remember, I wrote in my reporter's notebook.

> *Beverly was insisting on Caleb going to private school next year. I wanted him in public school. Dave threw his hands up in the air. If she wants to pay for it, just send him to private school, he said.*
>
> *That's not the point, I said. I was angry, so mad that my insides wanted to boil over, that I wanted to slap Dave.*

Then, the next night, *I was Kelly lying in bed, alone, staring at the clock. I felt this intense sense of loneliness that threatened to suffocate me. Dave came in at ten-thirty. I heard the sound of his footsteps, and then felt his breath on my neck, felt the wash of relief swarm over my body. "Sorry I'm so late," he whispered. I leaned into him.*

She called me a few more times, but I still didn't return her calls.

"You're going to have to talk to her eventually," Will said one night, when she called during dinner.

I heard Beverly's voice. *You can't let Will around the children.* And I felt the anger that welled up inside Kelly when she and Dave fought about his mother. "It's not that," I said to Will. "I just don't feel like talking to her right now."

"She's your sister," he said quietly.

"I know," I said, but I didn't pick up the phone.

Eighteen

On Saturday morning, Will and I took the train down to the city, and then we walked the four blocks to Kat and Danny's apartment. It was chilly outside, and Will and I hung on to each other's arms for warmth. "This is going to be interesting," I said as we walked up the steps to their historic-looking duplex.

"Yes." Will nodded, blowing into his hands to warm them.

I rang the bell, and Sarah Lynne flung open the door, her almost three-year-old sister, Arabella, behind her, clinging to her skirt.

"Hey there." Will bent down to their level and patted each girl on the head. "Are we going to have a fun weekend?" Sarah Lynne shrugged. Arabella retreated further. Will reached into his coat pocket and pulled out two Hershey's Kisses. He handed one to each girl. Their eyes looked back at him, wide with something, wonder maybe? And I wondered why I hadn't thought to bring candy.

"Girls," Kat called out. "Don't bother them, or they'll change their minds."

She opened the door wider and ushered us inside. "No we won't," Will said, emphatically.

Kat hugged him, then leaned in to hug me. "Are you sure about this? We don't have to stay the night."

I pictured Grant's hand on her arm. "Yes you do," I said. "You have a good time, and don't worry about us."

"I owe you." She squeezed my hand.

Danny walked out of their bedroom, a suitcase in tow. "The numbers are on the fridge. In case you need us."

"We won't," Will said. I nodded, in awe of the way he actually seemed comfortable in this situation, whereas I felt totally out of my element, trying to put on a show so Kat and Danny could get back to a good place. I knew it was silly, that the two things really weren't connected, but still, I kept thinking if they could fix things, then Will and I could, too.

"But if you do," Kat echoed, "the numbers are there."

They leaned down and hugged and kissed the girls, and Kat immediately put her sunglasses on and looked away from me. *She's sad*, I thought. *She's going to miss them.*

Three games of Candy Land, two hours of Barbies, and four episodes of *The Wiggles* later I was exhausted. During episode four of *The Wiggles*, Sarah Lynne dragged Will around the room, dancing and singing to all the songs, while Ara climbed up into my lap on the couch and started sucking her thumb. It was starting to get dark outside, and I knew it was almost time for dinner, but I couldn't take my eyes away from him: Will hopping around, all six feet of him, wild and wacky like the crazy Australians on TV. Was this what parenthood was all about? I wondered. Acting like the Wiggles? If that's what it was, then maybe Will *was* ready to be a father.

Ara leaned into me, her warm little head against my chest. It was a strange feeling, the way she'd attached herself to me so easily, so quickly. I'd played with Caleb and Jack and Hannah before, but never alone, without Kelly, and never for more than half an hour at a time.

Ara put her hand on my arm and twisted my watch— delicate and gold—a present from Will on a birthday a few years back, in what felt like another lifetime. "Aunt Jen," she whispered. She leaned back and looked at me. "You're so pretty. I like your curly hair."

I laughed. "Thank you," I said.

"I want to look just like you when I grow up."

I took a look at her straight red hair and her freckles, her tiny little pug nose, and her rosy cheeks, and I knew she was going to look mostly like Danny, with just a little smidgen of Kat. "Okay," I told her, because I didn't want to ruin it, that little-girl innocence that still allowed her to believe that anything was possible.

Later that night, after pizza and baths for the girls and bedtime stories for both of them—*The Berenstain Bears* for Sarah Lynne, and *The Cat in the Hat* for Ara—Will and I moved around quietly in Kat and Danny's guest room.

Will lay down on the bed, his clothes still on. "I'm exhausted," he whispered. "I don't know how the Wiggles do it."

I laughed and sat down on the bed next to him. "You were great with them," I said. He nodded. "How did you get to be so good with kids?"

"I'm just a natural, I guess." He paused. "Didn't I ever tell you that I used to be a camp counselor when I was in high school?"

"No," I said. "I don't know. I don't think so." I tried to re-member if he had, and I knew that even if he had I'd tucked it away in the back of my mind, filed away under something I'd thought of as trivial, though now it seemed fairly important, who Will was, who he'd been.

"My parents were friends with the owners of the camp," he said. "I had the five-year-old bunk. Two summers." He paused. "There you have it, my child care résumé."

"It's more impressive than mine," I said. I wondered what might have happened if Will's parents hadn't died, if he might've kept at advertising or kept up at the camp and de-cided to become a teacher or something. I wondered if maybe the law hadn't really defined who he was at all, but only in the ways he'd let it, in the ways he'd needed it to, to allow himself to grieve.

"Jen," he whispered, reaching for me, pulling me close to him. "You were great with them. Ara loved you. Sarah Lynne renamed one of her Barbies after you." His voice drifted off, and I could tell he was falling asleep, just like that, with his arm around me. I shifted onto my side, and I snuggled into him, the way Kelly had into Dave in my dream. And I had the notion that I should feel happy, and yet, as I closed my eyes, I couldn't shake the feeling of dread.

I was standing outside, on the back patio, the cool wind whipping against my cheeks. I held up my camera, and I zoomed in on the lilacs against the snow. Pale purple and white, a swirl of cream and light.

I heard banging on the window, and I looked up and saw Caleb and Jack, their little faces pressed to the glass. I waved and blew them a kiss, but the banging continued. Where the hell was Dave?

I focused the camera on the flower, turning, turn-
ing, turning the lens until the shot was perfect, until
the petal of the lilac hung just the right way against the
snow. This is the January shot, I thought. The perfect
photograph to stare at during the bleakest month—
cold, yet hopeful. And just as I was about to press the
button, the boys burst through the patio door, shouting
my name, calling for me. I put the camera down and
closed my eyes. If I could just have five minutes. Five
minutes.

"Wake up." I heard Ara's small voice, felt her body jump next to me on the bed.

"Five minutes," I whispered, my voice, my head, thick with Kelly, Kelly feeling overwhelmed.

"I have to go potty," she announced. I opened my eyes and looked at the clock: seven-fifteen. I looked at Will, lying on his back, breathing evenly.

"Okay," I whispered, and I dragged my tired and aching body out of bed, and helped her find her way to the bathroom.

Ara stomped on the tile floor, doing a little dance before she sat on the toilet, which promptly awakened Sarah Lynne, who also really had to use the bathroom, and screamed for Ara to hurry up. "I'm going as fast as I can," Ara yelled.

"Why don't you use the other bathroom?" I suggested to Sarah Lynne.

She folded her arms and shook her head. "No. I'm going to use *my* bathroom."

"It's my bathroom, too," Ara protested.

"Come on, Ara," I prodded. "Can you go a little faster?"

She sighed deeply in a way that reminded me so much of Kat that it startled me. "Fine."

I felt my hands shaking. I was sweating, not sure what to do or what to say to hurry her up, nervous that Sarah Lynne was going to pee on the hardwood floor. But after a few minutes, Ara got up, and Sarah Lynne promptly ran to the toilet.

I took a deep breath. "Should we get dressed?"

Sarah Lynne shook her head. "We have to brush our teeth first."

After ten minutes of fighting over the tube of toothpaste, I found some clothes and managed to get them on the girls, despite both of them deciding they wanted to have a spontaneous dance party. Ara didn't like the outfit I picked out at first and started crying, until I let her wear red pants with a red sweater, despite my protests that they didn't match. "They do," she said. "Red and red."

"Don't even try to argue," Sarah Lynne informed me.

So I didn't. But I wondered where she'd gone, sweet Ara who wanted to look like me, and how she'd turned into this whiny little creature. I'd had a moment, leaning into Will last night, when I'd believed him, when I'd actually believed that maybe I could do this. I closed my eyes and thought about the perfection of the lilac on the snow, and then the chaos that broke the moment. And last night, with Will, felt very far away.

I heard footsteps, and I watched Will stumble out of the guest room, rubbing sleep from his eyes. He was still in his clothes from yesterday, and his hair was sticking up and uncombed. He looked almost handsome in the way he seemed to have come undone, defenseless in a way.

"Uncle Will," Ara cried. "Look at my outfit."

"And mine, too," Sarah Lynne said.

He gave them the thumbs-up. "Very nice," he said. "Who wants to watch the Wiggles?"

"I do, I do," the girls chorused. They ran toward the living room.

"I'll be there in a minute," Will called after them. He turned to me. "I didn't hear them get up." He offered a meek smile.

I shrugged, not willing to admit that I'd been feeling overwhelmed. "You looked comfortable. I didn't want to wake you."

"I was comfortable," he said, reaching up to tuck a stray hair behind my ear, and it occurred to me that I was also undone, my hair uncombed, my face unwashed, my teeth unbrushed.

"I'm a mess," I said.

He shook his head and reached his thumb up to stroke my cheek. "No you're not."

"Uncle Will," Sarah Lynne screamed from the other room.

"You'd better go," I whispered. "I'll make some breakfast."

After lunch, Sarah Lynne and Ara fell asleep on the couch, and then Will and I sat at the table, reading the Sunday paper. I made an attempt at the *Times* puzzle, but my brain felt too foggy to get more than a few clues. "Need some help?" Will asked, when he saw me put the pencil down.

I shook my head. "I'm too tired to think."

"Me too," he said, but even as he said it his eyes had a certain twinkle to them, so I knew he'd enjoyed this. Will was cut out to be a father. He grabbed my hand across the table. "Jen," he said, and I swallowed a lump in my throat, knowing what was going to come next. I thought about the way he'd felt as I leaned against him last night, his body warm and entwined with mine in a way that I'd felt completely whole, completely safe. And why couldn't that just be enough? "Jen, you're good at this. We're good at this."

I thought about a baby, about what it might be like to hold this small and perfect being, an entirely blank slate that we would be wholly responsible for. This thing, this innocent thing that would rely on us, that would need us. "Will, I . . ."

"Oh my God," Kat said. I hadn't heard her come in, but I turned toward the sound of her voice, grateful for the interruption. Her face looked radiant, aglow with something I hadn't seen from her in years. "The girls are both asleep."

"Will wore them out," I said.

I smiled at him, and he nodded; a flash of disappointment crossed his face, which he quickly turned into a smile for Kat. "Your girls are a lot of fun," he said.

"Well, whatever you two did, you need to sell it and bottle it to parents everywhere."

"You had a nice time?" I asked.

"Fucking fantastic," she said.

"I second that," said Danny, who walked in behind her, put his arms around her, and kissed her shoulder.

Nineteen

It was after six by the time we got off the train and into my SUV. Will put the key in the ignition and turned to look at me before turning on the car. "Let me take you out to dinner."

"I don't know," I said, dreading the possibility of finding our way back to that baby conversation again. "I'm exhausted."

"You owe me a dinner, remember?"

I had promised him a rain check the night of the auction, and I realized I was starving, so I agreed.

"Great." He paused. "Where do we go?"

It had been years since we'd gone to dinner anywhere but the club. And before that, in the city, we'd dined at the fancy restaurants that I reviewed, compliments of the magazine.

I tried to remember where'd I'd gone before I met Will, in college even. There was a bar named Henry's not too far from my father's old house, and there was a little diner just south of there where I'd gone with my friends in high school. "Where do other people go?" Will wondered out loud.

I thought of Lisa, Bethany, and Amber, the club; Kat, the city. Then I tried to remember where Kelly went. "You know, I think Kelly and Dave and the kids like Applebee's," I said. I knew there was one not too far from their house, at the edge of a little strip mall, across the street from Acme. I'd met Kelly and the kids there for lunch once.

"Yes." He nodded. "I just saw their commercial the other day."

We looked at each other and we both started laughing, this crazy, giddy, tired laughter. What kind of couple didn't know where to go to dinner? Kelly had made fun of me on more than one occasion for not dining anywhere but the club. *My God, you're like freakin' Barbie and Ken,* she'd retort with a dry laugh. *Actually, according to Sarah Lynne, I was freakin' Barbie,* I thought now. *So there, Kel, take that.*

Will turned the key and pulled out of the parking space, and then stopped the car. "Where the hell is it?" he asked.

I started laughing again, and it took a few minutes for me to stop enough to give him directions.

Applebee's was oddly crowded for a Sunday night. Families and high school kids milled all around out front clinging to their plastic buzzers that the hostess told us would blink and sing when it was our turn. Will and I sat on a bench out front and waited. Will put his arm around me and I leaned into him, and let myself enjoy his warmth.

After twenty minutes, Will jumped when our plastic buzzer buzzed and flashed red. And then we were led to a tiny booth near the back of the restaurant. "It's happy hour," Will said, sounding a little giddy as he picked up the menu. "I think I'll get a drink."

I looked at the drink menu, and had an instant craving for a margarita, even though it had been years since I'd drunk anything but wine. "I'm going to have a margarita," I announced. "On the rocks, with salt."

He nodded and smiled. "Perfect." When the waiter came, we ordered two, and we let ourselves be talked into a plate of half-priced nachos and two chicken something-or-other combo plates.

At the club, we drank only wine, and only red wine, Merlot or Cabernet: heart healthy, trendy, and a perfect pairing with filet mignon. Our appetizers were escargot or half-shell clams or shrimp cocktail.

As I took the first sip of my margarita, the salty-sour taste burned my throat and warmed my brain. Then, as I started munching on a nacho, I started to feel this odd sensation of warmth that made me feel like I was glowing.

Will drank his margarita quickly and I followed him, drinking it down too fast to enjoy the salty-sour combination and fast enough to feel a little dizzy. "Another round," he told the young waiter when he popped back around to check on us.

Will reached across the table for my hand, and underneath the dim Tiffany light fixture, his face hung in a shadow, so he looked only slightly familiar, like someone I'd once known a very, very long time ago. Like a man, a stranger, sitting at a half-circle booth in Il Romano, who I might have the possibility of falling in love with.

The second round of margaritas came, and we drank them more slowly through straws, one-handed, not letting go of each other across the table.

"You look beautiful, Jen," Will whispered, somewhere between the nachos and the chicken something-or-other.

"That's the margarita talking," I whispered. Because I
hadn't taken a shower since yesterday morning or even had
time to put on makeup today.

"No." He shook his head. "It's not." He paused. "Hey," he
said, taking another sip. "Tell me one thing you want." The
words rolled off his tongue, effortlessly, as if it was something
he still said to me all the time, something easy.

I paused for a minute, not knowing exactly what to say.
Then I shrugged.

"Just one thing," he whispered.

So I said the first word that popped into my head: "Love,"
I whispered. I gently squeezed his hand, as if it was my lifeline, my safety. He squeezed back.

Then the din of the crowded restaurant faded away, and
there was nothing else but me and Will. Will and me.

After dinner we walked around the strip mall until Will felt
sober enough to drive home. I held on to his arm, as we walked
slowly past the shops of Oak Glen, a T. J. Maxx, a PetSmart,
a Hallmark store. "Let's go in," Will said when we got to the
Hallmark. He opened the door before I could answer, so I followed him inside.

In the front of the store there was a display of tiny ceramic
figurines, anyone and everyone you could imagine molded
and painted and looking like exact replicas—cats and dogs,
teachers and doctors. I noticed a judge, and I suddenly felt
dizzy and closed my eyes for a moment to try to regain my
equilibrium.

When I opened them, Will was holding something, a figurine, in his hand. "I'm going to buy this for you," he said. He

opened his palm and held it out so I could see it—a man with his arm around a woman holding a sleeping baby against her chest. The woman had her head turned, and she was looking up, smiling at the man who smiled back at her.

"Will, don't—"

"Sssh." He put his finger to my lips. He turned the figurine over. On the bottom, it had a price tag, and a name, "The Perfect Family." "It is the perfect family," he whispered. Then he handed the figurine to me.

"You shouldn't buy this for me," I said, the lightness of the margarita now feeling very far away, and instead, my head was starting to feel dull, achy.

"I'm not trying to rush you," he said. "But I saw the way you were this weekend. You were so great. That's all I was trying to tell you before." He paused. "Just let me buy this for you as a promise, a reminder. A someday."

"Okay," I agreed softly. "A someday."

Between the margaritas and the weekend, Will looked exhausted when we got home. He lay down on the bed, fully dressed, and fell right to sleep that way for the second night in a row. I took my time in the bathroom, examining my face for something as I brushed my teeth. I wanted to see it there, something in my eyes, something that told me I could be someone's mother. But I only saw what I always did, green eyes, a little tired, a few new crow's-feet. I stared too hard for too long, searching for something, and the glare from the bathroom lights started to hurt my eyes, started to make my own image feel too bright, unreal, so I had to look away.

I slipped under the covers and turned away from Will. I felt him shift, lean toward me, and put his arm around me. He mumbled something in his sleep. My eyes were too heavy to really wonder what it was, to wonder if he was trying to tell me that he loved me.

And just before I drifted off to sleep, I thought about Kelly's lilacs.

> *I was standing in Kelly's house. There was noise every-where, colors, light, music. The sound of the bathwater splashing. I looked down and saw the splashing right in front of me: Caleb and Jack playing with a boat. Hannah deliberately slapping her hands on the water, soaking the front of my shirt. My head was pounding from the noise, the light, the sound of the word Mom over and over and over.*
>
> *The world skipped, like a broken record.*
>
> *And then there was silence. I was sitting in the dark in the rocking chair in Hannah's room with Hannah on my breast, sucking quietly and softly. This feeling overtook me, an overwhelming exhaustion, and then, when I looked down at Hannah, her pudgy soft little cheeks, puffing in and out and swallowing, there was something else. This overpowering sense of love, an emotion that filled up so heavily in my chest that I felt it swell, that I felt it about to burst.*

When I woke up the next morning, I got out of bed and found the figurine Will had bought for me the night before. *The perfect family.* I sat there just staring at it for a few minutes, just imagining what it might feel like to have that love from the dream, to have it forever, and not have to let it go once you were fully awake.

Twenty

Author D. H. Lawrence once said, "I can never decide whether my dreams are the result of my thoughts, or my thoughts the result of my dreams." I know this because, sitting home alone, with a notebook full of dreams and nothing else to do, I started Googling dreaming. There must be some logical and sensible explanation, I reasoned with myself. Maybe D. H. Lawrence had it right, because my thinking and dreaming became one and the same. I wrote his quote down on a scrap of paper, and left it sitting by the side of my computer. Which came first, I wondered, the chicken or the egg? The dreams or the thoughts?

I heard a ringing sound from far away, and after it came again, a second time, I realized it was the doorbell. I peeked out the window to see who it was. There, standing on the front stoop, her hair sticking out from under a red wool cap, her body swathed in a long red peacoat, was Lisa.

I closed my eyes and tried to remember the last dream

I'd had of her, and it came to me only in pieces. She'd been baking cookies, crying into the batter. I heard the doorbell ring again, and I ran downstairs to get it.

"Hi." She held up a red-gloved hand and waved. I noticed she was holding a tin in her other hand. "I brought you these," she said. *Hanukkah cookies*, I remembered. "Hanukkah cookies," she said.

"I know," I said. I closed my eyes, and I remembered the Star of David cookie cutter sitting on her counter. The tears that rolled down her face as she cut out little dreidel shapes, and I knew that I had an answer to D. H. Lawrence's question. My thoughts were a result of my dreams.

"You know?"

"I guessed," I said, and then quickly added, "Don't you make these every year?"

She shook her head, "No, I don't think—"

I cut her off. "Do you want to come in?" She looked surprised, as if she hadn't been expecting this, me, to be nice, as if maybe she'd expected me to slam the door in her face. And maybe I would've, if I hadn't known, if I hadn't been on the outside of her world looking in, enough to understand her, to feel her literal pain. If I hadn't understood it so completely that I wanted to reach over and hug her, despite everything else that had happened.

I had Lisa sit down at the kitchen table, and then I made some coffee and arranged the Hanukkah cookies on a plate. They were awful-looking—dreidels that were amorphous blobs, menorahs that looked more like crumpled fists. "I don't know that I've ever seen Hanukkah cookies before," I said. *At least not like these*, I silently added.

"Oh, well, for Chance and Chester's school. They have a

multicultural holiday day. Cookies for everything. Christmas, Hanukkah, Kwanzaa." She waved her hand in the air. "Anyway, I had some extras, and I thought of you."

I nodded, handed her a cup of coffee, and put the plate of cookies between us, though neither one of us moved to take one. Lisa and I had been the only two Jewish women in the Ladies Lunch Club, so what she said made sense. But I could feel that it was not the real reason for her visit. I stared at her, waiting for her to say whatever it was she'd come to say.

"How are you doing?" she finally said.

"I'm okay," I said, taking a sip of my coffee. The truth was, I didn't exactly feel okay, though I couldn't really put my finger on why. I guessed it was the dreams, the way they hung around in my brain all the time, strange half-truths. "How are you doing?" I asked.

She shrugged, picked up a cookie, and stared at it for a minute before taking a bite, and then said, "Look, I feel terrible about what happened. About my part in it. No one deserves that. You don't deserve that." She sounded nothing like Lisa the prosecutor, or the doubles partner, the one so eager to fit in at the club, or the one who cried into her cookie dough. She seemed both sure of herself and remorseful, and it occurred to me that as I'd dreamed about her, I'd already begun to forgive her. She seemed to take my silence as her cue to keep on talking. "You know, I never told you this, but Barry got sued for malpractice once. Back when we lived in New York. It got out, and no one wanted to go to him."

"I'm sorry," I said, feeling genuinely bad for her. "That must've been awful."

"It was," she said. "But his insurance settled the claim, we moved here a few months later, and that was the end of it."

I tried to imagine Barry and Lisa being ostracized the way

Will and I had been, and I wondered if that's why Lisa always tried so hard to fit in, because she knew what it was like to be me, to be the outsider. "The truth is, Jen, tennis has been unbearable without you. Tummy Tuck and her lipstick and her perfect little ass and her perfect little daughter. It's enough to drive any normal woman insane." She reached out for my hand. "I miss you. And this"—she picked up a lopsided Star of David with her other hand and held it out to me—"is my lame attempt at an apology. If you can forgive me."

I nodded, and I took the cookie, her peace offering. "I miss you, too," I said, the words gushing out of me, a relief. She leaned in and hugged me across the table, and she smelled like ginger and roses, a scent I associated with playing tennis, with fitting in, being a part of something.

"Oh God." She laughed when she pulled back. "Bethany and Amber spent forty-five minutes talking about their boobs yesterday. Forty-five minutes!" I imagined them standing there in the locker room at the club, lipsticks in hand. "Amber thinks hers are uneven."

"Time for another boob job," I said, realizing that I really didn't miss it at all, that locker room.

"I know, right?" She laughed again, but then she stopped laughing, and her face grew serious, dark.

"You should quit tennis," I whispered.

"Oh, Jen." She sighed.

"I've been going running," I said. "You should come with me sometime."

"Running?" She chuckled.

"We can jog," I said. "Or walk." She hesitated, and then I knew what it was. Lisa might have missed me, but she wasn't willing to give up her life, her own social standing. "I've been going to this park in Oak Glen, by my sister's house. It's nice there. No one knows who I am. You won't run into any of the other ladies from the lunch club. It's just a bunch of Oak Glen moms with strollers."

She thought for a moment, and then she nodded. "Okay," she said.

The next morning it was thirty-six degrees outside, but I bundled up in my parka, a hat, scarf, and gloves, and met Lisa in the parking lot of Oak Glen park. When I got there, she was sitting in her blue minivan waiting for me, and when she stepped out, I saw she was wearing a bright orange ski coat and matching hat and gloves.

"You know, I haven't run anywhere since college," she called to me, her cheeks aglow, maybe from the cold, or maybe because she was excited.

"We can walk," I said.

"No." She shook her head.

So we started jogging, down the same path I jogged every morning now, the trail littered with chunky moms and bulky strollers. After five minutes, Lisa was panting, and she stopped and hung her head between her knees. "Maybe we should walk," she huffed.

I slowed down and started walking with her, letting her set the pace.

We walked for a few minutes in silence, until we passed a woman with a double stroller, her little twins dressed in matching pink snowsuits. "Oh, twins," Lisa said to the mother. She looked up at us and managed a weary smile. "I have twins, too," Lisa said.

"Does it get easier?" the mother asked.

No, I thought.

"Yes," Lisa said, and I wondered, if this was easier, what

had she felt like before? "A little bit. It does. Mine are in kin-
dergarten now."

"Oh," the woman said. "It's nice to know you made it.
That someone survived."

Lisa nodded, and then we kept on walking. "Poor thing,"
Lisa said. "She doesn't even realize."

"Doesn't even realize what?" I asked, wanting to know,
this secret Lisa knew that the new mother did not.

"I haven't survived anything," she said. I wasn't sure how
to respond, so we kept on walking in silence. "Are you and
Will ever going to have kids?" she said after a few minutes.

"Maybe." I paused. "He wants to," I said. *Someday.*

"And you?"

"I don't know," I said. "I mean, you're always the one who
told me not to, who told me it would ruin me."

"Oh, Jen," she said, wiping sudden tears off her face with
her mittened hand. "It's so much more complicated than that.
So, so much more."

"What do you mean?" But either she didn't hear me or
she didn't want to answer because she didn't elaborate, and
we walked to the end of the trail in silence, pulling our faces
under our scarves, trying to keep warm.

Later that night, the herbs having washed an enormous sense
of calm over me, Will snoring lightly next to me, I closed
my eyes and thought about Lisa, thought about what it was
about having children that had made her life so hard, and
what about it hadn't.

I was cold, sitting half naked on the examining table,
a thin paper sheet covering my legs. "Hello, Lisa,"
the doctor said, as she walked into the room. "How

are you feeling today?" A petite blond-haired woman whose smile was tight and fake. I suddenly hated her, though I'd been seeing her for years, since I was pregnant with Chance and Chester.

"Fine," I said, the word catching in my throat, feeling like peanut butter on my tongue. "I'm fine."

"Good." She nodded. "Lie back so I can have a look."

I lay against the table, my feet landing clumsily near the stirrups, and I knew that there was something wrong. I could feel it in my stomach, in the way it turned and ached. The smell of alcohol and Lysol nauseated me.

I closed my eyes, and I wasn't sure whether I felt like crying or screaming. Or just running. Standing up and running out of here before she said it, before she told it to me, coldly and matter-of-factly.

This was the end of something. That much I was sure of.

Twenty-one

I woke up in the morning, sweating profusely, the feel of the doctor's table against my back still so vivid that for a moment, when I opened my eyes, I was surprised to find myself in my own bed.

"I'll stop home for lunch today," Will called from the doorway as he hurried to leave. "I have an appointment over here at eleven."

"Okay," I said, my words sounding far away and dulled, blurry, the way they had in the dream. "I'll see you then."

When he left, I rolled over and closed my eyes, and I willed it to leave, willed that image of the doctor's office, the feel of it, to go away. But it wouldn't. Maybe because it was something that was always right there, always right near the surface for me. Maybe part of what Ethel said about dreams being a window into the subconscious was right after all. Though I'd dreamed of Lisa, that person in the dream could've been me: Five years ago, she was me.

Nearly six months to the day after I'd met Will, I'd found the lump: a tiny little squishy thing no bigger than a pea. I found it in the shower, and I tumbled out in tears. "I'm going to die," I announced. Will stood there, half of his face covered in shaving cream, looking alarmed.

Will went with me to see Dr. Horowitz, who said it was probably nothing, but that they would biopsy it, just to be sure, just because of my family history. Will took the day off work to take me to the biopsy.

And there I was, in the hospital gown, in the cold, cold room, lying back against the table, smelling the putrid alcohol smell.

When it was over, after the needle had punctured my anesthetized and freezing flesh, after I'd gotten dressed, I'd wandered out of the room in a state of shock that felt something akin to frostbite, where you are so, so cold that you are numb; suddenly, there was no feeling left.

Will walked toward me and pulled me into a hug, and then he whispered into my ear. "Marry me, Jen."

"What?" It was something I thought he might ask me, someday. Someday on a beach, on a hillside, over a romantic dinner at Il Romano. Not then, not like that.

"You heard me. I want you to marry me."

"Will, I don't know." I pulled back. "I might die," I said.

"No," he said. "You won't. I won't let you. It's all going to turn out to be nothing." And it sounded like he actually believed it, that he was big enough, important enough, to be able to pull this off.

"Even if it is nothing this time, it might not be next time. I'm damaged goods," I said.

"Jen," he said. "I love you, no matter what." He paused. "I

want to be with you." He held me with his eyes, oceanic in depth and color. "Forever."

"Forever," I promised back, leaning into him, thinking that forever was not such a long time for a girl who might be dying.

The lump did turn out to be nothing. *Just a scare*, Dr. Horowitz called two days later to report. *But it's good to keep on top of it. Be cautious.* He recommended I start getting yearly mammograms and breast MRIs even though I was only twenty-seven at the time. *Early detection is so important.*

When I told Will, he wanted to celebrate, and he poured us both a glass of wine. "You can take it back now," I whispered to him, three glasses later, as I lay against him on the couch. "I'm not dying." *Yet*, I silently added. *Not yet.*

As an answer, he kissed me; his lips pressed so hard against mine that it felt like he wanted something from me, needed something. His hands rushed across my body, barely skimming my breasts before he was lifting my skirt up, on top of me, inside me.

Afterward I lay there and I wondered if Will had proposed because he really wanted to marry me, or if, in some way, he only wanted to save me, wanted to save me in a way that he hadn't been able to save his parents. And I wondered if I only said yes because I wanted him to, wanted to be saved, because before Will, no one had bothered to try saving me.

The phone rang, startling me out of my half sleep. I saw Lisa's name on the caller ID and picked it up. "Are you running today?" she asked.

I glanced at the clock and saw it was already after nine.

"Shit," I said. "I overslept." Then I realized it was Wednesday. "Don't you have tennis?"

"Yeah," she said. "I just felt like running today." She paused. "But don't worry about it. We'll go another time. I should've called you first."

"You're at the park?" I pictured her standing outside, shivering, waiting for me.

"I just thought you went every day."

"I do," I said, thinking of her on that cold, cold doctor's table and feeling terrible that she was waiting out in that freezing parking lot, all alone. "I can be there in twenty minutes," I said. "If you want to wait."

"There's a Starbucks across the street. I'll go over and get some coffee," she said.

Lisa was still sitting inside the Starbucks, nursing her cup of coffee, when I arrived, so I went inside to join her. I'd left the house so quickly that I hadn't had time for my coffee, and now I needed it. My head was hurting, and everything felt a little blurry still.

"You okay?" Lisa said. "You seem a little out of it. Are you sick?"

Sick. I shook my head. But maybe I was, on the verge of some kind of flu, or, a possibility that sunk in my chest, something worse. Maybe that's why I'd been feeling so strange lately. "I don't think I slept very well," I said, explaining the feeling away to both her and myself. "I had a weird dream."

She sighed. "I haven't been sleeping very well either lately. Must be something going around."

I offered a meek smile and blew on my coffee, wishing it would cool quickly because I was sorely in need of the caffeine. I thought of her, lying on that doctor's table, and I leaned over and grabbed her hand. "Bethany's pregnant. She called me last night to tell me," she blurted out quickly.

"Oh," I said. "Well, that's nice." I pictured her pushing *two* little angels in a fancy double stroller.

"Yeah, just what the world needs, one more little Bethany." Her voice cracked, and she sounded as if she was about to cry.

"Lisa, what is it?" I whispered.

And then she did start to cry, softly. I watched tears roll down her face. She pulled her hand away from mine and wiped her cheeks hard, faster than the tears were coming. "Something awful happened," she said, and I nodded for her to continue, even though I could smell that cold alcohol smell, feel that cold table against my back. That feeling, the smell of sickness, made me feel like I was going to throw up.

"My baby died," she said. "My baby died." She said it louder, as if that would make her believe it, make it feel more real. "I didn't want her at first," she said, "and I didn't always remember to take the vitamins. And then she died, and it was all my fault."

"Oh, Lisa," I said. "What happened?" But before she said a word, I knew, the blond-haired doctor's voice, the horrible aching in her stomach. And yet deep down, I shook with a sense of relief, which made me feel guiltier than I ever had before. Lisa wasn't sick. She was going to be okay.

"Barry and I had a deal," she whispered. "We had a freaking deal. I was going to go back to work when the twins are in first grade. One more year." She paused. "I couldn't start all over again, couldn't go through it all again. So when I found out, I wished that it wasn't true. And then it happened—I had a miscarriage. What kind of a person wishes her own baby away?"

"It wasn't your fault," I told her. I remembered Kelly telling me Dr. Horowitz told her that once, after she'd had a miscarriage herself, that miscarriages were surprisingly common, that they were nature's way of preventing deformities.

"It was," she said, with absolute certainty. "I wanted it to happen. I made it happen."

"You didn't make it happen," I whispered, and leaned across the table and hugged her tightly. Ginger and roses and coffee, and wet tears on my shoulder.

"I haven't told anyone else," she said, pulling out of the hug.

"Not even Barry?" She shook her head, and it made sense, the sadness, the isolation I'd felt in my dreams.

"Barry." She laughed, but the laugh caught in her throat, and when I looked at her there were tears streaming silently down her face. "Oh God, Jen, you should've heard Bethany going on and on about her perfect pregnancy. I just couldn't do it again, couldn't go back there today."

"Oh, sweetie. I'm so sorry," I told her, handing her a napkin to wipe away her tears. "I wish I could say something to make you feel better."

She reached across the table for my hand again and held on to me, as if I was her only lifeline.

Will was already home for lunch, waiting in the kitchen when I got back, spooning yogurt out of a container slowly. When I saw him sitting there, I felt this urge to hold on to him tightly and not let go, so I went to him and hugged him. "Sorry I'm late," I whispered. "I was with Lisa, and we lost track of time."

"Lisa?" He pulled back and wrinkled his nose. "I thought you weren't friends with them anymore."

"I'm not friends with *them*." I shrugged. "Just Lisa." He stared at me, narrowing his eyes, waiting for an explanation. "She apologized." I paused. "She could use a friend."

I grabbed a yogurt and sat down next to him. Even sitting, I felt the room spinning too fast all around me, and I thought about how Lisa asked me if I was sick. I closed my eyes, and when I opened them again the moment had passed, the room was still. I turned to Will. "How's your day going?" I asked.

He sighed. "Amber Tannenbaum. Short appointment."

"Yeah, what happened?"

"Oh, she pretty much told me I'd ruined your life and then slammed the door in my face."

"Oh, Will," I said, reaching out for his hand, but he shook me off. "She's a bitch. Everybody thinks she's a bitch."

"Even Lisa?"

"Especially Lisa."

He sighed. "I don't know if I can do this, Jen."

"What?"

"This job. This life. I don't know." *You*, I silently added for him, because I wondered if I was a part of it, the things he couldn't take anymore.

"Okay," I said softly. "Then what do you want to do?"

"I don't know." He stood up and ran his hand through his hair. "Dammit, Jen. This is not a career for me. This is not a life. I'm just trying to tell you how I feel." He paused. "Unlike you. You never tell me anything."

"What do you want me to tell you?" I asked, knowing that nothing I was going to say was going to calm him down, was going to make him feel better about Amber.

"Tell me what you're feeling."

"I'm feeling . . ." I paused, trying to figure out exactly what I was feeling in that moment, and something about my dream and my coffee with Lisa had driven deep into my core. I felt tired and listless and strange, not at all like my normal self, except, I realized, I wasn't even sure who that was anymore.

"Sad," I finally said, settling on this one emotion, though it seemed absolutely inadequate to really encompass all of my feelings.

"You're unhappy," he said matter-of-factly, repeating what he thought I just said. But when he said it that way it didn't seem right at all. "I should've seen it. Fucking Amber could see it," he said, his voice calm and even despite the fact that I could tell by the way his face was getting red that he wanted to explode. "Do you want a divorce, because if you do, just say it."

My head was throbbing, and I closed my eyes to try to make it stop. I thought about the cold stirrups against Lisa's feet at the doctor's office, the feeling of drowning in my head and in hers, and then I couldn't feel anything past that. I wondered if it was possible to feel a loss for something you never had, for something that was never really yours at all.

"I have to go," Will said, picking up his coat. "I wouldn't want to be late for an appointment."

"Will, wait," I called after him. But he didn't stop, and I heard the front door slam with a sickening thud.

I thought about the Will in my dreams, the one who'd been unhappy, sick, as a judge, the one who'd been jealous of Janice for being able to just walk away, and I wondered if he felt that way now, too. If, back in the car, he was popping Tums or throwing up his lunch. *Oh, Will.* I felt an ache for him in my chest. Where did it all go wrong? I wondered, and I wished he was still standing there so I could comfort him, so I could wrap my arms around him and tell him that nothing else mattered. A divorce was the last thing I wanted.

I dialed Will's cell, ready to let it all come tumbling out, that I wanted him to be here with me, that I wanted him to be happy. But after five rings, I got his voice mail, so I hung up.

My head was throbbing; it actually felt as if it might explode. I felt too tired to stand, to think anymore, so I decided I would take a short nap. I went upstairs and lay down on the bed, on top of the covers, fully clothed, not even bothering to take off my sneakers, and I closed my eyes. I wanted to dream about something nice, something happy, so I thought about Kat, about the glow on her face, brighter than a new suntan, when she'd returned from her night away with Danny.

I was standing in the City Style *offices, twirling a strand of blond hair between my fingers, tapping an unlit cigarette on my desk. The computer screen stared at me, blank, the blinking cursor taunting me. Think, think, think. I tapped the cigarette.*

I heard a rap on the door, and I jumped. Hank peeked his head in. "See ya tomorrow, sunshine."

"Yeah, yeah." I waved while mentally giving him the finger.

I heard Grant in his office, heard the timbre of his voice, deep and smooth as he talked to someone on the phone, though I couldn't exactly make out the words. We were the only two people left. It was seven o'clock. It was dark. The rest of the office lights were off except for ours. Don't go in there, I thought. Do not go in there.

I heard him hang up the phone, and I stood up. You're just going to say hi, just going to be friendly.

I stood in the doorway of his office until he noticed. I wondered if he could hear it, the way my heart was thudding in my chest, loud and furious. "Katrin," he said.

I nodded. "You're working late," I said.

"Again," he said.

"Again," I echoed.

"Have you had dinner yet? I was thinking about ordering Chinese, if you want some." He stood up and walked closer. I watched him, as if in slow motion. Come closer, I thought. No don't. Yes, I want you to kiss me. No I don't.

Then he was standing next to me, his mouth close enough to my ear to whisper, "Why did you really come in here?" He didn't wait for an answer to lean in, to kiss my earlobe lightly.

The kiss, the precision of it, electrified me. "Grant," I whispered.

"Sssh." He put a finger to my lips, and then he moved his finger and leaned in to kiss me.

"Jen. Jen. Wake up." I opened my eyes expecting Grant, but the easy familiarity of Will surprised me. He sat at the edge of the bed, his hand on my shoulder. "Are you all right? You look upset."

"I don't know," I said, disoriented. "What time is it?"

"Three-thirty," he said. "I just stopped home for a few minutes." He paused. "I'm sorry about earlier. About what I said. I shouldn't have let Amber get to me like that." I closed my eyes, and I saw Grant's face, Grant leaning in for a kiss. *Seriously, Kat. Seriously? What happened to Danny, to your weekend, to your marriage, to your girls? You can't just throw all that away.* I didn't want to just throw it all away.

"No. I'm sorry," I said. I sat up and hugged him, held on tightly. I inhaled the familiar pine smell of him, the warm feel of his cheek against mine. "I don't want a divorce," I whispered in his ear.

"Neither do I." He reached up and gently ran his thumb across my cheek, and then he held his face close to mine.

I leaned up and kissed him softly on the lips. "You didn't ruin me," I whispered. "Just the opposite." He kissed me, harder, more insistently than I'd kissed him, and I pulled him on top of me on the bed.

"I'm sorry," he whispered in my ear. "I have to go. I have an appointment at four. And then I have to go to a dinner retreat in the city." He kissed my neck, and let his fingers linger to trace the outline of my collarbone.

"Okay," I whispered, bringing his mouth to mine again.

His mouth turned slowly and carefully the way it might the first time you ever kissed someone, the way it might when you wanted to taste another person, when you wanted to drink them in.

When he pulled back again, he looked me in the eyes and smiled. I remembered the way his smile had once made me feel like I was melting, and the way it sort of felt like that right now.

Twenty-two

The next morning when I woke up, Will was already gone. He'd come in late last night, and I'd woken for only a minute when I heard him getting into bed. And then I'd felt him kiss my shoulder and put his arm around my waist, and I'd rolled into him and fallen back into a deep sleep.

I couldn't remember dreaming last night, but the dream about Kat and Grant from yesterday afternoon still felt so fresh in my head. So over breakfast, I hastily wrote up some wedding announcements. They weren't due until the end of the week, but I had four announcements that took me less than an hour to compose. While I did it, I sipped my coffee slowly, and then I took a shower and got dressed. I left Will a note in case he stopped home for lunch again. *Gone to the city. Be back for dinner.* I thought for a minute, and then added, *Love, J.*

I sat next to a woman holding her baby on her lap on the train. The little girl was quiet and sat calmly sucking her thumb. Until she started trying to grab my leg. "Stop it," her mother said, but the girl kept grabbing. I shifted in my seat. "I'm sorry," the mother said to me, moving the little girl farther away, so she was grabbing her mother's leg instead.

"That's fine," I said. The woman smiled at me, this odd smile of relief and sadness that reminded me, in a way, of Lisa. "How old is she?" I asked.

"Seventeen months," she said.

"That's a good age," I said, though really I had no idea if it was or not. "And she's very well behaved." It was true, despite her attempts at my leg. Most babies I saw on the train were screaming or jumping on the seat.

"She's my little angel." The mother sighed. "What about you?" the woman asked. "You have any children?"

"No." I shook my head. And because she kept staring, I added, "Not yet," as if I owed this stranger some sort of explanation.

When I walked into *City Style*, Kat's office was empty, so I knocked on Hank's door. "Where's Kat?" I asked him.

He shrugged. "Not my turn to watch her," he said.

"I have these." I held up the folder that contained the wedding announcements, as if it was something important, top secret documents that were necessary to hand deliver, even though I normally just e-mailed them in on the due date. "I'm going to wait in her office."

"Be my guest." He didn't even look up from his computer screen.

On my way back to her office, I swung by my old office, Grant's office. It looked the same, tiny window in the corner, messy desk off to the side. Had it not been for the ultra handsome Grant sitting in my old chair, his feet up on the desk, the phone cocked between his ear and his shoulder, I might've felt like I could've walked back in and taken it over again, this oddly carefree life that used to belong to me, the Jennifer Daniels me: the one who only sometimes remembered to check her breast for lumps, who did the *Times* crossword puzzle at her desk, e-mailing answers back and forth with Kat so it looked like we were working, who enjoyed spontaneous sex with Will so much that she couldn't stop thinking about it the next morning, couldn't stop glowing into her coffee.

Grant cleared his throat. He'd hung up the phone and had noticed me standing there. "Hey there—"

"Jen," I said.

"Kat's friend."

I nodded. "She has an interview this morning," he said. "She should be back soon." It bothered me that he knew more than Hank, that he knew too much. Why the hell would he know her schedule, unless they were talking, unless he was waiting for her to return? "You can wait in here if you like." He paused. "This used to be your office, right?"

I nodded. "If you're not busy," I said, stepping past him, not waiting for his answer.

"Sorry about the mess." He started moving things around on the desk. "I bet you kept it neater than this."

I hadn't. My life as a reporter had been nothing like my life as a housewife: messy, hurried, bogged down, filled with too much caffeine and too much alcohol and not enough sleep. With time on my hands I'd become a neat freak, and I felt a little jealous looking at the mess, at the sloppy way life could unfold, could strike you in insane and beautiful ways that you would sometimes not expect, the way it had struck me that night I'd first met Will.

I sat down across the desk from Grant and stared at him

closely. He leaned back in his chair and folded his arms across his chest. He was gorgeous. I would give Kat that. He had a nice square jaw, an easy manner, deep blue eyes that were a shade lighter than Will's, and he smelled like a combination of coffee and citrus. "So, Jen, tell me. What made you leave this job?"

"I don't know." I shrugged. "My husband wanted to move to Deerfield, and I didn't feel like the commute."

"You guys have a bunch of kids?" he asked.

"No." I frowned, annoyed at being asked this question twice in one morning. Why did kids have to be a measure of everything, success, happiness, failure?

"Oh," he said. "It's just—it's a great job." I nodded. It was a great job. Amazing. Free dinners, movies, and shows, with very little expected in return except for an opinion on all of the above. "I hear you've been looking for some freelance work."

I knew what he was really asking, whether I was here to try to reclaim the job from him. The truth was, I realized, sitting here again, that I actually didn't want it. I'd left the job not because we'd moved to the suburbs, because Will became a judge, because Will thought we should have a family soon, but because I'd found the lump. The benign lump. But the lump, all the same.

After the lump, as I'd sat at this desk and typed up my reviews, it hit me that there must be something more, something else for me. This, this job, couldn't be all there was. Though, I thought now, I still hadn't exactly found it, whatever else there was for me. For a while I'd thought it had been my deceptively simple life in Deerfield, but maybe deep down, I always knew that wasn't what it was either. "Don't worry," I finally said. "The job's all yours."

"I'm not worried," he said.

"Though you can do me a favor."

"What's that?" He leaned in across the desk, so his face was close to mine, almost uncomfortably close, because I could still remember the feel of his lips on Kat's ear, the feel of his breath on her skin. And thinking about it made me feel nervous and a little bit tingly, the way I'd felt in the dream.

"Stay away from Kat," I whispered.

"Kat's a big girl," he said, sitting back, away from me. "She can take care of herself."

"What's that you're saying about me?" The sound of Kat's voice from the doorway made me jump, and I turned around and smiled sheepishly.

"She was just asking where you were." Grant lied easily, in a way that made me distrustful of anything that would come out of his mouth.

"Well, I'm here now."

"Nice to see you again, Jen." Grant nodded at me.

I nodded back, but I shot him a look that I hoped would make him think twice about Kat.

Back in Kat's office, I handed her the folder of announcements. "You didn't have to come all the way down here for this," she said.

"I know." I nodded. "I wanted to see you. I thought we could get lunch."

"I can't." She shook her head. "Fucking lunch meeting with Hank today."

I made a face. I remembered the lunch meetings with Hank, incessantly long and boring, where he handed out assignments and made fun of people who actually dared to— gasp—eat their lunch while he was talking. It was something that I didn't miss, that made me happy not to be a part of this place anymore. "I'm sorry," I said. "Do you have a few minutes now? To talk."

"Not really," she said, gesturing for me to sit down anyway. "What's on your mind, hon?"

"You," I said. "What are you doing, Kat?"

"What?" She looked confused.

"With Grant."

"What are you talking about?" Her eyes narrowed to slits. "What did he say to you?"

"Nothing," I said. I almost blurted it out. The truth. The whole truth. About the dreams, about knowing everything now, knowing too much. But there was no way she was going to believe me, and besides, it didn't matter how I knew, only that I did. "Kat, you have Danny and the kids." I thought about the way Ara had held on to my watch with her tiny delicate fingers, the way she'd admired my curls, the way her warm body felt snuggled into my lap, and I felt desperately sad for what might happen to her if Kat and Danny split up, if they both buried themselves in work and other people even more, and what it was like to lose one parent, and then lose another. "I'm just worried about you."

"Jen, look. I appreciate your concern. I really do." She paused. "But come on, you've spent the last four years in some fancy-schmancy suburb with all your rich-bitch friends. Suddenly they've had enough of you, and you come running back here?"

"It's not like that," I said, though what she said stung, maybe because it was partly true. I'd never meant to leave Kat behind when I left the city, but she became a working mom and I become a woman of Deerfield, and there was not too much to say to each other the few times a year we did talk, when our calls were filled with awkward slow silences and discussions of things we remembered from the past.

She leaned in closer. "I know you've been through some shit this year. Will fucked up. Big time. And you didn't leave him. Good for you, Saint Jen. But I'm not a fucking saint, okay?" She paused, pulled a cigarette out of her purse, and tapped it on the desk. "Just get out. Get the fuck out of my office."

I sat on a bench in the train station, Kat's words echoing in my head. *Saint Jen.* Was that really what she thought of me, that I was a martyr for staying with Will, that there was nothing else there? My head was throbbing and I rubbed my temples, willing the pain to stop.

A little girl, Ara's age, ran past my feet, dropping her book on the ground. I picked it up as her mother came tumbling after her. "Here." I handed it to the mother.

"Thank you." She smiled, scooped up her daughter and the book, and sat on the bench across from me. "*Goodnight Moon,*" the woman read the title of the book.

I closed my eyes, and it hit me in this flash, my mother sitting on the edge of my bed, reading that book to me. I couldn't have been more than five years old. I could hear the soft, sweet sound of my mother's voice—a memory that flashed back for only a few seconds and then I knew it would disappear just as quickly.

When I opened my eyes, the woman was gone, and I was sitting in the train station, all alone.

Twenty-three

Icame to the realization that if a moment could change your life, then another one could change it back, just as quickly, just as irreversibly. I would stop taking Ethel's calming herbs, and the dreams would stop, the windows into other people's lives would shut.

But without the herbs, I found myself lying awake, staring at the ceiling, listening to the quiet hum of Will's snore in my ear, and when I finally did fall asleep, my sleep was fitful in short and anxious bursts, so no amount of coffee or jogging could clear the fog from my head the next morning. Mid-week, Lisa called and canceled our jog, saying she wasn't feeling up to it this week, so I stopped going by myself, too. I was too tired for the exercise, and I realized I was feeling even worse off the herbs than I'd felt on them.

I sat in front of the computer screen, vowing to go back to that novel I'd started when we'd first moved here, but after searching, I couldn't even find where I'd saved the file. I opened up a new document, and then I stared at the blank screen for a while, but my mind was so foggy that I couldn't think of anything to write.

I got the *Deerfield Daily* and scanned the help-wanted ads, looking for something that might interest me. I did find one thing, a nonprofit agency that was looking for a part-time grant writer, but I didn't have the energy to dust off my résumé, fix it up, and send it out. And besides, I wasn't even sure if this was what I wanted.

I went into my bedroom, opened my jewelry box, and took out the figurine that Will had bought me, "The Perfect Family." I spun it around in my fingers. *The perfect family*, I thought. *And all that can be yours. Just pop out a baby, and voilà.*

Maybe the only difference between me and everyone else I knew was that my problems with Will were seemingly obvious; my embarrassments had been splashed across the front page of the *Deerfield Daily*, while their pain was private, undetectable to the naked eye. Like the couple made of glass, frozen with these slick smiles on their faces.

If only you were real, I whispered to the woman before putting her back into my jewelry case, *you'd be a mess, too.*

By the end of the week, I was so tired, so listless, that I stood in the bathroom debating what to do. Maybe I could take the herb and force myself not to dream, not to think before I went to bed. Once Kat had done an article on breathing techniques for relaxation, where you were supposed to focus on every individual part of your body, focus on making it become heavy and tired until your whole body succumbed to rest. *Kat.*

I thought about the way she'd looked at me, and then, sleep or no, I considered washing the whole container of herbs down the sink. I held the bottle in my shaking hand, but my decision was interrupted by a knock at the door.

I put the herbs back into my medicine cabinet. "Come in," I said.

Will opened the door and walked in. His face was drawn, tired or sad or maybe both; I couldn't tell. "Everything okay?" he asked, and I noticed I was gripping the sides of the sink, as if I needed it to stand, to hold me up.

"Yeah," I lied. "How was your day?"

"Fine," he said. "Fine. Fine." He paused. "I'm going to have a drink. Do you want one?"

"No thanks," I said. He turned to walk out, and I reached out for his hand. "Wait," I said softly. "What are you having?"

"Scotch." And then I knew something was wrong. Will never drank scotch unless he was upset, unless there was something he wanted to drink to forget. I wondered if there had been another incident, another bitch slamming a door in his face. "Are you sure you're all right?" I asked. He shrugged my hand away. "Okay," I said. "Pour me one, too. I'll be down in a minute."

He left, and I stared at my face in the mirror. I pinched my cheeks to give them some color, smoothed out the curls with my fingers. *Who the hell are you?* I thought, and I wondered without the dreams, without a job, without friends, without a husband who worked incessantly, if it might finally be the time for me to figure it out.

Tomorrow, I promised myself, and then I went downstairs to have my scotch.

Will built a fire, and we drank our scotch on the couch. At first we sat at opposite ends, watching the nightly news, Gary Adams smiling bigger than a clown on crack. "I hate this guy," I said to Will. "We should change the channel." But neither one of us felt like moving to do it, so we watched him.

"Look at him," Will said, finishing the first scotch and pouring himself another. "He smiles and his face doesn't even move. It's like he's not even human."

"Botox," I said. "Lots and lots of Botox."

"I don't get it," Will said. "Why would a person willingly inject themselves with poison?"

I shrugged, and I handed my empty glass to Will so he could pour me another. "Vanity," I said. And then I thought about my former friends Bethany and Amber, and their perfect boobs and flat stomachs. "Fear."

"Fear?" He handed me back the scotch and I sipped it, ignoring the burning in my throat that ricocheted to my lungs and made it almost hard to breathe.

"Getting old. Getting ugly. Not wanting to lose something."

"Hmm." Will considered what I said. "What a strange way to try to hold on."

After the news was over, we watched *Extra*, and I drank another scotch.

I crawled over to Will's side of the couch and put my head in his lap. Will stroked my hair with the hand he wasn't using to hold his glass. I closed my eyes and let the warmth of the fire, Will's hands, radiate through my body, and I could almost forget about everything else. "Jen," Will said, after what felt like a very long time. He started massaging my temples. "I don't give a crap about weeds."

"I know," I murmured. I kept my eyes closed, and I was beginning to feel drowsy. I knew I should say something else, something more encouraging or helpful or interesting, but I was too heavy, too exhausted to think.

I felt Will shift me so I was leaning against him, and I felt him kissing me. I kissed him back, and I pressed my body into him. I wanted him, more than I had ever wanted anything, and I closed my eyes and felt his hand on my pants, tugging at my waistband.

"Jen," I heard Will whisper, from what felt like very far away. "Jen, are you awake?"

But I was too tired to answer him, too tired to show him how much I wanted him, so I didn't, and I leaned against him and fell into a deep and blissfully dreamless sleep.

When I woke up, it was still dark.

The fire had burned down to tiny glowing embers, I had a blanket draped over me, and I saw Will had moved to the love seat.

But I heard it, a horrible wailing sound, an alarm clock, no, a siren. "What time is it?" Will moaned, and I noticed the bottle of scotch was empty, that he must've finished it after I fell asleep, which worried me for a minute, until I heard the wailing noise coming closer. I stood up and walked into the kitchen to check the time. "Six," I said, and then I went to look out the front window, to determine the source of the terrible wailing.

Will walked up behind me, and when his hand touched my shoulder, I closed my eyes, remembering how much I'd wanted him last night. "I'm sorry I fell asleep," I whispered. I leaned against him, and he wrapped his arms around me, and kissed the top of my head lightly.

"An ambulance," he said, just as I, too, noticed it, pulling up next door. "My God, at Lisa and Barry's house. I hope they're all right."

Lisa.

★ ★ ★

Will insisted on going with me to the hospital, even though I protested, even though I reminded him he would be late for work. "It doesn't matter," Will said, as he rifled through the cabinet for aspirin. "What's this?" he asked, holding up a bottle of herbs.

"Nothing," I lied. "Here. The aspirin's in the drawer."

He offered one to me, but even though I had a splitting headache, I declined. The headache felt like penance, felt like something I deserved. Because I knew, even before I got to the hospital, what had happened, what she had done.

No, that's not true, I didn't know exactly what had happened because I hadn't dreamed it. I didn't know if she'd slit her wrists in the bathtub, taken too many pills, or jumped out her attic window. But I knew, because I'd been her, in a dream, for a few moments. I'd felt what she was feeling, the pain, the numbness, the incessant heaviness of doom.

Will and I found Barry in the waiting room. He sat in a chair in the corner, his head in his hands, and it looked like he'd been crying. Will put his hand on Barry's shoulder, and Barry looked up at us. He nodded. Then he shook his head.

"What happened?" Will asked, and it amazed me the way Will's voice exuded nothing but kindness. Here was Barry, a man who used to be Will's friend, who used to play golf with him. Here was a man who'd not even extended to Will so much as a phone call, a kind wave when he'd been indicted, and here Will was in return. I put my hand on Will's arm, to steady him, to steady myself.

"It's Lisa," Barry finally choked out. "She's—"

"Is she all right?"

"I don't know," Barry said. "She wouldn't wake up. She just wouldn't wake up."

Will sat down next to him, and I sat on the other side. On the TV hanging from the ceiling, *Regis and Kelly* came on, bantering back and forth about something I was only half listening to. I watched Kelly Ripa shake her hair off her shoulders, as she said something about her husband and one of her kids, and I thought, *Now there's a woman who really has it all together.* Or did she? I wondered if, underneath it all, if there was something. Another man she wanted to kiss, a pregnancy she thought she hadn't wanted, a mother-in-law who came between her and her husband. Did we all have it, that something that made us broken beneath the surface?

"Mr. Rosenberg." The sound of the doctor's voice startled me, and I looked up. The doctor was a slight woman, very petite, almost childlike, and she did not look like someone who could withstand the rigors of medical training. She motioned for him to follow her to a more private spot in the room. "It's okay." Barry nodded at her, and then looked at me and Will as if he was afraid for us to leave him alone.

She cleared her throat. "Your wife is awake now."

"Oh thank God," Barry said.

"We pumped her stomach." She paused. "Seems she took an entire bottle of Valium. But luckily you got her here in time."

Barry shook his head, not able to process what I already knew. Will shot me a quizzical look. I turned away. "Why would she do that?" Barry said, and I marveled over how you could walk through life married to someone and not even know them, not even understand them in the slightest. Like Will and I had done. A few months ago, neither one of us had noticed that the other one was drowning.

The doctor said something about a psych evaluation and about holding her in the hospital for observation. "Can I see her?" Barry asked.

The doctor nodded, then looked at me. "Are you Jen?" she asked.

"Yes."

"She's been asking for you." She turned to Barry. "Maybe it's better if you let Jen go in first."

I looked at Barry, whose eyes looked a little more downcast than they had a few moments ago. "You go ahead," I said. "I'll wait."

"No." He shook his head. "You heard what the doctor said." He paused. "She's asking for you."

I followed the doctor down the long white corridor to Lisa's room. She didn't say a word to me, didn't tell me what to say or not to say to Lisa. When we reached the room and I thanked her, she only nodded.

I stood at the doorway for a moment, staring at her. In her hospital bed, Lisa looked older and limp like a rag doll. She was hooked up to an IV and a heart monitor, equipment that had a familiar look in a hospital that had a familiar smell to the one my mother had been in after her mastectomy. Standing in the hallway, I felt twelve years old again, and terrified, the sharp scent of the Lysol bringing tears to my eyes and making me feel a little dizzy.

Lisa turned to look in my direction, so I walked into the room. "Hi," I said, trying to make my voice sound steady and even, though inside, I felt it quaking.

"Hi." Her voice sounded scratchy, and she grimaced when she spoke.

I sat down in the chair next to the bed, and she reached her hand out for me, so I held on to it. "Does Barry hate me?" she said.

"No." I shook my head. "No. I think you scared him." I paused. "And you scared me, too."

Tears welled up in her eyes and ran slowly down her cheeks. "I'm sorry," she said. "I just thought, I thought . . ." She paused for a minute, an attempt to compose herself. "Yesterday was my due date."

"Oh, Lisa, I'm so sorry," I said. "But you have to know it wasn't your fault."

She shook her head. "That's what the doctor said, but she didn't know what I was thinking, that I wasn't trying." She paused. "A baby girl," she said. "I could've had a baby girl."

I felt her pain, in my heart, in my gut, a cold, sharp sensation, an icy prong of fear that came in realizing that what you wanted and what you got were sometimes two separate things. "You could try again," I said.

She shrugged. "I don't even think Barry would want another baby. And I'm supposed to go back to work next year . . ." She let her voice trail off. "Everything is just so hard now."

We sat there not saying anything for a few minutes, letting her words hang in the air, until finally I said, "Did I ever tell you about my mom?" I knew I hadn't. I never talked about my mother, not with anyone, barely even with Kelly.

"No."

"She died when I was thirteen. Breast cancer."

"Oh." Lisa wiped her cheeks with her free hand. "I'm sorry. I didn't know."

I nodded. "Afterward, my father worked all the time. My sister went to college. I basically spent high school cooking my own Ramen noodles and eating them by myself in front of the TV."

"Oh, Jen," she said.

"You have two boys," I said. "Two beautiful boys, who desperately need you. More than you know."

"Need me?" She let out a dry laugh. "They need the Wii, and their Razor scooters."

"They need their mother," I said. "They need their mother." My voice cracked on the word *mother*, and I felt tears forming in my own eyes.

"They need their mother," Lisa whispered back. She squeezed my hand.

"Barry really wants to come in," I said. "You should talk to him, tell him."

She shook her head. "I can't," she said.

"Lis, he's not going to blame you."

"You don't know that," she said.

She was right, I didn't know for sure, but I knew that the way Barry had looked, sitting in the waiting room, said something, that despite any differences or distance the two of them had, Barry still loved her. Barry did not want to lose her.

Twenty-four

When we got back from the hospital, Will showered and left for work, and I decided to take a nap. My head ached and my mouth was dry, and I wished I'd just taken the stupid herb instead of drinking so much scotch.

I took one now, with a bathroom cup full of water, and then I crawled into bed. As I closed my eyes, I thought about Lisa, lying in the hospital bed, an island, not wanting to let Barry in. And then I thought about the way I'd felt last night, drunk and exhausted and lying on top of Will. I had to let him in. I didn't want to be Lisa. I didn't want Will to feel like Barry, just standing there, from a distance, watching, so undeniably helpless.

I was sitting at my desk, staring at the piles of paper in front of me, staring at them, but not really seeing them. It was late, already pitch dark, and the only light shin-

*ing in the office was the moonlight and the tiny halogen
lamp on my desk.*

*I picked up the Post-it note that Janice had handed
me before she left. The Brew—nine P.M., it read, in
Janice's neat curlicue handwriting.*

"Do you know where this place is?" I'd asked her.

*She'd shrugged. She hadn't. "I can Google it for
you, Judge," she offered.*

*"No." I held up my hand. "That won't be neces-
sary."*

*"Everything all right?" she asked, resting her hand
on her pregnant belly and cocking her head to the side.*

"Of course." I forced a smile.

"Are you sure? You look a little pale."

*I shook my head. "Now don't you worry about me.
You go home and get some rest."*

"Judge, I—"

*I held up my hand. "Janice, really. That's all for
today."*

*And now the office was quiet. So quiet. And dark. I
fingered the Post-it note and checked my watch. Eight-
thirty. I felt the bile rising in my throat, my palms
sweating, my heart beating rapidly in my chest.*

Time to go.

Time to go, I thought, opening my eyes. I was expecting it
to be dark, but it wasn't. The midday sun streamed into the
room, hurting my eyes, the brightness nearly blinding me,
making the room feel white and shapeless, and reminding me
again that I should never drink that much scotch. *Time to go
where?* I wondered. *Where had Will been going, and what had*

made him so anxious? I knew exactly where the Brew was, a bar not too far from where I'd grown up. But why would Will have been going there?

I got up and took a shower and got dressed. Then I made some coffee. But I still couldn't shake the dream, get the feeling of Will, of the depth of his anxiety, out of my head. Why hadn't I ever asked? Why hadn't I ever just talked to him? But then I realized that someone else had. So I finished my coffee, grabbed my car keys, and started driving toward Janice.

I'd been to Janice's home only one other time. Will and I had stopped there once, on the way to the club for a Friday night dinner when Will had been picking up something he'd left at the office.

She lived in a townhouse, just on the edge of Oak Glen, the identical-looking brick units a stark contrast to the neighborhoods of McMansions where we were. Luckily she lived in an end unit, in the first row, so I had no trouble remembering which one it was.

I parked out front, and then waited in the car for a moment. I'd never liked Janice. Not that there was anything inherently wrong with her, but it had always been clear to me that she'd had a crush on Will. It was there in her eyes, every time I saw her, in the dopey way she looked at him, and looked away from me, never wanting to meet my gaze. It was there in her mousy little voice when she called him Judge, like he was the king of her universe. I closed my eyes and thought about Will, about lying against him last night, wanting him, his hands skimming my waistband. *Will.* I sighed and got out of the car.

I stood on her porch for a minute before ringing the bell. I knew it was rude, to show up here like this. I should've called—though I didn't have her number, and I certainly didn't want to ask Will. So I took a deep breath, and I hit the doorbell.

"Mrs. Levenworth," she said when she saw me, unable to hide her surprise.

"Are you busy?" I asked. "Can we talk?"

She opened the door for me to come inside.

The inside of the townhouse was sparsely decorated, very minimalist and plain, which, I thought, reflected Janice's personality nicely: beige walls, beige furniture, oak shelving. "Can I get you some coffee?" Janice asked, seeming oddly eager to please.

"No." I shook my head. "I won't stay long. And I'm sorry I didn't call first."

She gestured for me to sit down. "It's okay. Rose is sleeping."

Rose. I'd nearly forgotten about the baby. *Cute. With pudgy cheeks*, as Will had said that night that felt so long ago. "How's she doing?" I asked.

"Good, getting big. She's rolling over on her own now, and smiling. She has the cutest smile—" She stopped talking and smiled at me. "I'm sorry. Listen to me going on. I'm sure you don't care."

"No," I said. "I do." I noticed that Janice seemed more animated than I'd ever seen her—when she was talking about Rose, her entire body seemed to light up, and she went from a beige to a red, or at least a soft pink. "It's nice to see you so happy," I added.

"Motherhood agrees with me," she said. I nodded. "But anyway, what do you want to talk about?" She averted her eyes again, and I knew she knew that there was only one reason for me to come here, one person I would want to talk about. I nodded again in response. "How is he doing?" she asked softly.

I thought about the way he'd needed to drink that scotch, the way he'd whispered to me almost on the brink of sleep that he hated his life as a weed control salesman. "He's been better," I said, being more honest than I'd meant to be walking in here.

"I heard he's working in landscaping now." I nodded. "Judge Levenworth."

She seemed to be blinking back tears, and I felt this strange need to comfort her, so I put my hand on top of hers. "He'll be okay, Janice."

She nodded. "I know."

"But I just wanted to ask you one thing." I paused. "Was Will happy as a judge?"

She shrugged. "I don't know." She paused, as if really truly thinking about it for the first time. "He was a good judge." She lowered her voice to a whisper. "But that's not the same thing, is it?"

"No." I shook my head. "I don't think it is."

"He had a lot of Tums," she said. "And coffee." She thought about it some more. "And he did seem a little sad, near the end. A little anxious, maybe."

I wished I could go back in time to that moment, that I could stay awake and wait for him to walk in after a long day, that I could go to him and ask him how he was feeling and what he was thinking, that I could go to him, loosen his tie, and start kissing him, the way I'd kissed him last night.

I swallowed hard, and then choked out, in barely a whisper, "Do you think he actually did something wrong?"

"No," she said quickly. "Absolutely not."

I nodded. "Of course he didn't."

"I've been racking my brain about it for months. How did it happen? Was it something I did? Did I do something wrong?"

"You didn't," I assured her, though I had no idea if this was true.

"He's just such a good person. He doesn't deserve this." She paused. "Did he ever tell you about my morning sickness?" I shook my head. "It was terrible. And you know a lot of bosses wouldn't care how you're feeling, they'd just want you to do your job. But not him. Whenever I was sick he told me to go home and rest, and then he did my work and his own. I'd ask him about it the next day, but he'd just tell me to take care of myself. Not to worry about it."

We were interrupted by the sound of a baby crying, amplified, though somewhat far away. She held up the baby monitor, which I hadn't noticed until then was clipped to the side of her sweatpants. "Rose is awake," she said. "Wait here. I'll go get her. You can meet her."

"I—" But before I had time to choke out a no, she had left the room. I sat there, staring at the beige wall, thinking about her resounding no, in response to my question about Will. She had such absolute confidence in him. I thought about Will, doing her work for her when she was sick, and I felt guilty for even asking the question. But there had been something off, something not totally right. I'd felt it there in my dream, and I wondered if, in my dream world, I could see Will more clearly than Janice had been able to in real life. I wondered if Janice's vision was more than a little clouded.

I looked up, and she was standing in front of me, holding on to the baby, her face illuminated, aglow with a wash of pride and love. I thought about the way Kelly had felt breast-feeding Hannah, and I smiled. "Do you want to hold her?" she asked me.

"Yes," I said, not sure where my response came from, because in my head, I'd been thinking no. She put the baby into my arms, and I felt her soft flesh against my own, smelled her baby powder smell. I brushed her fine hair from her face, and then without even thinking about it, I leaned down and stroked one of her pudgy little cheeks. Will had been right. "She's beautiful," I said.

Janice nodded. "This is what it's all about," she told me. "This, right here."

When I got back in the car, I noticed I had a new voice mail. I hoped it was from Will, because I now really wanted to hear his voice. But as soon as I heard the annoying crackle, I knew it was from Sharon. "Hello, Jennifer. Your father and I are going to be in town in two weeks, and we're going to have a little party. Call me back, and I'll let you know the details." She paused. "I hear you're not talking to your sister. What's that all about?"

None of your business, I thought, as I hit the delete button. There was no way I was going to that party. No way I was going to watch her and my father stare at me and Will, disappointment hanging so heavy in their faces that it would make me want to crumble.

I drove by Kelly's house on the way home, tempted to get out of the car and ring the doorbell. I knew she was home. Her red minivan sat in the driveway, the hood dusted in snow that was now a few days old.

"So," I imagined saying to her. "Dad and Sharon are having a party." I tried to remember if my mother and father had ever had a party, and I couldn't think of a time when they had.

Once, before our grandparents died, our mother had thrown a surprise party for their anniversary, but I couldn't remember our father being there. In fact, I think he might have been at work, missed the whole thing.

"I know," Kelly might say back, rolling her eyes. "But of course we have to go."

"Why of course?"

"Come on, Jen. Grow up."

I wondered if maybe I'd just missed it, the obligation gene, the sense of duty Kelly felt to our father and Sharon, to Beverly, whereas I felt nothing. I was empty.

I heard a rumbling and looked up and saw the garage door starting to roll up, and then before she could see me, I hit the gas and sped away.

By the time I got home, Will was already there, lying on the love seat the way he'd been this morning when I'd awoken to the sound of the ambulance. He had his eyes closed, but when he heard me walk in, he said my name, softly.

I went and sat down next to him, on the edge of the love seat. I thought of my dream and Janice's resolve. "How are you?" I whispered, wishing I'd asked him months ago, wishing I'd stopped to notice him the way Barry should've stopped to notice Lisa.

"My head hurts," he whispered.

"I'll get you a glass of water and some aspirin," I said. I hesitated for a moment, and I touched his stubbly cheek with my thumb.

He opened his eyes, and sat up a little. "You don't have to do that. I'll get it in a little bit. Just lie with me," he whispered. He moved toward the back of the love seat, making room for me. So I lay down next to him, turned on my side, and curled my body into his. He stroked my hair back, and after a few moments he said, "Crazy day, huh?"

I thought about Barry in the waiting room and Lisa in the hospital bed, Janice holding on to Rose, and Sharon's acerbic voice. "Crazy," I said, marveling at how the world felt so still, right here, lying in his arms.

"You feel so nice," Will whispered into my neck. "Let's just lie here forever."

"Okay," I agreed, and I leaned in closer to him, close enough so every inch of my body entwined with his.

Twenty-five

Lisa was in the hospital for a week, and when she returned home, I made sure to stop by and check on her every morning on my way to jogging in the park.

"Amber's getting her tits done," Lisa told me one morning, as I sat at her kitchen table and watched her empty her dishwasher. I was the only one to know what had really happened to Lisa, which, for some reason, made Lisa open up a little bit more about the other women.

The rest of them only knew what Lisa had told them, the story she'd concocted, that she'd simply been dehydrated, too much running around, too much stress, too much exercise (and I thought it was funny that they bought that last part). But why wouldn't they? Apparently the women had been feeding one another bullshit for as long as I'd known them, probably longer, and maybe I had been a part of that, too, pretending like Will and I had had the perfect marriage, pretending like I was above having children, like I was the one doing something good in running the auction, when, really, all I was doing was passing the time.

"Barry's doing it?" I asked.

"His partner," she said. "Do you think life would be different as a D cup?"

"No." I shook my head. I couldn't imagine how that would solve anything. "Absolutely not." Though I certainly had wondered how life would be different without breasts, how I would feel if I had them taken from me. And that seemed like it would make life eminently different for some reason.

"Barry suggested I get mine done a few weeks ago." She laughed. "But he was really sweet last night. He apologized. He said he didn't mean that I needed it, only that he was trying to help." She paused. "He actually felt guilty about it, as if that were the reason . . ." She let her voice trail off.

I knew she hadn't told him the truth, and I wondered if she ever would. It seemed clear to me, having visited her life in dreams, that telling Barry might be the only real way for her to break out of this. She blamed herself for so much, and I guessed that Barry would blame her for nothing, that Barry could make her understand that it wasn't her fault. And then I thought about Will, about his life as a judge, and how we never told each other anything. "You have to talk to him," I said. "You have to let him in."

After my run, I had a splitting headache again, and when I got home, I took two ibuprofen. Then I saw the mail and a note that Will must've left on the table when he'd stopped home for lunch. *CALL ME IF YOU WANT ME TO PICK UP DINNER. I LOVE YOU. I love you.* Right there in all caps, so bold and so obvious, it made me want to cry. I picked up the phone and dialed his number. *You have to talk to him*, I'd told Lisa. *You have to let him in.*

"Hi," I said softly, when he answered. "You busy?"

"Sort of," he said. "Just walking into an appointment."

"I saw your note."

"Do you want me to get something?"

"No," I said. "I have a chicken." I paused. "I just wanted to say hi."

"Oh," he said. "Hi. Can I call you back in twenty minutes?"

"You don't have to call me back. I didn't mean to bother you."

"You're not," he said. "But I have to go."

"Will." I said his name forcefully, afraid he might hang up before I said it. I heard his breath, slow and steady on the other end of the line. "I love you, too."

After we hung up, I noticed the mail on the table. Sitting on top of the pile was a thick manila envelope, the return address telling me it was from *City Style*. As I ripped open the package, I thought about Kat and Grant, pictured them having drinks at a bar, as she leaned into him. And then I wasn't sure if it was something that I dreamed or something that I imagined, because the image in my mind felt foggy, unclear, which only made my head start throbbing more.

Inside the envelope were the handwritten brides' forms, and a note written in Kat's large scrawling handwriting— which simply read: *Deadline: Feb. 14.* I turned the piece of paper over, looking for answers, looking for something else, but that was absolutely all it said.

So she was still sending me work—she didn't totally hate me. I knew if she wanted to, she could've easily asked the intern to write these up, so it sort of felt a little like an apology, or at least an opening. But an opening for what? I wondered. She obviously didn't want my advice, and maybe she was over my friendship. In fact, maybe she just felt sorry for me.

I thought about Ara and Sarah Lynne, about Ara's tiny little fingers on my watch, her warm body in my lap, and then I took the forms from Kat and went to the computer to type them up. I had over a week, but I knew finishing would give me an excuse to talk to her again. Still, I sat there for a while, staring at the blank screen until everything was blurry and my head was pounding again. But nothing came to me, no words at all.

Twenty-six

The next week I had my annual doctor's appointment with Dr. Horowitz. I always dreaded it, something that seemed to creep up on me every February, almost something of a surprise, though clearly it wasn't. But this year I dreaded it even more than usual because I hadn't been feeling like myself lately. And as I sat in the waiting room, I had this nervous pit in my stomach that something was wrong, that Dr. Horowitz was going to give me bad news.

I drummed my fingers nervously against the edge of the chair, too terrified to read my copy of *City Style*, though I pretended. I opened it up to Kat's article, "Fifty First Dates," which detailed fifty different places you could go on a unique date in the city. I stared at her byline and her photo until it made me dizzy, until I could almost see her frowning the way she had that day in her office.

"Mrs. Levenworth," the nurse called out, and I jumped,

because it felt like it'd been a long time since someone had called me that.

As the nurse checked my blood pressure, I felt my pulse beating fast and steady in my head, my neck. "A little high." She frowned.

"It always is." I laughed nervously. "Doctors make me a little nervous."

"Oh," she said. "White-coat syndrome then. Well, I'll let the doctor know."

I didn't bother to tell her that Dr. Horowitz already knew, that Dr. Horowitz had seen me clutching Kelly's hand in my mother's hospital room when he'd come in to visit after the mastectomy. That Dr. Horowitz had been the one to first reassure me that my lump was probably nothing, and then, when it was, to recommend annual breast MRIs.

"Jennifer," he said breezily as he walked in, his easy manner calming me slightly, but not much. "How's your family?"

"Great," I said, which didn't feel like such a lie anymore, though I imagined he must've read about Will and thought it was.

"Have you been keeping up with your breast self-exams?" I nodded. "Good. Then let's check everything out."

I lay back against the cool table and held my breath as he palpated around my breasts checking for a lump I might have missed. *Please don't find something. Please don't find something. Please don't find something.*

"Totally normal," he said, and I exhaled. "I'll get you a slip for your MRI, but I don't feel anything to worry about." He moved to the end of the table to do the rest of the exam. "Any other problems?"

"No." I shook my head, not wanting to mention the headache that wouldn't go away, or the dreams that wouldn't stop coming, not wanting to give him a cause to search harder, to find something else.

"And are we planning on getting pregnant soon?"

"No," I said. "I don't know."

"Well, I'll write you a script for prenatals, just in case. It's better to start taking them before you conceive. Then as soon as you get a positive test you can call our office and set up an appointment." He reached for his prescription pad and scribbled on it, then ripped off the page and handed it over. The way he laid it all out, so officiously, so matter-of-fact, it was as if it was all decided for me. He'd written the same prescription last year, but I'd declined it, telling him I was sure I wouldn't need it yet, that I would call him if I changed my mind. But now I thought about what Lisa had said, about not always remembering to take her vitamins, about feeling that that was to blame for her miscarriage, and though I didn't think it really was, I accepted the prescription from him anyway.

"I don't even know if I'll use it," I said. "If I'll ever have a baby."

He nodded, all business, not reacting to whether I ever would or would not have a child. I imagined the way Will's eyes would look if I announced that to him, the truth, so openly, and I knew they would mist up, that he wouldn't even be able to look at me. "How old are you now?" Dr. Horowitz asked, glancing down at my chart.

"Thirty-three."

"Well, we recommend that if you know you want to have a baby, it's better to do it before you hit thirty-five. After thirty-five the risk of Down syndrome increases." He paused. "Not to rush you," he said, "but sometimes, timing is everything."

I nodded, thinking about the way people always talked about hearing their internal clock ticking, and I wondered if the sound of mine was just drowned out by something else; fear, maybe. "Are you still thinking about genetic testing?" he asked.

It was something he'd brought up every year since I'd found my lump, the possibility of learning whether I had the breast cancer gene, of learning whether my mother's cancer was random or whether it was also preprogrammed in me, my destiny. But I'd never been able to decide whether it was better knowing or not knowing, so I always waffled, telling him I'd think about it. Once I'd asked Kelly about it, if she thought about having the test. She'd waved her hand in the air and said, "Oh, Jen, you can't worry about every little thing. You could be hit by a bus tomorrow." I'd nodded, but I'd been thinking, *But Mom wasn't hit by a bus, and getting hit by a bus is not carried in a person's DNA.*

"I don't know," I finally answered him, wondering if having the test might just be better than not knowing. What if it was not my destiny to die? What if my mother's cancer, my father's disappearing act had been nothing more than a fluke after all?

"I'll tell you what," Dr. Horowitz said, looking neither pleased nor displeased about my noncommittal answer. "I'll write you out the slip for the lab work, and then you'll have it if you decide you want to do the test."

So I left his office with two little pieces of paper in my hand, both of them, maybe, having the ability to decide my future.

When I got home, I finished the wedding announcements. I'd been torn between wanting to get them done, to have an

excuse to talk to Kat, and not wanting to get them done, because I wasn't sure what I would say to her when I did get the
chance. Now I had no choice; they were due tomorrow. When
I finished, I attached them in an e-mail to Kat, which, even
though I'd already rehearsed it in my head all week, I wrote
and rewrote three times, before deciding just to simply write:
Sorry. Can we talk? xoxo, Jen.

I sat there and stared at the screen for a minute, knowing
she was probably at her desk, that she would probably hear
the click of the e-mail and open it up right away. *Please respond*, I willed her.

Exactly three minutes later, she wrote back. *Can we meet for
coffee? Downstairs? 3:30?*

The train station was empty in the middle of the day, and
the train wasn't crowded either. I leaned my head against the
window and closed my eyes, feeling my head throb, as if
it had its own painful pulse. *I should call Ethel*, I thought.
She would have something to give me. I'd been putting it off
because I was worried she would tell me it was a side effect of
the calming herb, that she might even tell me to stop taking
it, and that was something I couldn't risk doing again. I felt
like I needed the herbs now, needed them to figure everything out.

When I opened my eyes, the seat next to me was taken,
and I recognized the mother and daughter who sat there. The
girl still had her *Goodnight Moon* book, and she held it tightly
to her chest. Her mother stared in the other direction, so I
couldn't meet her gaze.

The girl looked at me, and I smiled. "That was my favorite
book when I was a little girl," I said.

She hesitated before speaking, and I imagined that her

mother, who clutched her ever so tightly, must've warned her more than once about talking to strangers. But then she said a line from the book, no louder than a whisper, so I almost couldn't hear her.

I closed my eyes again and heard the same words in my mother's voice, heard her voice so vividly in my head that it gave me chills.

When I opened my eyes, because I felt the train stopping, the girl and her mother had already stood up and walked away, and the sound of my mother's voice had once again completely left me.

Kat was already sitting outside the coffee shop when I arrived at exactly four minutes before three-thirty. She was bundled up in a gray wool peacoat with a red scarf, hat, and gloves, and I watched her take a drag from her cigarette.

"Hi," she said, when she noticed me. She dropped the cigarette and squashed it with her black high-heeled boot. "We can go inside. It's freezing out here."

I nodded, appreciating the gesture. It was cold, but I also knew she wouldn't be able to smoke inside.

Inside felt astoundingly familiar—the smell of rich coffee, fireplace, and muffins—and not just because I'd been here so recently in my dreams, but because Kat and I had come here so often when I used to work here, every afternoon, just around this time, just around the time when the day was starting to feel stretched too long, and we were getting weary in our dimly fluorescent lit offices. We'd both order skinny lattes, and then linger at a table in the corner for twenty minutes or maybe even half an hour, our reporter's notebooks open in front of us, so it looked like we were working, even though we rarely ever had.

We walked up to the counter now, and Kat ordered first, a decaf chai tea. Tea. And decaf. *You're a different woman now,* I thought. And though it should've seemed obvious, I still found this surprising.

"I'll have the same thing," I echoed, wanting to show that I, too, had changed, had become someone a little worldlier or a little wiser, though really, I would've much rather had the latte, much rather been that girl who could sit in the corner and laugh, and blow off work, and feel as though the heavy things in life were too far away to bog me down.

We stood by the counter waiting a few moments for our drinks, not saying anything, Kat kicking the tile floor with the pointy toe of her boot. After the barista handed us our chais, I followed Kat to our former usual table.

"So," she said, blowing on the hot tea and then taking a small sip, keeping her eyes on the tea the whole time.

"So," I said back. I took a sip of my tea, which was too sweet and burned my throat. I tried not to grimace as it went down. It wasn't really the hot tea but the quiet between us that really bothered me. "Are you still mad?" I finally said, when I couldn't take the silence anymore.

She shook her head. "No, I'm not mad." She sighed. "You were right. I knew you were." I nodded. "But I just didn't want to hear it, you know?"

"Oh, Kat," I said. "I shouldn't have brought it up like that. I should've stayed out of it." I left out the part about how hard it was to mind your own business when dreaming as a person made it feel like it completely was your business. "And just so you know, I never left you for my friends in Deerfield. It wasn't like that."

"I know." She waved her hand in the air. "I was just jealous."

"Of my Deerfield friends? Don't be," I said, thinking that

if only she knew, *if only she knew*, the way the perfect surfaces of their lives were even more cracked and worn than hers. At least with Kat, what you saw was what you got—loud and sometimes brash and sometimes too abrasive—but she put it all out there anyway.

"No." She shook her head. "Of you. I was jealous of you."

"Of me?" Maybe she couldn't see me any more than I'd been able to see her before I'd started dreaming. "That's silly."

"No," she said. "You had the balls to quit your job, and move to the suburbs, and go after what it was you really wanted in life. And me?" She laughed and rubbed her fingers nervously together, as if running them over an invisible cigarette. "I'm still here."

She'd mistaken my quitting for living out my dream, rather than what it really was: pretending, playing house, playing judge's wife, playing high society lady. "You have nothing to be jealous of," I said quietly. "If anything, I'm the one who should be jealous of you. You have direction, a career, two beautiful girls." And maybe I had been a little jealous of her, before I'd dreamed about her, that was, before I knew that those things, the satisfying career, the so-called perfect marriage, the children, did not equal happiness.

She shook her head. "They are beautiful, aren't they?"

"Yes," I agreed again. "They are."

"It wasn't about Grant, you know," she said. "It was never about him." I nodded, waiting for her to continue. "I hate my job," she confessed. "It bores me. I think that's why I let myself pay so much attention to him—I needed something to get me out of bed, some reason to keep coming to work."

Maybe Kat had always been bored. She'd been the one initiating our e-mail crossword puzzles and our coffee breaks, and I'd willingly gone along. She was infectious, and I'd loved every minute of it. Maybe it was being friends with Kat that had made me feel alive, not the job, and I felt relieved that I hadn't been able to get the job back after all. "You could quit," I suggested.

"I know," she said. "But it's not that easy." She paused. "This is all I know. All I've ever done." She finished off her tea and then looked at me and smiled. "I mean, it's one thing to be a crappy parent if you're at work all the time. But what if I'm always home, and I still fuck it up?"

"You won't," I said.

"How can you be so sure?"

"I can't." I paused. "But you won't. I know you won't." I thought about the way Sarah Lynne and Ara both were beautiful and loving little girls, and I knew that despite what she thought, Kat was already doing something right.

"Well, I'm fucking up my marriage," she said.

"So am I," I agreed, but as I said it, I considered whether I still was, or whether Will and I had turned some sort of corner.

"Oh please," she said, rolling her eyes. "You and Will."

"You and Danny," I said right back, even more emphatically.

"I know." She sighed. "You know why I never actually fucked Grant?" I shook my head, wanting to hear, because I had already just assumed that she had. "It was something that you said."

"Me?" I considered the power of the herbs, the dreams, to have allowed me to change something, to change the course of Kat's life, and the throbbing in my head was now temporarily feeling worth it.

"Yeah," she said. "Something you said at your wedding." *My wedding. So it had had nothing to do with the herbs. The herbs had changed nothing real.* "You were getting dressed in that dressing area, and I was pinning your veil in your hair. We had some champagne, and you lifted your glass to toast. And then you said, 'To me and Will having even just a glimmer of the spark that you and Danny have. Or something like that."

I nodded. I had a vague recollection of champagne, a lot of it, and blathering something about wishing Will and I could be as great as them, something I'd always been afraid wouldn't happen, that no matter what, we'd never shine as brightly in a room as the two of them.

"Anyway," she said, "I better get back up there before Hank sends the police." She rolled her eyes. She stood up and leaned in and hugged me close, so very affectionate and un-Kat-like. I hugged her back, held on tightly. "I'm sorry," she whispered in my ear, and then: "Thank you."

"No," I whispered back. "Thank you."

That night, as I lay in bed, Will curled up behind me and wrapped his arms around me, and then this feeling of utter calm came over me, this feeling that everything was going to be all right. Maybe what Kat said was true, maybe we were Jen and Will. Will and Jen. An us. A we.

"I saw your prescriptions on the counter," Will whispered softly in my ear, as if he was reciting a love poem, something romantic. The calm dissipated, and it was instantly replaced by this cold blast in my chest and the return of my throbbing headache. It was a stupid thing to do, leaving them out like that, leaving them there for him to see, when I hadn't decided what to do about either one of them. I'd been so caught up in meeting Kat that I'd forgotten all about them.

"It's no big deal," I whispered back. "Dr. Horowitz gives them to me every year. Just in case."

I waited for him to protest, to make it a big deal, but all he said was "It's good to have options." Then he curled in closer. "I'm coming home early tomorrow. I planned something special."

"Why?" I whispered, feeling warm and drowsy again.

"It's Valentine's Day." He lifted up my hair and kissed my neck. "Will you be my Valentine?"

"Of course," I whispered, wanting to ask him to be mine back. But I was too tired and the words caught in my throat. Instead my mind had drifted back to the genetic tests, and I wondered if whatever doomed me also doomed Kelly, if the two of us were linked in a terrible way. For a moment I missed her.

"Kelly," Beverly said, "the kids need new clothes. You can't dress them like this to go to a party." I picked Hannah up from her crib. She sucked her thumb, and she looked adorable in her Old Navy jeans and pink sweater. "A girl should wear a dress. To a party, for heaven's sake. I'm embarrassed for you."

"Bever— Mother," I corrected myself. "It's too cold for her to wear a dress."

"Tights," she said. "Wool tights, dear. That's how Kathleen always dresses the girls."

I was sure the girls had tears in those wool tights within five minutes from screaming in a tantrum on the floor, but I decided not to mention that, because I knew it wasn't going to help anything.

"And really, when are you going to get her ears pierced? Kathleen got the girls' ears pierced at six months."

"I don't want to get her ears pierced when she's so young," I repeated for what felt like the thousandth time.

She shook her head. *"Just because she has two older brothers doesn't mean she can't look like a little girl, you know."*

"Hey there." Dave poked his head in.

"Dave, come in here," Beverly said. *"We need a man's opinion."* I rolled my eyes at him. He pretended not to notice. *"Now don't you think your daughter should wear a dress to a party?"*

"Sure," he said. *"A dress is nice."*

"Or jeans and a sweater are fine." I glared at him.

He put his hands in his pockets and shifted nervously. *"I don't know,"* he said. *"I'm not good with this fashion stuff. I'll leave it up to you ladies."* He leaned in and kissed me on the head, but I shrank back. *You bastard,* I thought.

I looked down, and when I looked up again, the room had changed.

We were sitting in a big, airy dining area at the Deerfield Inn, the same room where Dave and I had our wedding reception. Hannah bounced on my lap, in a dress, and Caleb and Jack squirmed in their chairs on either side of me. *"I'm hungry,"* Jack whined, ignoring the steak on his plate.

"I have to pee," Caleb announced.

"Can you hold it?" I said. He shook his head.

I tried to get Dave's attention to help with the kids, but he was across the table, deep in conversation with Mark Fitzmaurice, the accountant for Daniels and

Sons. "Do you want me to take him?" Beverly asked.

I didn't, but I also didn't want to drag three children in there by myself. "Thanks," I told her, not feeling thankful at all.

As they walked out, my father and Sharon went up to the front of the room. Sharon tapped her glass of rum and Coke with a butter knife. "Listen up, everybody," she cackled. "Donny and I have an announcement to make."

The room got quiet, except for Hannah, who pounded on the table with a spoon. "Well," Sharon said, "after all these years, Donny is finally making an honest woman out of me." Shit. "He's asked me to marry him, and I've accepted." She leaned up and kissed him quickly on the lips, and I had to look away. I felt this overwhelming sense of nausea.

Beverly walked back in, holding on to Caleb. "What's all the ruckus? What did I miss?"

"They're getting married," I said, swallowing the rest of my glass of wine too quickly.

"Oh, how nice for you, dear." Beverly patted me on the shoulder. "Now you'll have two mothers."

Hannah was still pounding with the spoon, and the noise, the news, made my head want to explode, made me want to stand up and scream.

Two mothers. Beverly's words echoed in my head. Two mothers.

No mom. Mom is dead, dead for so long that she has been forgotten, and every piece of where I came from has nearly been obliterated.

Twenty-seven

I woke up with a pounding headache, my heart exploding in my chest. Kelly's thoughts were still so fresh in my head, it was as if they were my own thoughts: *Every piece of where I came from, obliterated.* My father and Sharon were getting married.

The clock said seven-thirty, and I heard Will in the shower. I figured I had about an hour, maybe two, until the phone rang, until Kelly called with the news, and I debated whether I was going to answer it.

On one hand, I knew I couldn't stay mad at her forever, but on the other hand, when she called, the call would be full of obligations, musts. Must help plan the wedding. Must attend. Must be a bridesmaid. Must write a toast.

Maybe deep down Kelly felt the same way I did—she hated Sharon, she was angry with our father, she still couldn't really get over the death of our mother—though it had been nearly twenty years. On the surface, Kelly wouldn't let it show; she would do all good things expected of one's daughter. That was Kelly, the person who called Beverly Mother.

And yet a part of me still wanted to answer the phone, wanted to hear my sister's voice, wanted to bitch with her about how Sharon would be a crappy stepmother. Because sometimes, no matter how mad you were or how much you wanted to hate her, your sister was the only other person in the world who felt exactly the way you did.

Will came out of the bathroom still wet and wrapped in a towel from the waist down. I closed my eyes and inhaled him, the pine aftershave, and then I opened them again and watched him for a moment before he turned, before he noticed me. His curls were dewy, and his broad shoulders were lined with drops of water. He saw me, and he smiled, this incredible, soft smile that he reserved only for me, a smile that brought me back to when we were first dating, a smile that seemed to say everything he was thinking about me, everything good. "You're up." He walked over and kissed me lightly on the lips. "Happy Valentine's Day."

"Happy Valentine's Day," I murmured, but as I leaned in to kiss him back, his face swirled in front of me, and I closed my eyes.

"Don't forget," he said. "Be ready by four, okay? And wear something nice."

Something nice. Not to go to the club or an auction, but to go out, with him, on a real, bona fide date. I felt a surge of something warm through my chest as I watched him walk toward his closet, watched the way his strong arms moved as he opened the door.

I thought about Kelly, and the way she wanted to get Dave's attention and couldn't get it. And here I had Will. No other family, no job that kept him away at all hours anymore.

Just Will. One hundred percent Will. Maybe we could have a baby. Maybe Will would be nothing at all like my father, now that he was no longer a judge. This Will would be around to help, to give love; this Will, the one who came home early for Valentine's Day and planned something special, the one who left me notes on the table with the word *love* in them, and sometimes came home for lunch just to spend time with me. Not Judge Will, who hadn't even remembered to give me a Valentine's Day kiss two years running, who'd had Janice send me an expensive bouquet of roses that I was sure she had picked out and he had never even laid eyes on. No, this Will, the one walking out of his closet now in khakis and a blue sweater, was clearly different.

"What are you thinking?" Will asked. "You look so serious."

"Oh, nothing." I shook my head. "You look nice."

He walked over and sat at the edge of the bed. "I'm going to make some coffee. Meet you downstairs in a few minutes?" He traced the edge of my cheek with his thumb, and I closed my eyes for a minute, leaning into the warmth of his hand.

After I cleaned up from breakfast, I got dressed and wandered over to Lisa's. She was still her pajamas when I arrived, and she looked like she'd forgotten to take a shower yesterday—her hair sticking out like a wild woman's.

"You and Barry doing anything for Valentine's Day?" I asked.

"Oh shit." She sat down at the kitchen table and put her head in her hands. "I forgot."

"Well, I was going to go pick up something for Will, if you want to come."

"I should bake him something," she said. "Barry loves my cakes."

"Lisa," I said with mock seriousness, "I have something very, very important to tell you."

"What?" She looked up.

"No one loves your cakes. Your cakes are a disaster."

She looked at me, and then she started laughing, and she couldn't stop, until tears started rolling down her face. The tears kept coming, even when the laughter stopped. I leaned in and hugged her, and for a few moments, we sat there in her kitchen, holding on to each other.

We ended up in the Villages of Oak Glen, the same shopping center with Applebee's, because I knew there was a Hallmark store there where Lisa and I could pick out cards, and I also knew we wouldn't run into any of the other ladies of Deerfield, for Lisa's sake.

Lisa and I walked down the aisles, laughing at the sappy cards. Then she pointed to a section that said, "Baby's First Valentine's Day." She didn't say a word, just pointed, but I could see the way her face fell, the way any trace of laughter dissipated into dust.

"Oh, Lisa," I said.

"I never thought this would be my life. I mean, who ever thinks this when you get married, that you're going to wake up every morning feeling so shitty?" She paused. "Well, you know." I nodded, because in a way I did. Or at least I had. I thought about the way I'd felt this morning, watching Will walk across our bedroom, and just thinking about it again now, I felt a little breathless.

She picked up a card. It was burgundy with two interlaced hands and the words "Love Is Forever." "Does anybody believe in this crap?" she said. "Love is forever." She sighed.

"I don't know." I shrugged, thinking about my father and Sharon, about the way she'd swirled her rum and Coke and announced she was being made into an honest woman. It did seem to make a case for the contrary of love lasting forever, the way he'd quickly abandoned my mother as soon as she got sick, and now he was willing to promise forever to someone else. But then I thought about Will again, standing by his closet door, wet from the shower, and how I'd felt a swell in my chest, a feeling I thought had died, but perhaps had only been buried somewhere.

I picked out a card for Will that had two interconnected hearts on the front, and on the inside simply read: "You + Me = Love." Nice. Elegant. Mathematical. Straightforward. I knew he would like it.

As we walked up to pay, I noticed the table with the figurines that Will had found the last time we were here. I saw "The Perfect Family," and then next to that, there was another one, a figurine with the same couple. In this one the baby was older, a child, a little girl Ara's age. The man stood with his arm around the woman; she leaned her head into his shoulder, and the little girl stood dressed in a pink dress with a pink bow in her hair, staring up at them with what could only be described as blatant love and admiration.

I picked the figurine up and turned it over to read the name. "Afterglow."

"What's that?" Lisa asked. I showed her. "Oh please. Nobody's that happy. In real life, the woman would've gained twenty pounds, the girl would be screaming, and the husband would be at work."

I nodded, and though I knew she was probably right, that this figurine only captured a moment, a frozen one at that, and that it didn't show what lay beneath the surface for these people, for this family, I took it up to the cash register and bought it anyway.

When I got home I ate lunch, and then I took a long bath. I shaved, moisturized, perfumed, straightened my hair with a straightening iron, put on a little mascara and some lipstick, and then I put on the red dress that I'd worn to the auction last year.

If I closed my eyes I could remember her, the Jen who'd walked into the club frozen, holding on to Will's arm as if we were both statues, that Jen who'd stood up in front of the wealthy people of Deerfield, who'd announced bids and prizes into the mike, the Jen who'd sat at a table with her friends, carefully cutting into her food, laughing at the appropriate moments, adding a comment at the right time. Had that been fun? Had I enjoyed that? I couldn't remember, now, any feeling of joy from that night, not even the smallest bit. Even the excitement I'd felt when we counted up the donations at the end of the night was muted. It was something, maybe, but nothing real, nothing to make the pain of losing someone, a person, a mother, to breast cancer, subside.

But the dress was gorgeous. I'd bought it in the city, at a boutique just down the street from *City Style*. It was a one-of-a-kind, hand-dyed, hand-spun red silk, with a strapless interlaced bodice and a knee-length silk skirt.

"What do you think?" I remembered spinning in front of Will. He'd sat in his study, looking through a pile of briefs.

"Very nice," he'd said, without looking up.

Tonight, just as I was looking for my shoes in the closet, I heard Will come into the bedroom, and when I walked out, he stared at me. His eyes moved all across my body, up and down the length of the dress. "Wow," he said. "You're stunning."

I felt my pulse quickening, my face turning hot, and I felt a little nervous, like first-date nervous. It seemed absolutely insane, to have that feeling after so many years together, but I had it nonetheless.

He walked toward me and touched my hair, which had grown back nearly to my shoulders. "It's straight," he said.

"Do you like it?"

He nodded and leaned in and kissed me softly on the lips. "Just let me get changed, and I'll meet you downstairs."

Will came down dressed up in a suit, clean-shaven, looking so much like Judge Will on his way to work, yet looking nothing like him at all. This Will had bright eyes that stared at me with this quiet intensity, a tender sort of glow that I wasn't sure I'd ever really seen from him before, not even when we were first married.

"You look nice," I said.

He reached for my hand, and he led me out to his car. He opened the passenger door for me, and then, once I was sitting down, pulled a scarf from his pocket and tied it around my eyes. "So you'll be surprised," he whispered, barely grazing my ear with his lips as he said it.

On the ride, I closed my eyes behind the scarf, listened to the din and hum of traffic, the sound of the soft jazz saxophone Will had put on the radio. At one point Will put his hand on my leg, and I felt calm, warm, a feeling that everything was going to be all right. I wasn't worried about dying or dreaming, and I almost felt like I could be lulled to sleep.

What I guessed was about forty-five minutes later, the car slowed down and came to a stop in a parking space. "We're here," Will said. He pulled the scarf off gently, and I blinked to focus my eyes.

We were in the parking lot of Il Romano, the restaurant

where we'd met, had our first blind date. And had never been back to since. After my review, the restaurant took off, and it was nearly impossible to get a table.

"How did you manage this? On Valentine's Day?"

"I have my ways." He smiled.

Not only did Will manage a table, but the same one in the corner, the small half-circle booth that we'd shared on our first date. "This is so nice," I said, genuinely surprised and overwhelmed by his thoughtfulness and a little amazed by his ability to pull it off. "Thank you."

Will put his arm around me, and I leaned into him. When the waiter came over, Will asked if I minded if he ordered for us. "No, go ahead," I said, surprised because it wasn't the sort of thing he usually did. Even at the club we'd both always ordered for ourselves.

"Do you know what I ordered?" he asked, after the waiter had gone.

"Antipasto, chicken marsala, Chardonnay—"

"Our first dinner together," he said. "Do you remember?"

It was funny that he remembered it to a T, that easily, when I really had to think hard to remember, and I'd been the one to write the review. What I remembered with precision: Will's eyes as he'd stared at me across the table, bright and smart and sexy and warm. The food, not so much. "How do you remember that?"

He shrugged. "I wrote it down."

"You did?"

He nodded. "I was looking through some of my old things last week, and I found it, on a yellow legal pad." He paused. "Do you want to know what else I wrote down?" I nodded. He cleared his throat and starting singing, softly, *"Hey there, you with the stars in your eyes . . ."* It sounded different in his voice now than it had that night, after he'd had too much wine, and he'd serenaded me on the walk home from the restaurant. He'd commented on the real stars in the cool night sky and the pretty green color of my eyes, and then he'd started singing.

"Oh, Will." I reached for his hand now. "I'd forgotten about that." I'd almost forgotten the way another person could surprise you, the way they could instantly and irrevocably make you feel that there were actually stars in your eyes.

"Here. I have something for you." He pulled a tiny box, wrapped in gold foil, out of his pocket and handed it to me. I carefully tore off the wrapping paper, and as I opened the box I felt a spark of something; nerves, excitement.

Inside was a pair of diamond star earrings tucked into black velour, sparkly enough to be real stars against a dark night sky. "Oh, Will," I said again. "They're beautiful." I paused. "You shouldn't have. I mean, how can we afford these?"

"Sssh." He put his finger to his lips. "Try them on."

I took the tiny pearls out of my ears and put the new stars in. "What do you think?"

He nodded, kissed my earlobe, and tucked a strand of hair behind my ear.

I thought about the figurine sitting in my purse, still in the Hallmark bag, still unwrapped, and then I knew I had to give it to him. "I have something for you, too," I said, fishing through my purse, and then handing him the bag.

He took the figurine out, looked at it, and smiled. He turned it over and read the bottom. "Afterglow," he whispered.

"Do you recognize them?" I pointed to the couple.

"The Perfect Family?" I nodded. "It's beautiful, Jen," he whispered. "Thank you."

Twenty-eight

When we got home, full of good Italian food and warm from the candle glow and the wine, Will stood at the bottom of the steps and held out his hand. I took it and followed him up slowly. I felt this overwhelming sense of tenderness, almost the way I felt when the herbs calmed me and lulled me into a deep and dream-filled sleep. Only for the first time in a long time I wasn't at all tired.

We stepped into the bedroom, and Will pulled off his suit jacket, then his tie. He ran his hand down my back, slowly unzipping my dress.

I pulled it down in the front and then stepped out of it, so I was standing there in front of him in only my red strapless bra and red underwear. "You're so beautiful, Jen," he whispered, reaching to unhook my bra, then tugging down the waistband of my underwear.

He leaned in to kiss me, and I felt that nearly forgotten urgency, the one I'd felt when we first met, when I had to be with him at that moment, no matter where we were or what we were doing. He kissed my neck, then my shoulders, and he pulled my bra the rest of the way off.

I unbuttoned his shirt and pulled it off him and threw it on the floor. Then I leaned closer to him, so we were standing bare skin to bare skin. His chest was warm and electric.

He took off his pants and pulled me on top of him on the bed. "Jen," he whispered in my ear. "Jen. Jen."

I felt him, so close, so warm, this rush of pleasure in my body, in my brain. There was this feeling of overwhelming desire; I'd been wanting him for so long that I couldn't wait another second. I kissed him, and as I pulled him inside me, I heard him moan my name softly.

I'd forgotten how good he felt when we were together, really together, not the halfhearted attempts at getting pregnant, not the polite, him-on-top, me-still-half-asleep, six A.M. sex. But this, our bodies warm, flailing, melting against each other, the sheets.

Afterward I lay completely still on top of him, our sweaty skin blending into one set of flesh, our two selves blending into one. He wrapped his arms around me and kissed my hair. "Tell me one thing you want," he whispered.

"You," I whispered back, not hesitating at all this time but saying the first thing, the first word that popped into my head.

"I love you," he whispered.

"I love you, too." And I realized, lying there, that I'd never loved Will for what he did, but who he was, and how I felt when I was with him. That none of the rest of it mattered, if he was a lawyer or a judge or a seller of selective herbicides.

I was sitting inside a bar, my suit hanging heavy against my back. I swilled scotch in a highball glass

and checked out the football game that played out over-
head, on a TV that hung underneath a sign that read:
"The Brew." The Eagles fumbled. Idiots, I mumbled.

"That fucking McNabb." The bartender shook his
fist. I finished off my scotch and motioned for him to
pour me another one. "You drinking alone?" he asked.

"No," I said. "Not quite."

I watched the door nervously, hoping that he
wouldn't show, that Jude Marris would've snorted one
too many lines of coke and forgotten. But no such luck.
Just after the Eagles gave up another touchdown, he
walked in, carrying a briefcase close to his chest as he
squeezed his way through the crowded bar.

"Will," he said.

"Judge," I corrected him.

"Yeah." He snorted. "Judge."

He put his briefcase on top of the bar and slid it
toward me. I peeked inside; not legal briefs but cash,
stacks of it, stacks like I would've seen only in a movie.

In the moment before panic hit me hard, gripped my
chest as if it was squeezing it directly, I almost wanted
to laugh at how cliché this was—cash in a briefcase,
for Christ's sake. "It's half," Marris said. "You'll get
the other half after." He stood up, folded his hands in
front of his chest in an attempt to look menacing, but
he still looked like a little jerk-off. "Don't fuck with
us, Will."

"Jen." Will shook my shoulder lightly, then harder. "Jen,
wake up." I opened my eyes and saw his face, looming large
above me, fading against the morning light, then illuminat-
ing, as if suddenly struck by sunlight. Then I saw the cash in

the briefcase. *Don't fuck with us, Will.* I shook my head, trying to clear it of the image, trying to make it disappear, not be real. It wasn't. It couldn't be.

I felt the sheets against my naked skin, which was warm and still a little tingly from the night before. *That was real. That was real.*

"Jen," Will said again, and I noticed for the first time that he was holding my cell phone in his hand. "It's your sister."

"I—"

"You really need to talk to her this time," he said, and he put the phone into my shaking hand.

Twenty-nine

Hearing Kelly's voice, hearing it stretched and tight and muffled into tears, was almost more surreal than hearing Gary Adams that morning on the news, telling me that Will had been indicted. Hearing Kelly choke out that Dave was in the hospital, that Dave might be dying, felt like it could not be real, could not be happening.

"What do you mean?" I asked, flabbergasted, my brain still foggy from the dream. I could still smell the smoke and the beer from the inside of the bar, feel the thin, dirty paper of the money between my hands.

"He just collapsed in the kitchen," she said. "And he wouldn't get up."

I took a deep breath. "Where are you now?"

"St. Francis Hospital. In the waiting room. The doctors haven't come out. They haven't told me anything." She started sobbing into the phone. *St. Francis.* A hospital I hadn't been in since our mother was there twenty years earlier: radiation, chemo, mastectomy, chemo again. All at St. Francis.

"Take a deep breath," I said. "What can I do? Tell me what I can do."

"Can you come here?" she asked.

"Of course. I'll be there in twenty minutes."

"Oh, Jen," she said. "I'm sorry. I'm so sorry. I never should've said anything to Dad. I don't know what I was thinking. I—"

"It doesn't matter now," I said, and none of it did. I felt a little guilty for not having called her back, for staying so mad for so long. And hearing her voice, hearing her panic and her worry for Dave, my heart ached for her. "Just stay calm," I said. "Everything's going to be fine. I'll be there soon." I snapped the phone shut, and I held it there against my cheek for a moment.

"What is it? What happened?" Will asked. "She called three times before I answered, and when I picked up she was crying." He paused. "You were in such a sound sleep. I almost couldn't wake you."

To sleep, perchance to dream. But not this. Why this? I told Will what Kelly had said, and that I needed to rush to get to the hospital to be with her. "You go ahead to work, and I'll call you," I said, feeling newly awkward around him. I'd felt too much last night, then dreamed too much, and now I knew too much to really process or understand any of it.

He looked me solidly in the eye and said, "I'm coming with you. I'll drive." Then he wrapped me in a hug and whispered in my ear, "I'm sure Dave's going to be fine." He stood back, stared at me deeply, and he smiled. I knew what he was thinking, that last night had been amazing. He brushed my cheek with his thumb, and he leaned in and kissed me softly on the mouth.

It's what I was thinking, too, and for a minute I kissed him back. But then I thought about the dream, the money. "I have to get dressed," I said, pulling back. "I have to go."

In the car on the way to the hospital, Will and I didn't talk. The only sound was the roar of the heat trying to warm us in the chilly February air. I stared straight ahead and twisted the diamond stars that were still in my ears. *How did you get the money to pay for these, Will?*

Oblivious to my thoughts, he drove carefully and slowly through the slushy streets, keeping his eyes on the road.

When I walked into the waiting room, I didn't notice Kelly at first, but I saw my father, his arm around Sharon, who was drinking what looked to be a cup of coffee, not a rum and Coke. He looked right at me, but as soon as he caught my eye, I looked away. Then I heard Beverly's voice coming in the door behind us, the high-pitched sound of it, shrill like a wild animal, emitting something that was a cross between a cry and a scream. Kelly emerged from somewhere behind my father, still in the red sweatpants she'd probably slept in, her hair frizzy and piled on top of her head in a messy bun.

She saw me, and we walked toward each other. "Thanks for coming," she said. I reached in to hug her. She was cold, and she smelled like coffee, and I held on to her tightly, almost afraid to let her go.

"I'm so sorry," I whispered, and I was. It had been stupid, childish, ignoring her calls, staying mad at her for so long. She stood back and squeezed my hand.

"Do you know anything?" Will asked her.

"No." She shook her head, tears welling up in her eyes.

"He's my whole life, Jen." She looked at both of us as she said it. "I can't live without him. I can't."

"He's going to be fine." I hugged her again, wishing I could really comfort her, that I could really make something better for her. I wished I could dream the future instead of the past, wished I could know for sure. Because I knew Kelly was right, she couldn't live without him. *Please God, let him be okay.*

We sat down in a row of hard plastic chairs, Will on one side of me, Kelly on the other. Will put his arm around me, and I wondered for a moment what it would be like if it was Will who had collapsed instead of Dave. Tears instantly welled up in my eyes. I couldn't lose him. Couldn't lose Will. Couldn't. I leaned my head on his shoulder, and I leaned in so close that for a few minutes, it was easy to forget about the dream, easy to remember the way he'd felt against my body last night.

My father paced nervously, while Sharon walked over and stared at me and Will. She started to say something to me, then stopped. *Yes, I know, you're engaged,* I thought, surprised at her restraint, at her ability to check her good news, to understand that this was not the place nor the time. *And yes, I missed your party.*

"Where are the kids?" she finally said, to Kelly, not to me.

"They were still sleeping. My neighbor came over to the house to wait with them."

"That old lady who lives next door?" I asked. She nodded. Her next-door neighbor was seriously something like ninety years old, wrinkly and hunched over. Caleb and Jack could probably literally plow her over with one of their monster trucks.

Will cleared his throat. "Do you want me to go over there and stay with them?" he asked.

Beverly coughed loudly from the row of chairs directly

behind us. "Oh," Kelly said. "I don't know. I'm sure Alice
will be okay for a little while."

Will looked at me, and I pictured him holding the briefcase of money, and then dancing to *The Wiggles* with Sarah
Lynne, carrying Ara on his shoulders. *Whatever you did*, I
thought, staring at him now, *you are not a monster.*

Beverly stood up and shot Kelly a look. I thought about her
demanding that Hannah needed to wear a dress and get her
ears pierced, and I wanted to punch her.

And then a doctor walked out through the double doors.
"Mrs. Kaplan."

"Yes," Kelly and Beverly said in unison. They both stood
and moved toward the doctor, who rubbed his chin, seeming
increasingly perplexed.

"I'm his wife," Kelly said, as she approached the doctor.

"*I'm* his mother." Beverly edged her way just slightly in
front of Kelly. I was tempted to grab Beverly by the hair and
pull her back toward the rest of us, but I suppressed the urge.

The doctor shook his head and kept talking. "Dave suf-
fered a massive heart attack. He's stable now, but we think
he may have some blocked arteries. We're still running some
more tests, but I want to prepare you. He's probably going to
need bypass surgery."

"He's thirty-seven," Kelly gasped. *Will's age.* "That can't
be right."

"Well," the doctor said. "We see it more than you think.
Early onset heart disease. Could be genetic or lifestyle-
driven." He paused. "I'll come out when we know more." I
remembered that Dave's father, Stan, had had a heart attack
some years back, and it struck me, the way Dave had been the
one who'd succumbed to his bad genes, not Kelly.

"Oh, my baby," Beverly said. "Can I see him?"

The doctor nodded. "One at a time and not too long. He's still groggy."

Kelly blinked back tears and nodded resolutely. I put my arm around her. "He's going to be okay," I said. "The doctors are going to fix the problem, and then he's going to be fine."

"Kelly," Beverly interrupted me. "I'm going back to see him first, and then you can go."

"But I think I should—" Kelly started.

"Dear, I'm his mother. Someday when your children are grown, you'll understand. I'll come back out for you when I'm finished." She walked toward the area the doctor had indicated, not even waiting for a response.

"Why do you let her walk all over you like that?" I asked.

"I don't," Kelly said. "She's just upset, and . . ." I thought about the party dress, about Beverly's insistence that Will shouldn't be around the children.

"That's your husband," I said. "That's your husband in there."

"Oh, Jen, don't you think I know that?" Tears welled up in her eyes again.

"You're strong," I said to her. "Be strong." She sat back down in the chair and buried her head in her hands. "Kel," I said, "Dave wants you in there, not his mother."

I felt a tap on my shoulder, and looked up to see Sharon's big nose, practically in my face. "Jennifer, when you're done with your sister, your father has gone to the atrium and would like you to go speak with him." I glared at her. "Well," she huffed, holding her hands in the air. "Don't shoot the messenger."

Kelly looked up. "She'll be there in a minute, Sharon."

Sharon walked back to her seat, and I shot Kelly a look. "What?" She shrugged. "If I'm going to tell Beverly to go to hell, the least you can do is talk to Dad."

"She's right," Will said, putting his hand on my shoulder. "Do you want me to go with you?"

"No." I sighed. Because I knew having Will there would only make things worse.

As Kelly walked back to attempt to see Dave, I wandered toward the atrium.

I still remembered where it was, still remembered sitting on a long green couch sharing a yogurt with Kelly while our mother was in surgery, still remembered the feeling of dread, the sinking like a weight in my stomach, the sinking that came with knowing that life as we knew it would never be the same again.

The atrium had been updated in the past twenty years. The green couch had been replaced with two red velour armchairs, the cold white tile replaced with warm maple hardwoods, looking oddly similar to my living room. *How strange*, I thought, *hardwoods in a hospital*.

My father sat in one of the red armchairs, and other than him, the room was empty. I guessed it was too early in the morning for patients or visitors.

I tried to recall the last time I'd talked to him, the two of us in a room alone, and I couldn't. It might have been just before I met Will and just before he met Sharon. I'd gone back to his house for dinner one night, and Kelly and Dave had canceled at the last minute. He'd made steak, and the two of us had sat in relative silence, knives clanking against the edge of my mother's china. "How's work?" he'd asked.

"Good," I'd said. "You?"

"Good." He'd nodded.

And now here my father was, sitting in a red chair, wanting to talk to me. "Jenny." He stood up when he saw me. I tried not to look at him, tried not to meet his eyes, to see the disappointment that I knew would be there. "Why don't we have a seat?"

"I'm fine," I said, not wanting to give in, even the smallest bit.

"Okay," he said. He wrung his hands together.

"Look, I know you and Sharon are getting married, okay. So if that's all, I should get back."

"Your sister told you?"

"Yeah," I lied.

"You know I love Sharon," he said. *Good for you*, I thought, but I didn't say it out loud. "And I loved your mother, too. I did."

"You had a funny way of showing it," I said, my dry laugh coming out dangerously close to a sob.

"It was hard for me." He closed his eyes. "Watching someone you love in so much pain. I couldn't . . . Seeing your sister out there like this, it's killing me." I felt his words intensely, and turned my head so he wouldn't notice the tears welling up in my eyes. I wished for a moment that I could dream about my father, that I could be him for a night, feel the sharpness of his pain the way he felt it twenty years earlier.

"Okay," I said softly. "I really should get back."

"You've made up with your sister?" I nodded. "Good." He put his hand on my shoulder, and it was such an odd gesture coming from him. His hand was large, the skin wrinkled, dry, and cracked. The hand of a stranger, and yet the weight of it on my shoulder did not feel strange at all. "I just want you to know. I never cared that you were married to a lawyer or a judge or . . . I just wanted you to be happy. Are you happy, Jenny?" He didn't pause long enough for me to answer; his words tumbled out, hastily, as if he'd been holding them in so long that, finally, now that they were escaping, there was no stopping them. "I know I could've been a better father. I know I've made mistakes. But I've always loved you and your sister."

Love was a funny thing. That much I knew. "Okay," I whispered, part of me believing it, the other part of me really wanting to.

"I'm sorry if I don't always say it. If I haven't been there as much as I should've been." He sat down, as if suddenly it was too much for him to keep on standing, as if he was too old. When I looked at him, he did seem old. His hair and beard were nearly all white, his belly sagged out over his jeans, the skin under his eyes fell in folds. When had he gotten so old? "I know I handled everything all wrong with you girls after your mother died." He paused. "It's just you—you remind me so much of her. You always did. Your hair, eyes. Your expressions." He put his head in his hands. "You have your mother's smile."

"I do?" I sat down next to him. I never thought of myself in terms of my mother, only in terms of what I'd lost when she'd left me. I never thought that I was like her in any way except for a genetic curse, and then I felt this new pain, this inability to remember her completely.

"She would've been so proud of you, both of you girls."

"Do you really think so?" I whispered.

"I do," he said.

"Thank you for telling me this," I said, because this new information about my mother felt like a gift. He nodded and smiled, and I smiled back. *My mother's smile.*

"I want you to come to my wedding. You and Will. July 20, down in Boca."

Dave had just had a heart attack, and my father was thinking about his wedding? I wondered if Sharon had put him up to this, if she'd told him to get me when my defenses were down. I could just imagine her whiny little voice. *What will everyone think if Jenny doesn't come to the wedding? It was bad enough that she missed the engagement party.*

"That's what this is about?" I asked, feeling close to tears, my head throbbing so badly that I felt tears might break me. "Your wedding?" His smile slipped away, quickly replaced by the oh-so-familiar frown of disappointment. I sighed. "I really do have to get back. Kelly needs me."

"I know," he said, his voice coming out barely louder than a whisper.

When I got back to the waiting room, Beverly was wrapping herself in her fur coat and dragging her husband out by the arm. "What did you say to her?" I whispered to Kelly.

"What did Dad want?" she asked back, as if she hadn't even heard my question.

"Do I have Mom's smile?" I asked her.

She thought about it for a moment, and then she said, "I don't know. I'll have to find a picture. It's hard to remember her smiling."

Thirty

By noon, Dave was moved into a room, and the doctors determined that he did indeed need a triple bypass that would be performed the next day.

Kelly asked everyone to leave, because she was planning on spending the rest of the day with Dave. Alone. "Do you want me to watch the kids?" I asked. "Bring you anything?"

"No." She shook her head. "The kids are going to Beverly's."

"Beverly's?" I asked, wondering exactly what she'd said to her mother-in-law while I was in the atrium with our father.

"They love it there. They'll think it's a vacation." She paused. "Can you please come back tomorrow morning, and sit with me? During the surgery."

"Of course." I nodded. "And if you think of anything else, just call me."

"It's scary," Will said to me, as we walked carefully over ice patches in the parking lot.

"He's going to be all right, though? Don't you think?"

"He's tough," Will agreed. "And he has so much to live for." We got into the car, and I put my hands in front of the vents to warm them. "But I mean, Jesus Christ, he's my age," Will said. "Just to think that it can all be taken away from you. Just like that." I thought of the briefcase in the bar, of the way the money felt, of the disgusted feeling that Will felt when he'd touched it. "It's not the same, Jen," he said, as if he could read my mind. "Life. Life is short. Life is delicate."

I thought about what my father had said, about me being so similar to my mother. "I always thought I would die young," I said, feeling almost a little relieved that the truth, my fear, was finally out there, out in the open. "I mean my mother did, and I already had that lump."

"It was benign," Will said.

"But still." I shrugged. "Your destiny is your destiny." I paused. "I mean, didn't you ever think you might die in a car accident, after what happened to your parents?"

"No." He shook his head. "It was an accident. A fluke." He put his hand on my leg. "Lightning doesn't strike twice in the same place," he said. "God forbid."

"We can't help who we are. What we're made of. I mean, maybe Dave just has bad luck of the draw. I think his father had his heart attack in his forties."

"He'll pull through," Will said. "I know he will."

Neither one of us said anything else for a while. I stared out my window, at the white, frosty world swirling by, so white with snow that it looked like the world was blank, like there was nothing out there. Will gripped the steering wheel hard and stared straight ahead. When he turned into the driveway, he stopped and cleared his throat. "Is that Lisa?" he asked. "On the porch?"

I looked up and saw her, the red peacoat, the red hat. She was sitting on our stoop and shivering.

"Oh thank God you're all right." Lisa rushed toward me as I got out of the car. "When you didn't stop by this morning, I tried to call. I left you five voice mails."

I opened my purse to look for my cell phone and realized I must have left it in the bedroom. "I'm sorry," I said. "My brother-in-law, Dave, had a heart attack. We were at the hospital."

"Oh shit," she said. "Is he okay?"

"He will be. We hope."

Will walked in through the garage, and Lisa and I followed behind him. "I'm going to make some coffee," he said. "You ladies want some?"

"None for me." Lisa sighed. "Coffee's on my no-no list now."

"I'll have some," I told him. He leaned in for a quick kiss and went toward the kitchen, while Lisa and I sat down on the couch in the living room.

"Wow," Lisa said. "I'm amazed."

"Why?"

"You two. The way he looks at you." She shook her head.

I thought about the Will who had touched me last night and then about Will in my dream, about the money in the case, the way Lisa had said, only a few months ago, *That permanent disbarment is some serious shit.* Then something Lisa had said a few minutes earlier struck me funny. Coffee was on her no-no list now. Since when?

"Lisa," I said. "Are you—?"

She cut me off before I could finish. "I don't know how it happened," she said. "Well." She laughed, sounding almost giddy. "I know how it happened. But it was only one night. Last month. And it's not like we were trying."

"Does Barry know?" I asked her.

"No." She shook her head. "Not yet." She reached out for my hand. "I'm terrified it will happen again."

"It won't," I told her.

"You don't know that."

I thought about what Will had said in the car. "It won't," I told her, feeling so sure in my heart that for her what had happened really had been a fluke. "Lightning doesn't strike twice in the same place."

After Lisa left, Will and I sat close on the couch and sipped our coffee. I leaned into him, the warmth of his body radiating over me. I thought about Lisa, and the new little life that had sprung up inside her, that I knew was going to bring her back to life, too. I considered that if I got pregnant, our little babies would grow up together and play together and go to school together. It all seemed like a very nice fantasy, if I didn't let myself think about the other half, about what people in Deerfield believed that Will had done. Or the absolute truth, whatever that might be, of what Will had actually done.

Part of me wanted to know this truth, and part of me didn't want this moment, this one small fantasy, to end. Will put his hand on my leg. "I'll take the rest of the day off," he whispered. "We can get back into bed."

"No, I shouldn't. What if Kelly needs something?"

"We'll take the phone with us," he said, stroking back my hair, kissing my neck.

He might be a criminal, I thought. *You don't even know him at all.* He leaned over and kissed me on the mouth, softly at first, then harder.

I stopped thinking, and I kissed him back.

★ ★ ★

I was lying naked, on my side in the bed, Will's arm around me. I stared at my phone on my night table, willing it to ring, willing Kelly to need something. It stayed silent.

I heard Will's soft and easy breathing in my ear. *Don't fall asleep*, I willed myself, and then, when it was clear that I was going to, I chanted Kelly's name, over and over again in my head.

But in the seconds before sleep, I had a thought not about Kelly, Kat, Lisa, or even Will. But about myself. About this strange feeling I had, a feeling that settled in my stomach and washed over my body, a sudden and intense melting, like sunshine hitting snow.

I was lying in a bed. I looked around. White walls, small TV hanging from the ceiling, and a sign by the door, "St. Francis Hospital: Rules for Visitors."

"Do you know where you are?" a woman asked.

"Yes." I nodded. "What happened?" I asked. "Where's Dave?"

"Dave?" she said. "Can you tell me your name?"

For a minute, I was stumped. Who was I? Lisa? Kelly? And then I caught a glimpse in a mirror hanging over a sink, and I was myself. Jennifer Daniels Levenworth.

"Do you know your name?" the woman repeated.

I nodded. "Jennifer," I said. "Jennifer Daniels Levenworth."

"Very good," she said. "What's the last thing you remember?"

I remembered Will's hand running up my thigh, and then feeling him inside me. But I wasn't going to tell her that, so I said, "Dave. My brother-in-law had a heart attack. That's why I'm here. Isn't it?"

She shook her head. "Do you remember getting your hair washed at the salon? Pierce Avenue, I think."

I nodded. "That was months ago," I said. I heard Jo's voice in my ear. "Isn't that your husband?"

"Yes," she said, seeming oddly perplexed. "It was."

"Who are you?" I asked.

"I'm Ethel," she said. "Ethel Greenberg." I looked at her. She was no Ethel Greenberg. She was middle-aged with red curly hair, and verging on morbidly obese.

"You're not Ethel," I said.

She pointed to her name tag, which clearly read in bold red letters "Ethel Greenberg." "I'm a social worker," she said. "I've been checking in on you. Trying to help your family and your friends. Your husband." I looked around for him, for Will. "He went home to get some dinner," she said, as if she could read my mind. "But he's been here with you, a lot." She paused. "You're lucky, you know, to have someone like that." I thought that I should ask her why I was here, and how long I'd been here, but before I could say anything, I heard a knock at the door.

"Come in," Ethel said. I looked up, and there was Will. Tall, handsome, curly-haired Will. "There he is," Ethel said, smiling. "He can't stay away."

He saw me staring, and he ran toward the bed. "She's awake," he said to Ethel. Then to me, "You're awake."

"Yes." Ethel nodded. "It's only been a few moments. I'll go get the nurse and leave you two."

Ethel waddled out, and Will took her place by the bed. He buried his head in my chest, and when he sat back up, he was crying. "Jen," he said. "Jen. Jen." He paused. "I've been so scared of losing you."

He put his hand on my earlobe and fingered a star earring.

"Hey there, you with the stars in your eyes," I sang softly.

"You heard me," he said. "You heard me sing it when I put them in your ears last night." He paused. "Ethel said you could hear us, but I wasn't sure."

"Of course I heard you," I said. "In Il Romano." In the dim wash of candlelight, I'd watched the stars glow.

"The doctor said you were dreaming. You were dreaming, Jen. You were here last night. You've been here for a while."

I shook my head. "I'm so tired," I said. "I'm sorry. I need to sleep."

He squeezed my hand and leaned down and kissed my cheek. "Just promise me you'll wake up," he said.

Thirty-one

J en," Will said, shaking my shoulder. "Wake up."
    It took me a moment to react, and then I opened my eyes
and looked around. Blue curtains, maple hardwood floors,
blue damask comforter. My bedroom. The first glow of day-
light peeked through the window. "What time is it?" I asked.

"Almost seven," he said. "You slept all night. You must've
been exhausted. I tried to wake you for dinner, but I couldn't
get you up."

I sat up, realizing that my stomach was empty, that I hadn't
eaten anything since dinner at Il Romano. "I'm starving," I
said.

"Do you want me to make you something. Eggs? While
you get ready to go to the hospital."

The hospital. The dream came back to me and hit me,
crushing me like a boulder rolling all too quickly down the
side of a mountain. And then I remembered what Ethel had
said, about that philosopher who'd dreamed he was a butter-

fly, and then when he awoke, wondered which it was, if he was a man dreaming he was a butterfly or a butterfly dreaming he was a man. *The mind plays tricks on you*, Ethel had said. *Sometimes things are not as they seem.*

"No, no eggs," I said. "I'll just grab a granola bar."

"Well, at least let me make you some coffee." He paused. "And I can come with you, if you want."

"No." I shook my head. "You should go to work. I'll be fine."

He hugged me and whispered into my hair, "If you need anything, you call me."

"I will," I agreed.

While Will went downstairs to make coffee, I called Ethel and left her a message, telling her I was stopping over in forty-five minutes. It's not so much that I wanted answers—though I did—but that I wanted to see her, see that she was still there, in her converted garage among her shelves and shelves of pill bottles. I wanted to make sure she was real.

I rang the bell on Ethel's garage first, and when she didn't answer, I walked up to the front door of the house and rang that one. Two rings later, she opened the door in her bathrobe, holding on to her cup of coffee. "Jennifer," she said, sounding surprised to see me.

"I left you a message," I said.

She held open the door and ushered me to come in. "What is it?" she asked. "Is everything all right?"

"I need you to tell me what you meant, that thing you said about the man and the butterfly." She looked perplexed. "The man dreaming he was a butterfly—"

"Oh, that," she said.

"I mean, how do you know the difference?" I lowered my

voice to a whisper. "I'm not sure I know the difference." I wondered if this was real, standing here with Ethel, or if I was dreaming now, if what was real was me in the hospital for whatever reason.

"Oh, Jennifer. We need to get you off that herb," she said. "I meant for it to calm you, and look at you, you're a mess over these dreams. I want you to stop taking them immediately." She paused. "And I want to check your meridians, see where all this anxiety is coming from." She put her hands over my stomach. They were warm and solid hands. "Could be the liver."

I wondered when Ethel checked my body, my meridians as she called them, with her electrical impulses if she could figure out why my dreams had gone crazy, telling me the truth about other people, or maybe just the truth about myself. "I have to go," I told her. "My sister's husband is having surgery this morning, and I promised her I'd be there."

"Okay." She nodded. "I have an opening on Friday. Stop back then, and we'll check everything out." She paused. "You should embrace your dreams, Jennifer. You're very lucky. People who dream can figure things out, can dig deep into their subconscious in ways that other people cannot." She paused for a minute, as if wanting to let what she'd said settle in the air. "Namaste."

I saw Beverly and Stan first, sitting in the waiting room, Beverly huddled into her husband, her fur coat on her lap. "Where's my sister?" I asked. Beverly ignored me, and Stan pointed in the direction of the atrium. I nodded a quick thank-you toward him, then stopped. "If you guys are here, where are the kids?"

"With your father." Stan shrugged.

I pictured Caleb, Jack, and Hannah throwing simultaneous tantrums, in a circle around Sharon, and my father sitting idly by. But I didn't know that for sure. I had absolutely no idea what kind of grandparent my father really was, a thought that made me feel a little sad.

In the atrium, Kelly sat in one of the red chairs my father had been in the day before. "Hey," I said, waving. "You all right? I saw Beverly and Stan in the waiting room."

She shrugged. "It's her son. I can't tell her not to be here."

"I know." I nodded.

"Do you remember waiting here, when Mom was in surgery?" I nodded again. "Do you remember how it felt?"

"I was terrified," I said. "But I pretended not to be because you were so calm."

"I wasn't calm," she said. "I wasn't calm."

"Dave's going to be fine." I reached out for her hand.

We sat there for a little while in silence, until I finally said, "Do you want me to get you something to eat, or some magazines to read?"

She shook her head, then shrugged. "I don't know. Maybe some magazines. To pass the time."

"I'll go down to the gift shop."

"Tabloids," she said. "Something really trashy."

"Of course."

I remembered my way to the gift shop, just down the hall from the atrium. I remembered Kelly and I had walked in there together, just after our mother came out of surgery. We'd pooled a week's worth of lunch money and had bought her a miniature teddy bear with a "Get Well Soon" stick balloon in its hands.

Our mother had gushed over how much she loved it, over how it made her feel better already, and I could still remember the nausea I'd felt swelling in my stomach, seeing the bandages across her chest, the stiff way she sat up in the bed.

I shook the memory away. I hated it when the bad ones came, when the good ones seemed to be buried in my mind so deep that I had a hard time locating them, even when I wanted to. *Her voice. Her smile.*

Then I looked up, and at the other end of the gift shop by the door, I saw the woman from my dream. The faux, fat Ethel Greenberg. She was dressed in a red tent dress that clashed with her red curly hair. She caught my eye, and she smiled, then walked out the door. I turned to run after her, to glimpse her name tag, but by the time I got to the hallway, she was already gone.

As I walked back into the gift shop and picked through the tabloids, I considered my options.

A. I was dreaming now. In reality, I was the one in the hospital.

B. I was awake now. My dream last night had been a combination of things my psyche had dug up, a fat woman I'd probably seen in the hospital yesterday. I had been taking an herb for the last several months that somehow allowed me to experience moments of my friends' lives.

Either possibility felt mildly insane. I could not be dreaming now. How could I be? Everything felt so real, the smell of Lysol and urine in the hospital corridor, the sounds buzzing over the intercom.

Everything else had felt real, too, all the moments I'd been inside my friends' heads, their bodies, their minds. And the moments when I hadn't—the aftermath of these moments—Lisa taking too many pills, Kat drinking her chai tea, Will kissing me with passion.

I paid for the magazines and walked back to the atrium to

find Kelly. But the room was empty, so I walked back to the waiting room.

When I got there, I saw Beverly holding on to Kelly, Beverly sobbing. I pulled Kelly away, and Beverly fell onto Stan. "What happened?" I asked.

Kelly shook her head, as tears streamed down her face. She tried to speak, but she couldn't. I hugged her, let her hold on to me, let her cry into my hair, until finally it was Stan who said it. "A stroke," he whispered, as if the words didn't make sense, even to him.

Thirty-two

I called Will to come pick me up because I felt too shaky to drive. My head was pounding, and I heard Stan's words ringing in my head over and over again. This could not be real. This could not be happening. This had to be a dream.

Will walked into the waiting room, and when I saw him, I ran to him, fell into his chest, felt his arms around me, smelled his pine smell. "Where's Kelly?" he asked.

"She already left with Beverly and Stan to go get the children."

"The children," Will echoed, his voice thick with something I'd never heard from him before, a sense of loss and regret that came across much deeper than anything he'd felt after losing his career in law.

"I don't know how they'll survive it," I whispered to him, all the same knowing that they would have to, that Kelly and I had had to.

"They will," he said. "Children are resilient."

"This is why," I whispered. "This is why I never wanted to have children."

He pulled back and looked confused, then mildly alarmed. "Dave?"

I shook my head. "Parents die," I said. "It's not fair." I started crying for the first time, sobbing into his shirt.

"Jen, you're not making any sense," he said. But I was; it made perfect sense to me. Why bring someone, another person into the world, when we were all such imperfect beings, all riddled with disease or prone to accidents? Why make someone love you, someone young, someone helpless, when all of that love could be taken away? Just like that.

"It wasn't you, Will," I said. "It was never you. You were never the reason why."

"No." He shook his head, resolute. "It was. I was never home. I was never there for you."

"I never let you be," I said softly. I could've told him not to run for judge. I could've said no to moving to Deerfield. It wasn't really that I was scared he would resent me for it. No, I was afraid of something else altogether. I was afraid to let him get too close, to let him love me too much. Because then, when something happened to me, he'd be shattered, left with nothing.

"Come on." He held on to my arm and pulled me toward the door. "Let's get you home."

Will had come in his Daniels and Sons truck, not even taking the time to get his own car after he'd gotten my call. His new devotion to me seemed astounding. "Here, let me help you up," he said. I let him, his hands holding on to me feeling like the only thing holding me together.

★ ★ ★

When we got home, Will wanted to make me something to eat, but I was too tired to eat. This feeling of exhaustion overtook me, and all I could do, all I wanted to do was sleep. "You're still tired?" Will said, unable to hide his disbelief.

My whole body felt heavy, and my head ached. It was the way Lisa had felt, as if I were moving under water, trying so hard to push my way through something so thick, so heavy.

"I'm worried about you," Will said.

"Dave is dead," I said. The words sounded awful and so final when I heard them in my voice. "Just let me sleep."

I curled up under the covers, and I immediately felt myself drifting off.

I was lying in the hospital bed. I saw the white walls, the TV hanging from the ceiling, the mirror over my sink. I heard someone, and I turned and saw Fat Ethel sitting by the bed. "You're back," she said.

"What do you mean?"

"You fell back into the coma." She stood up. "Quite the anomaly you are. Keeping us all guessing." She shook her head.

"Coma?" I asked. "What happened? How did I get here?" I sat up too fast, and my head was killing me.

"Whoa, slow down," she said. "You remember that morning in the salon?" I nodded. "Jennifer, you had a stroke." A stroke?

"When you were getting your hair washed," she said. I heard the water, rushing, rushing in my ears, the way it had that morning in the salon. "It happens sometimes if the neck is overextended, a blood vessel can burst. It's called a beauty parlor stroke."

"But that was months ago," I said.

"Yes." She nodded. "You've been in a coma since then." She paused. "We weren't sure if you were ever going to wake up. And then you did. And then you went back out again."

"Is this real?" I asked her. When she didn't answer, I tried another question. "Where's Will?"

"I think he had to go to work." Work. "But I think your sister is here."

As if on cue, there was a knock on the door, and Kelly stepped in. She saw me, and she smiled brightly. She looked different. Thinner. Her hair was much shorter, chin-length. "Oh thank God," she said, glancing quickly at me, then at Fat Ethel.

"I'll be back to check on you," Ethel said, and then it was just Kelly and me in the room.

"How are you feeling?" Kelly asked. Her eyes, like saucers, gave her away. She was worried. Kelly reached up and smoothed back my hair, such a motherly gesture.

"I'm still so tired," I said. "Do you mind if I close my eyes?"

"Just promise me you'll wake up," she said. "I need you."

When I woke up the next morning, it was snowing. I got out of bed and watched the flakes fall plump and gracefully from the sky like white-winged butterflies floating past our bedroom window. Will must've heard me get up, because I heard his footsteps behind me, felt his arms around my waist. He kissed the top of my head.

"What if you hadn't gotten indicted?" I whispered to him. "What do you think would've happened to us?"

"I don't know, Jen," he said. "I honestly don't know." He paused. "But the job wasn't the reason why we fell apart."

"I know," I said, spinning around to face him. "It was my fault."

"It was both of us." He touched my chin softly with his thumb.

"I didn't want you to get too attached. In case something happened to me."

"The lump was benign," he said. "It didn't mean anything." He paused. "And even if it did, it wouldn't have changed how I felt about you."

"Sometimes, I wondered," I said out loud, for the very first time. "The way you proposed to me. If you really meant it, or if you just felt you needed to save me."

"I really loved you," he said. "I really love you."

After Will went downstairs to make coffee, I walked into the computer room, sat down, and quickly Googled "strokes and hair salons." Article after article came up, of something, a rare phenomenon, exactly what Fat Ethel had said in my dream, the beauty parlor stroke.

I clicked on the first one and scanned through words: *hyperextended neck, carotid artery tear, blood clot.*

It was a real thing, and how had I known that? I must've read an article about it before, I reasoned. As Ethel said, dreams were only our subconscious coming out, coming through. But no matter how hard I tried, I couldn't remember ever having heard that term before, *beauty parlor stroke.*

I walked into the bathroom and turned the shower on, undressed, and stared at my naked body in the mirror.

I am real, I thought. *Right now, I am real.*

★ ★ ★

When I got to Kelly's house, everyone was already there. Sharon answered the door and ushered me in, the absence of her chiding almost disconcerting, almost unreal. After a minute she said, "Thank God for the children."

"Why would you say that?" I frowned.

"Well, because they're a part of him. Without them he really would be gone forever."

I'd never thought of it that way before, that without me and Kelly, every single scrap of our mother would've evaporated into dust. I thought about what my father had said at the hospital, that I was a lot like her, and for the first time, I considered that something Sharon said might have had some merit.

In Kelly's living room, Beverly sat on the couch still wrapped in her fur stole, talking loudly on her cell phone to what seemed like Dave's sister, Kathleen. My father sat opposite her on the love seat, while the kids sat on the floor, entranced, watching *The Wiggles*. "Where's Stan?" I asked, but nobody answered me.

I closed my eyes, and I saw the way his mouth had moved so slowly yesterday in the hospital waiting room. *A stroke.* A stroke.

"Your sister's upstairs," Beverly said, when she hung up the phone.

I found Kelly lying in her bed, in the dark. "Kel," I whispered. "Are you okay?"

"Jen," she said. "You're here."

"Of course I'm here." I walked toward the bed and sat on the edge, next to her. The memory of the day our mother died flooded my brain, sudden and vivid and irrevocable: Kelly and I sitting on her bed after we knew she was gone; Kelly putting her arm around me and telling me that everything was going to be fine. *I don't believe you*, I had said.

I know, she'd whispered back. *But we'll have each other.*

Dave had walked into the room, sat down on the other side of her, hugged her, pulling her toward him, away from me. And that was the moment when I first understood I would never have more than a piece of her, that all I'd really have to rely on completely was myself. A thought that had utterly terrified me.

"Jen," she said now, "I can't do this alone."

"I know," I told her, knowing how hard it was, how I had felt alone for so long. "But you're not alone," I whispered. "You have me. We have each other." I heard her voice in my dream, *I need you.*

I lay down on the bed next to her, watching the ceiling for a while, staring at the way the fan stood still, listening to the rumble of the heat coming through the vents. I closed my eyes and wished I could take it all back, all the jealousy I'd had of her and Dave, all the moments I'd spent hating her just a little bit or fighting with her. Because now I knew, her happiness had nothing to do with mine; I had always been the one getting in my own way, keeping other people at a distance.

The snow had started to accumulate as I left Kelly's, but I knew I had to stop at Ethel's, even though the roads were slippery. I hoped she would read my meridians right now, tell me what it was exactly. Maybe it was my liver, as Ethel had thought the other day, or maybe I had a brain tumor. That would explain it all, the crushing headaches, the dreams, the slippery grip I now felt I had on reality.

"How's your brother-in-law?" Ethel asked, as soon as I

walked into her office. This time, it seemed she was expecting me, though I wasn't supposed to come back until Friday.

"He's dead," I said.

Ethel nodded, a nod of resignation, as if it was something she already knew, as if she were a fortune teller, not an herbalist. I looked around the room and noticed right away that it was different, that the shelves were nearly empty, the herbs half packed into moving boxes scattered carelessly around the cement floor.

"You're moving?" I asked. She nodded. "You can't move," I said.

"Lie down, Jennifer." She pointed to her makeshift medical table.

As I lay down, I said, "You can't go. I need you."

She shook her head. "No," she said. "We're almost done here."

Ethel hooked up the machine, attaching the electrodes to different parts of my body, one at a time. My liver, my lungs, my kidneys, my heart, all came up clean. And then she checked my brain. "Ahh," she said. "Here is the problem."

"What is it?" I asked, alarmed. "A tumor?"

She shook her head. "Lie back," she whispered. I did what she said, and I heard her rummaging around on the shelves, and in the boxes, clinking through bottles of herbs, until she found what she was looking for.

"Will this help?" I asked her, as I felt her rubbing a foul-smelling tincture on my temples. "Will this help me know what's real and what's not?"

"Jennifer," she said. "Close your eyes." She continued rubbing. I felt my body relax, the way it did before I took the calming herbs, before I was about to dream. "You know what is real," she said. "You are in control of your own destiny."

No, that didn't seem right. Not when there was so much out of our control.

"Not death," I said. "Not dying."

"Sometimes," Ethel said softly, "you just have to choose to want to live. Choose it completely, with your mind, your body, your spirit." She continued rubbing, and for the first time my headache began to subside. "Just embrace it," she whispered, and for a brief moment it was not Ethel's voice that I heard at all, but my mother's, so soft and small and so uniquely hers. "You control your destiny. You control your destiny," she said. "Just trust what your mind already knows. Trust it completely. You know what is real."

This is what I know is real: Will. I love Will.

And that was the last thing I remembered thinking before the darkness.

Thirty-three

I opened my eyes, and Will was standing there, by the window, watching the snow. He turned and smiled at me. "Good morning," he said.

A steady sense of relief washed over me as soon as I saw him. "Will," I said, my voice croaking out, slowly, scratchily.

He walked toward the bed, and he took my hand in his, brushing my knuckles lightly with his fingertips. "Good news," he said. "You can go home soon."

"Home?" I echoed.

"Ethel's going to set you up with some physical therapy."

"Physical therapy?" I pictured Ethel rubbing my temples.

"You'll need to regain your strength," he said. I looked around, saw the hospital rules for visitors on the door, and then I realized that was not the Ethel he meant. *Your subconscious plays tricks on you. Everything is not what it seems.* "But the doctors say you'll be back to playing tennis by summer."

"Tennis." I thought about Amber and Bethany applying

their lipstick in the mirror, and I knew I never wanted to go back there, not even if they still wanted me. *You are in control of your own destiny.* That was not a life. That was not the life I wanted.

He leaned closer. "Jen, there's something I need to tell you."

I nodded. "Dave is dead," I said, remembering the feeling of Kelly lying next to me on the bed.

"Dave?" He frowned. "No."

"Are you sure?"

He frowned again. "Dave is fine, but his father passed away a few days ago."

"Stan." I pictured his face, the way it contorted as he said the word *stroke*. "Did he have another heart attack?"

Will nodded. "You really could hear us. The doctors were right."

I wondered what else I heard, what was real and what wasn't. "Will, who else was here besides you?"

"Your sister, of course. And Kat and her girls, and Lisa came by a lot. Your dad and Sharon came by a few times, and Dr. Horowitz stopped by once. Oh, and so did Janice."

I thought about my father, about the way his voice had sounded when he told me I had my mother's smile. Had I really heard him say this?

"And of course Ethel. My goodness, she's been a godsend, that woman."

I heard a knock at the door, and I looked up and saw Fat Ethel standing there. She walked in, breathing heavily as if the move from the door to the bed was too much for her. She hugged Will, then leaned in and hugged me. "I just wanted to wish you luck," she whispered in my ear.

"Thank you," I said, still feeling uneasy around this Ethel, the fake one who seemed astoundingly real to Will.

"Namaste," she said.

I pulled back, startled for a moment, and then I said, "You know, I always wondered what that meant, namaste."

She leaned up and smiled. "It is a coming together," she said. "Of mind, body, and spirit. A recognition of this in one another."

Choose it completely, with your mind, your body, your spirit, I heard the other Ethel saying.

"That makes sense," I said. "That makes perfect sense."

After Ethel left, I fell asleep. I didn't dream, and when I woke up, it was dark, and I was still in the hospital bed. Will was sleeping in a blue vinyl chair, his mouth open, his neck askew. "Will," I whispered into the darkness. "Will."

"Hmmm?" he murmured softly, smiling, even in his state of half sleep, as if he had been waiting for me to call to him forever.

It occurred to me that the last thing he remembered, he knew of us, was our nonargument when I goaded him on about Janice's baby. Thinking about our life, our relationship then, brought tears to my eyes. I thought for a moment that we'd gotten it all back, and yet what if none of that had been real?

"Will," I whispered louder.

He opened his eyes. "What is it? Are you feeling okay?"

I patted the space on the bed next to me, wanting him to get in beside me, wanting him to hold me, the way he had in what I was beginning to understand was only a dream world.

He stood up and walked toward me, and he sat at the edge of the bed. I grabbed on to his hand, held it tightly. "I've had a lot of time to think or dream or something," I whispered.

He nodded. "I hate the way things were between us before. I don't want to go back to that."

"That's what I was trying to tell you earlier," he said, leaning in closer, stroking my cheek with his hand. "I'm not a judge anymore."

"You got indicted. And there was money. In a briefcase?"

"Indicted?" He chuckled. "No, but you really did hear me didn't you?" I shrugged. "The money in the briefcase." He sighed. The image, the moment in the bar still felt resoundingly clear to me. I held my breath, waiting for the truth, and it was strange the way I felt as if I'd been waiting for it forever, though I guessed the absolute reality was, it had been only a few seconds.

"You know it wasn't about the law anymore. It was all so corrupt. Lawyers wanting to buy me, and the Feds wanting to use me to catch them. That's why I had that money—it was all a setup. And I'd had enough." He cleared his throat. "That and you being here. Well, I just couldn't do it anymore." He lowered his voice to a whisper. "I couldn't be away from you." He paused. "I've been working a little bit for Dave, selling weed control of all things. He and Kelly insisted. They said I needed to get out of the hospital a little bit. You're not mad, are you?"

"Oh, Will," I said. "I never cared that you were a judge. I just want to be with you. I just want us to be us again."

"Me too," he whispered, lying down on the bed next to me, leaning in close, putting his arms around me, the way I'd dreamed him doing. "Me too."

My first night at home, I checked my medicine cabinet for any signs of herbs before getting into bed. But there was nothing there. Somehow, it was Western medicine that saved me, brought me back to life. Back into a real life.

Will and the doctors said I would make a complete recovery, that what happened to me was a fluke, and also the result of a poorly set up washing station at the salon, something for which Will said we could sue, but I'd already told him that it felt like the wrong thing to do. My neck had simply been at the wrong angle, and something had snapped. Something had to give. As Ethel the herbalist once told me, or maybe it was Ethel the social worker, a small crack was rarely just a crack, but the result of something bigger, something worse, lying just beneath the surface.

Now I got into bed, and I cuddled up next to Will. I rubbed his leg with my foot, which did feel oddly Jell-O-y, and probably in need of more physical therapy. I thought about my jogs in Oak Glen park, and how they'd felt so real. But I knew they weren't, or my legs wouldn't feel this way. Maybe I would start jogging there, though, and maybe when I was over there, I'd stop by Kelly's more often, too.

Will rolled toward me, and he stroked my cheek with his thumbs, just like he had on Valentine's Day. "I'm so glad you're home," he whispered. "I missed you so much."

"Make love to me," I whispered back, wanting to recapture it, the magic I'd felt that night.

"Jen, I don't know. The doctors said to take it easy for a while—"

I cut him off by kissing him, and rolling on top of him. I pushed my body into him. He groaned, and ran his hands across my back.

Then we were naked, tangled up in each other, my body warm and tingling the way it was on Valentine's Day. Will snored lightly, and I lay there, with my eyes wide open. I was afraid to sleep here, in my own bed, where I remembered falling asleep and dreaming so many times. The dreams themselves still seemed so incredibly real, so incredibly close.

So I got out of bed, made my way into the kitchen, and made myself some coffee. Then I wandered into the computer room and checked the drawer where I kept my dream notebook, only to find it filled with a few empty reporter's notebooks.

There was one notebook, though, sitting by the computer on the desk. I flipped through it, but it was not filled with the dreams I so vividly remembered writing down, but instead notes for the last article I'd written for *City Style*, about Chinese medicine, herbs, and a little old Jewish lady who'd practiced it. As I flipped through them, I remembered: I had visited her once, all in the name of journalism. She had checked my meridians and told me that she'd felt something there, underneath, and she'd even given me herbs. But I'd never taken them, never gone back. I'd written the article, and then promptly fell into my life in Deerfield.

I flipped through the rest of the notepad, and these notes were followed by some shopping lists and some auction phone numbers. And, on the very last page, scrawled messily, there was an idea for a novel and some quotes about dreams—one by D. H. Lawrence wondering whether dreams resulted in thoughts or vice versa, and one about an ancient Chinese philosopher who once dreamed he was a butterfly.

I remembered what it felt like to write my own dreams down, how it had felt oddly free, to write something again, to write something that was purely mine, entirely for me. I wished that had been real, that I had that notebook here with me now.

I turned on the computer, and in the glow of the half moonlight, I opened up a fresh document and started to type, before I forgot, this crazy story about what was real and what was dreaming, about how much you could know about another person and about yourself, about the difference between being a man and being a butterfly, and how sometimes there was no distinction, no visible difference at all. *The transformation of things*, I heard Ethel say.

I typed until morning, until I heard Will's alarm go off, heard Will's footsteps coming toward me.

"You're writing again," he whispered, sounding equal parts astounded and relieved.

"Yes," I said. "I think I am." I looked up from the computer to smile at him, and suddenly the exhaustion overtook me.

Will followed me into the bedroom and lay next to me on the bed. He held my hand and stroked my palm with his fingers. His touch made me feel alive, awake again. "What now?" I whispered. "You can't sell weed control forever." I was stating a truth that I had never been able to bring myself to say in my dream world.

"I don't know." He shrugged. "Maybe I could."

"Tell me one thing you want," I whispered.

He hesitated, then said, "I think I might like to work with kids. Be a teacher." He almost put it out there as a question, because I knew he knew that the old Jen, the one he last remembered being here on that warm October day, would've scoffed at the idea.

"That's a good idea," I said. "I think you'd be good at that."

"You know, summers and weekends off. Good hours." He paused. "We'd probably have to move."

"That's okay," I said.

"But I want to be around more, if we have kids," he said. "And even if we don't, I don't want to miss everything."

"Good." I rolled over, so my body was leaning close into his. "I don't want you to."

"What about you?" he asked. "What's one thing you want?"

"This," I said, snuggling in closer to him. "You. And I think I do want to write still, finish that novel."

"That's two things." He laughed. "No fair." He paused. "I want you to have it all, Jen, everything you've ever wanted."

"I know," I said, feeling groggy again and too close to sleep to really make the words come out the way they were supposed to.

"Sweet dreams," he whispered, kissing my hair.

Let's hope not.

If I dreamed, I had no memory of it when I woke up, feeling utterly rested, my head completely clear and not throbbing at all. Will lay next to me, awake, and I wondered if he'd been watching me sleep.

"Are you hungry?" he whispered. "Can I make you something?" I was hungry. Starving. So I nodded and thanked him. "Stay here," he said. "I'll bring it up to you in bed." Part of me wanted to protest, but I saw the way his face, his eyes lit up, and I knew that this would make him happy, taking care of me.

He stood up, and I noticed, for the first time, the two little porcelain figurines teetering on the edge of his night table just behind his alarm clock: "The Perfect Family" and "Afterglow."

This sense of panic overtook me as I wondered which reality I was in. I heard Ethel's voice. *Was he a man, dreaming he was a butterfly, or a butterfly, dreaming he was man?*

"Where did you get those?" I asked Will, pointing to the figurines.

"Oh, these?" He shrugged, picking them up. "I bought them for you in the hospital gift shop. Here." He handed them to me. "They're yours. They're silly, but . . ."

I heard Ethel's voice again: *You make your own reality.*

"No," I said, taking them and holding them between my palms. "They're not silly at all."

Thirty-four

It is swampy in Boca Raton in July, and I sit in my white folding chair and fan myself with the program. "Do you want a drink?" Will asks. "I can get you a water from inside the hotel."

"Yes." I rest my hand on my growing belly. "We're thirsty."

He kisses my forehead. "I love you," he whispers.

"I love you, too." I watch him walk away, watch with wonderment that he still looks cool and perfectly calm, his hair just a little curlier from the humidity.

I take my phone out of my purse and check for messages, and I sigh when there aren't any. Lisa is due any day, and she promised to text me as soon as she goes into labor.

Just as Will gets back, the music starts, and Dave turns around from in front of us, holding the video camera steady. Kelly walks out in her lavender bridesmaid's dress, holding on to flower girl Hannah, and flanked by ring bearers Caleb and Jack.

"Too bad your father didn't want Sharon to stress you out," Will says, "or you could've been up there, too."

"Ha," I say. "Too bad."

Kelly looks overwhelmed, but when she sees Dave, her face lights up, and she blows him a kiss.

Sharon and my father walk down the aisle together, their arms linked, their faces glowing in a sheen of sweat and maybe love.

And then they stand under the chuppah, vowing, in front of the rabbi, all their senior friends, and us, to love, honor, and cherish each other in sickness and in health.

Will catches my eye at that part, and I smile at him. I wonder if my father will be able to do it this time around, and though I'm not a fan of Sharon's, I'm still rooting for him to change, rooting for him to be the man that he thinks he might be able to be.

We've been talking more since I woke up, and though our relationship is still far from perfect, I can't get over the fact that he came to visit me in the hospital, that he was there for me, in a way he never was for my mother. Maybe that was his way of apologizing, and maybe mine is simply showing up, not missing his wedding, not missing what might be a moment of happiness for him. I now understand how easily happiness can come and go.

Before I filled his prescription for prenatal vitamins, I took Dr. Horowitz up on his offer to get the genetic testing. I wanted to choose to live, to choose completely, as Ethel had said, and knowing seemed like the best way to do it.

The test came back negative, but as Dr. Horowitz said, it did not mean for sure that I'd never get breast cancer like my mother. "There are no real promises in life, Jennifer," he'd said. "No guarantees." That, I understood.

As Kelly once said, I could always get hit by a bus, and having a stroke as I got my hair washed, I kind of did. Yet, somehow, I am still here, still breathing and healthy. As Ethel said, I'm the only one who can take charge of what I want. I'm in control of my own reality, my own destiny.

I look up when I hear clapping, and then I watch as my father breaks the glass with his foot.

I hear my cell phone buzz in my purse, so I take it out, my heart beating quickly in my chest in anticipation for Lisa. But I see it's a text from Kat instead, who is only two states away at the beach in Hilton Head with Danny and the girls. *Bored out of my fucking mind! Who said staring at the ocean is relaxing??? Can't wait till U guys get here!! Danny and the girls say hi. XOXO.*

"What's that?" Will leans over my shoulder.

"Kat." I laugh. "She's bored at the beach. She says she can't wait for us to arrive."

"Oh, you know she's loving every minute of it." He laughs. Just after I woke up, Kat quit her job and got a part-time one with the *Inquirer*, doing a column about motherhood that she can write from home. *This is all your fault, you know*, she called me and said, just after she got the new job. *You making me reevaluate what the fuck I was doing with my life.*

I thought about our conversation in the coffee shop, and though it still felt entirely real to me, I knew what she was really referring to was my coma, my long period of, as Kat put it, scaring the shit out of everyone.

I hear the booming sound of Dave's laughter, and Will and I both look up. Dave has Caleb on his shoulders, while Kelly clings to Jack and Hannah.

I look at Will, who stares at them, with this intense look of joy and admiration and want. He puts his hand on my stomach. "Is she kicking?" he asks. "Does she like weddings?"

As soon as his hand hits my stomach, I feel the soft kicks, the spiral jabs like uneven dance moves. It's as if she knows that he's out here, waiting for her.

It's the first time he's felt her move, and his face lights up with this boyish sort of elation. "She's actually in there," he whispers.

"She is." I laugh.

He shakes his head. "Sometimes, I think this is all a dream," he says.

"No." I shake my head. "It's definitely not."

I take Will's hand, and then we walk inside the hotel together, holding on tightly to each other, neither one of us willing to let go.

A⁺

AUTHOR INSIGHTS, EXTRAS & MORE...

FROM

JILLIAN CANTOR

AND

AVON A

Reader's Guide Questions

1. When Jen's husband, Will, is first indicted, she decides to stick by him, at the cost of her friendships and her country club life. Do you think she does the right thing? And why do you think she would believe in him, even though their relationship is on rocky ground in the beginning of the book?

2. How do you feel about the way the people in Deerfield treat Will and Jen after he's indicted? Are they right or wrong in doing so? Did you initially feel bad for Will when he's forced to go from judge to salesman, or did you think he got what he deserved? If you were friends with Jen, would you have reacted to her similarly or differently from her friends in the book?

3. Jen and her sister, Kelly, both still feel residual aftershocks from their mother's death, even though it happened twenty years earlier. How do they handle their grief in different ways? How do you think Kelly and Jen both live their lives differently than they might if their mother had lived? Is Jen right to still be angry with her father, or do you agree with Kelly that at a certain point she needs to let things go?

4. Why do you think Jen is afraid to have a baby? Is Will right, that she's not sure she wants to have a baby with him, or is it something else?

5. When Jen begins dreaming about her friends, sister, and husband, she begins to see that she was wrong about each one's happiness. How does learning these intimate things about those around her begin to inform her choices about her own life? How do you begin to see the characters differently after learning more about them through Jen's dreams? Is it true that we are each flawed in some way? Do you believe that, beneath the surface, we all have something lurking there that we don't tell our friends, siblings, or even spouses?

6. Which character do you identify with most, Jen, Lisa, Kelly, or Kat, and why? Do you agree or disagree with the choices these women make about being mothers and wives?

7. At one point in the book, Ethel tells Jen about "the transformation of things," about the man who dreamed he was a butterfly, and then woke up unsure whether he was a man dreaming about being a butterfly, or a butterfly dreaming he was a man. How does this idea inform your understanding of Jen's situation? Why is the book called *The Transformation of Things*? What are the ways in which Jen transforms herself?

8. Jen spends most of the book dreaming about other people in her life, learning secrets about them. But how did you feel when she started dreaming about herself? What did you believe to be her reality, and what did you believe to be her dream world? Did you notice any clues throughout the book that Jen might be awake when she was "dreaming" or vice versa?

9. Twice when Jen takes the train into the city, she comes across a little girl reading *Goodnight Moon* with her mother, a book Jen vividly remembers reading with her own mother. Who do you think this girl is, and why do you think these scenes are in the book?

10. How do the figurines that Will and Jen give each other act as symbols for what they want in life and with each other? Why do you think Jen finds the figurines at the end of the book?

11. Are Will and Jen right for each other? Do you think that they have both changed enough to make their marriage work by the end of the book? Why or why not?

Q&A with Jillian Cantor

Where did you get the idea for this book?

When I first sat down to write this book, my idea was to write about a woman whose husband was indicted, and who was then ostracized from her life. This idea came to me after I'd read a bunch of news articles about politicians caught up in scandals, and I began to wonder about their wives, who, at the time, were hardly even mentioned. Then a friend told me about a woman she'd met who was the wife of someone involved in a scandal. My friend mentioned that the wife seemed very nice, but she also wondered out loud about how people must be treating the wife differently, in light of what her husband allegedly did. The story, for me, sprung from there, as I thought about that woman, that nice woman whom I'd never met. I thought about the fact that she'd done absolutely nothing wrong (and maybe, neither had her husband). I thought about what it would feel like to be her, to feel everyone staring at her and judging her.

And so I came up with Jen, a completely fictional woman in a similar situation. I thought it would be interesting to place her in a marriage that was less than perfect, even if it appeared perfect from the outside. I thought it would be interesting to see what might happen to this marriage after her husband's fall from grace, and her being ostracized by her friends. I thought it would be interesting if her husband's indictment actually ended up being the best thing that could've happened to her marriage, and her life. I got here, in part, because I wanted to think about these political scandals through the eyes of a wife, and in part because I am an eternal optimist—deep down, I believe that good can come from even the worst thing and that there must be some husbands and some wives who would weather this storm and come out on the other side stronger.

Why and how did you decide to include the dreams? Why do you think they were important in this particular story?

I wrote the first one hundred pages of the first draft of this book quickly, over the course of just a few weeks, but, aside from the first chapter, these pages were very different from what you see in the book now. These first one hundred pages were dreamless. Then, at around page one hundred, I got stuck. I wanted Jen to transform, to realize that things weren't always what they seemed in her own life and the lives of her "perfect" friends, but I wasn't sure how to get there.

And then I wrote a scene where Jen was distraught about not being able to go to the charity auction, and she had a dream about it. A very vivid dream. I am a vivid dreamer myself, especially when things in my own life are in turmoil, so it made sense for me to include this. But I was still stuck with where to go with the book, until, a few days later, it occurred to me (in the shower—because, really, this is where I get all my best ideas): What if Jen's dream about the auction was real? What if she read the details verbatim in the paper the next day? What if Jen dreamed real things about other people's lives, even while what she thought she knew in her own life was really a lie? From there, I went back and rewrote the first one hundred pages to include the dreams, before moving on.

Writing the dreams ended up being my favorite part of writing this book. I loved the idea of Jen being able to see beneath the surface of other people's lives, to see that she wasn't the only one with imperfections in her life, that underneath, her friends' perfect lives, her sister's perfect family, her husband's perfect job, that they, too, were flawed. In a way, it was like wish fulfillment—I'm guessing many of us have, at one time or another, wondered what goes on beneath the "perfect" exterior of other people's lives. I know I have.

I also thought about the idea that Jen's situation, her husband's indictment, the falling apart of her marriage and her social life, would all feel very surreal to her, maybe dreamlike. And so it seemed fitting to me that there'd be some confusion between dreaming and reality in the book.

How did you come up with the idea of a beauty parlor stroke? Is it a real thing?

I'm certainly not a medical expert, and the details of the stroke and the effects in the book are written with my own fictional liberties. But I did once read an article about something called a beauty parlor stroke.

I have sort of an odd interest in rare medical phenomena. Whenever I see an article about one online, I can't stop myself from reading it (and then usually also worrying that it might happen to me. I'm a little bit of a hypochondriac, too!). But one time, a few years back, I happened to click on an article about this, this beauty parlor stroke. I found it bizarrely fascinating, but then I forgot about it.

When I was almost finished writing the first draft of this book, I found myself stumped about how to end it initially. At about the time I was contemplating the last few chapters, I went to the salon to get my hair cut. As I was getting my hair washed, I noticed my neck was in a really uncomfortable position, and all of a sudden, I remembered that article I'd read on the beauty parlor stroke a few years back. After a brief minute of worrying I might have one, it occurred to me that Jen had been in a hair salon in the beginning of the book—yes, I'd actually unknowingly placed her there before I'd known exactly what was going to happen to her over the course of the book. And after I finished getting my hair cut that day, I went home and sketched out the ending for the first time.

Are you similar to Jen or any of the other women in the book? Are any of the characters autobiographical?

No, none of this is autobiographical. But I am a mom and a wife, and I do sometimes struggle with the same questions as the women in the book, questions of how to balance a career and motherhood and marriage (and how to, somehow, keep your sanity in the process). And although none of this is about my life, there are bits and pieces of me in here, within the characters.

Like Jen, I am writer, who has, at times, floundered to find her voice. Like Lisa, I seem to have the unfortunate inability to bake anything that looks edible, especially pineapple upside-down cake. Like Kelly, I'm married to my high school sweetheart, and I'm a stay-at-home mom. I can identify with Kelly's loud and messy house, her overwhelming love for her kids, and also the feeling of sometimes just wanting some time for herself to do something creative.

But even still, these characters are not really like me at all. Their lives are nothing like my life. I don't feel Kelly's sense of obligation to make everyone else happy. I am much quieter and more introverted than Kat or Lisa. I don't feel the sense of loss or emptiness or insecurity that Jen feels in the beginning of the book. And so they are all, in their own ways, complete figments of my imagination, even if I can see parts of myself in all of them.

Is Deerfield County a real place? Why set the book here?

Deerfield County is a fictional suburb of Philadelphia that I very loosely based on Bucks County, the suburb of Philadelphia where I grew up.

This seemed like the natural place for me to set the book, in a suburb rife with McMansions but also with older sections like the place where Kelly lived and Jen and Kelly grew up. It felt like the appropriate place for a woman like Jen to be ostracized. I also liked the proximity to the city and Jen's old life, and yet the fact that Deerfield seemed worlds away. Finally, I wanted to set the book somewhere where it would snow and be cold in the winter, because I liked the way the weather worked as a backdrop for Jen's mood near the end of the book, as she literally and figuratively had to tread over ice.

Deleted Scenes

As a writer, one of the most important things I do is revise my work. A lot. I wouldn't let anyone near a first draft of one of my books (I cringe at the thought!). My first drafts are often messy and filled with plot holes and infinite things that don't make sense. *The Transformation of Things* went through many, many revisions and drafts before I even showed it to my agent. And then, after she read it and gave me her insight, I put it through another major round of revision before the manuscript made its way into the world. In that final revision, I spent the better part of a month dissecting the dialogue bit by bit and focusing the book, which meant I had to make the decision to take things out that just didn't fit in the end.

One of these things I cut was a storyline and two dreams that Jen has of Bethany, in which Jen realizes that perfect Bethany and her perfect "Angel" daughter are not nearly as *perfect* as they seem. This first scene happened just before Jen takes the train into the city the first time, and then continues with a dream later that night.

. . . I saw Bethany pushing Angel in her Swedish pram around the block. She was practically right in front of my house when I walked out there, so I waved, because, really, I had no choice.

I was surprised when she stopped, when she peered at me, as if she wanted to actually chat. "Hey stranger." She waved me over.

I walked toward her. Angel peered out from behind the shade of the pram and stared at me, as if she, too, was trying to decide whether I was worthy of her smiles. I thought about the way my nephews, Jack and Caleb, had been at her age, and the way they and Hannah were now, rough and grabby in a way that reminded me of monkeys, and also an oddly endearing combination of whiny and sweet. My nephews and niece had sticky hands and skinned knees. They hugged a little too hard, and Hannah, unlike Angel, was hardly ever in a dress. And here was Angel, the surreal little alien baby, all dressed up and frilly like a doll.

"I miss you at tennis," she said. I didn't point out to her that I hadn't left willingly. "Lisa's paired up with Bets."

"Oh," I said. "Well, that's good." Betsy Weinstein was nice enough, but she famously—or perhaps infamously—had two left feet. I'd heard she'd always wanted a place in tennis club, and the ladies had always lied and told her there wasn't an opening. I found it almost funny the way my misfortune had opened up new doors for her, and the way the tennis matches must be oh so much clumsier without me.

"So I don't know how to say this," she said. "So I'll just blurt it out."

"Okay."

"Are you going to leave him?"

I wondered what it was with everyone asking me that, and why they even imagined that I would. Though we'd been having problems lately, I still couldn't imagine being alone in this world, being entirely without him. Shit happened. I already knew that, knew that the fairy-tale life we had in Deerfield wouldn't or couldn't last forever. Though I'd imagined it so much differently.

I'd imagined waking up one morning, finding a lump in my breast. Entering a dungeon of chemo or surgery or both, and then it would all be gone, this happy carefree existence of mine.

I shook my head. "No. I'm not going anywhere."

"Just FYI." She lowered her voice a little. "If you left him, everything would be different. I mean, everyone would understand, you know?"

I thought what she meant was that if I left him, I would be welcomed back, but it seemed like such a despicable thought that

I wasn't exactly sure how to even dignify it with an answer. So I just said, "Okay. Well, enjoy your walk."

And then I turned and walked into the garage, not even looking back to see if she was staring after me, her mouth agape with surprise . . .

Later that night, as I drifted off to sleep, I thought about what Bethany had said, that no one would blame me if I left him. And then I thought about the way he'd sounded this afternoon, on the cell, far away and tired and wanting something from me, something simple, a hello. *I don't want to leave him*, I thought. And I felt so sure in this moment that, deep down, I did still love him, but I was way too tired, way too heavy to move, to roll over and understand why or even verbalize it. But my last thought before I fell asleep was that I wished I'd told Bethany to go to hell.

Then I was dreaming.

> *There's a smell. Windex. Strong and pungent and burning my nose, just the way I like it. Like it?—I hate the smell of Windex. I spray it on the kitchen table, making neat circles with my neat little rag. My glass table—I don't have a glass table. I look down at my boobs, which are much larger and faker-looking than I'm used to, and then I know I am Bethany.*
>
> *Angel is sitting in her high chair, sucking on a sippy cup. I spray, spray, spray. Angel watches, doesn't say a word, doesn't speak. The doctor says she should be speaking now, that he wants me to have her hearing tested. I clap my hands loudly. She looks up, but she doesn't say anything. She just keeps on sucking.*
>
> *"You're a good girl, aren't you?" I say.*
>
> *"Dada," she says back. That's her one word. Dada. Kevin is barely here, and that's what she calls every goddamn thing in the house.*
>
> *I keep spraying even though the table is clean. I*

spray, and then I turn on the TV for Angel. "Mommy will be right back," I say.

I am starving. I've eaten only half a melon slice, and it's twelve-thirty. I want a piece of chocolate cake so badly that I salivate just thinking about it.

In my bedroom, I take my diaphragm out of the night table drawer and take it into my sewing room. I pick up a needle, and I start poking it, gently at first, then harder and harder, as if it were a pincushion, a voodoo doll. This hunger, this incredible hunger cuts my stomach so deep, like something I have never known, like something worse than the feeling you get from not eating.

And then, when I am finished. I put the diaphragm back in the box, back in my night table. Now I am in control.

And here's a second dream about Bethany that appeared closer to the end of the book.

I'm sitting in a waiting room. Cold and sterile, white and smelling like Lysol. A doctor's office. Angel sits on my lap, barely moving, just holding on to my arm, staring at my nails with wide-eyed wonder.

They call us back, and as I walk down the long, checkered hallway to the room, I feel this horrible all-consuming fear, this nausea. I know what they're going to say isn't going to be good. Isn't going to be anything I am prepared to hear.

"Hello, Angel." The doctor waves in her face. She doesn't react. I stare at him and smile. He's attractive, young, with thick blond hair and a pear-shaped face.

He averts his eyes. His mouth moves for a while, with no sound. I watch his lips. They're nice, supple lips, like lips you would want to kiss. And then I hear him say, "Asperger's syndrome."

The words echo and echo and echo, as if they're daring me to make sense of them.

The storyline continued from here, with Jen researching Asperger's syndrome a bit and finally even confronting Bethany about it, offering to help if she needed it.

So why did I cut these scenes? For starters, my agent pointed out to me that these Bethany dreams and her storyline really weren't necessary. And as soon as she said it, I realized she was right. This happens to me a lot in revision: Someone else will read the book and will say something to me so painfully obvious that I want to kick myself for not realizing it on my own. Yes, Bethany's storyline was only slowing the book down.

Bethany and Lisa were overlapping way too much in my earlier draft of the book. Lisa already asks Jen if she's going to leave Will, and she updates Jen about tennis, so it didn't progress the book forward in any way to have Bethany do it, too. Once I cut Bethany's storyline/dreams, I had more room to expand Lisa's, and I thought Lisa had much more potential as a character. She's nicer, more sympathetic, and though she makes some bad choices, I could see Jen getting past this and being her friend. On the other hand, even though these dreams changed Jen's perception of Bethany, Bethany herself didn't change, and in this version of the book when Jen tried to reach out to her, Bethany ended up telling Jen, in no uncertain terms, that she didn't want *her* help.

Which brings me to another reason that I cut this: Unlike the rest of the dreams in the book, these dreams didn't do anything to help support Jen's personal transformation. I liked that they showed a part of Bethany's story, but, then again, this wasn't Bethany's story. It was Jen's.

Was it hard for me to cut these scenes even though I knew it was the right thing to do? Was it hard to let this storyline go? I'll admit that it was, a little bit, anyway. A part of me wanted readers to know Bethany the way I did, but the other part of me, the part that realizes that the best of my writing comes out in revision, knew I needed to let it go. And sometimes that's really what revision is all about for me, just letting go of the individual bits and pieces of the book and cutting and rewriting and expanding the parts of the book that truly make it a story.

Alan Cantor

JILLIAN CANTOR was born and raised in suburban Philadelphia. She attended Penn State University, where she graduated with honors with a BA in English. She then attended the University of Arizona, where she received her MFA in fiction writing. While there, she was also the recipient of the national Jacob K. Javits fellowship. She's the author of two books for teens, *The September Sisters* and *The Life of Glass*. *The Transformation of Things* is her first novel for adults. She lives in Arizona with her husband and two sons.

Jillian Cantor